LITTLE GREED MEN

Book One of the Silverville Saga

A Novel by

KYM O'CONNELL-TODD
&
MARK TODD

For Mike — hope you enjoy your time in Silverville!

Raspberry Creek Books, Ltd.

RASPBERRY
CREEK

BOOKS

Mark

6-30-2018 Palmork

LITTLE GREED MEN

This book is a work of fiction. Names, characters, places and incidents either are products of the authors' imaginations or are used fictitiously. Any resemblance to actual events or locales or persons, living or dead, is entirely coincidental.

© 2013 by Kym O'Connell-Todd & Mark Todd

ISBN 978-0-9851352-3-2
Library of Congress Control Number: 2013936063

Printed in the United States of America

www.raspberrycreekbooks.com

Raspberry Creek Books, Ltd.
Gunnison, Colorado   Tulsa, Oklahoma

Cover Design by
Kym O'Connell-Todd

(This book was originally published in 2006 by
Ghost Road Press of Denver, Colorado,
under the title "The Silverville Swindle")

Also by Kym O'Connell-Todd and Mark Todd

All Plucked Up:
Book Two of the Silverville Saga
(Raspberry Creek Books)

The Magicke Outhouse:
Book Three of the Silverville Saga
(forthcoming from Raspberry Creek Books)

By Mark Todd

Strange Attractors
(Write in the Thick of Things)

Wire Song
(Conundrum Press)

Tamped, But Loose Enough to Breathe
(Ghost Road Press)

ACKNOWLEDGMENTS

A special thanks to our readers group, who commented on early versions of this book: Carmen Civitate, Kara Dalkey, Matt Gaylen, and T.L. Livermore. Thanks to W.C. Jameson, Ed Quillen, and George Sibley for reading the manuscript and offering advice. Our gratitude also goes to Egan and Vance Kelso, Chuck Pusey, and Dale Irby for providing technical information, and to Ashlin O'Connell for proofing portions of the novel during a bivouac on her way to the top of Mt. Rainier. We thank Matt Davis, Sonya Unrein, and Tess Jones, all of Ghost Road Press, who brought out the original work under the title of *The Silverville Swindle*. And lastly, we want to extend a special thanks to Larry Meredith and all the folks at Raspberry Creek Books, who made possible the revised and updated current version under its new title, and for giving a home to the entire Silverville Saga.

A final note: Even as we revised this latest edition, we still did our best to write a politically incorrect novel. If we failed to insult any specific group, we sincerely apologize.

We dedicate this novel to all small mountain towns struggling to find their place in the New West

LITTLE GREED MEN

PROLOGUE

Earl Bob Jackson had to piss. How was he to know it would be his last act on Earth?

He squinted into his windshield trying to see past the stripes of snow that glanced off his yellow Cadillac DeVille. The headlights managed to illuminate a ten-foot path in front of his vehicle, but beyond that, he could only guess what the terrain looked like. He was on a mountain pass – this much he knew – and although he sometimes felt like the car moved downhill, Earl Bob didn't think he had yet reached the summit.

"This road sucks," he muttered to himself. "This weather sucks. Colorado sucks."

What was worse, his bladder felt like a bloated dead cow about to explode in the sun. He'd seen plenty of those, although most of them, or what was left, rotted in the wake of mysterious circumstance. Cored rectums. Surgically excised lips. The usual stuff that accompanied mutilations.

Take that time he investigated the mass "murder" of a herd of calves in Ten Sheep, Wyoming. Those ranchers were mad as hell by the time they'd called him in. Whoever, or whatever, performed the work had really done a fine job. Earl Bob had found the calves picked with a clean precision. Not only were their rectums and lips gone, everything but the skeletons had been removed, leaving the bones as intact as a museum exhibit. No predators could have managed such a tidy scene. And no satanic cult would have taken the trouble. Besides, no one found footprints, just a patch of burnt sagebrush and grass nearby.

Why did his work always seem to take him to the middle of nowhere? Earl Bob unclenched one fist from the steering wheel, flexing his fingers. The radio vacillated between "Your Cheatin' Heart" and an irritating hum, punctuated with occasional blasts of Mexican mariachi music, depending on the turn of the road. But this late at night, he was willing to listen to whatever he could find. He dared not take his attention from the snow-packed pavement to fumble for his collection of gospel CDs. Fat fingers of snow reached across the highway in front of him, the wheels thumping each drift with a soft shudder that resonated in his bladder.

If this was springtime in the Rockies, Earl Bob wasn't impressed. This was nothing like the picture that joker from Silverville had painted for him on the phone. He hoped Buford Price's promises of success would be more accurate than his predictions about Colorado weather. Earl Bob recalled bits and pieces of those promises: . . . we've got a project that needs somebody with your kind of credentials . . . a good money-making venture . . . make it worth your while . . . pay all your expenses . . .

It was true. They did need Earl Bob's expertise to pull off this scheme. Besides, he was tired of working for government wages, tired of getting shuffled all over the country. Tired of exposing the UFO hoaxes of publicity-starved amateurs. Not that Silverville's plan wasn't the same thing, but if the town was going to cash in on what everyone wanted to hear, maybe it was time for Earl Bob to cash in, too.

He'd never miss those jerks in the investigative department. They didn't even give him a going-away party. Twenty years in government service was enough.

Now that cute little piece, Judy, was a different story. There were nights between road trips when he had enjoyed her company. He found himself telling her about his investigations, his problems, his complaints. Judy always listened as he settled his head against her soft bosom; he took comfort from her caresses and quiet words of sympathy. Earl Bob told Judy lots of things he never told anyone else. Things like how he had trouble urinating in public bathrooms. Like how he colored his hair to disguise the early signs of graying.

He had even told Judy about The Secret. How, as a reckless young driver in his boyhood home in Tennessee, he had once struck down a teenager at a crosswalk. Earl Bob had kept right on going, something he had never confessed to anyone – except, of course, Judy.

But when she moved her answering machine into his apartment, things began to look too permanent. He was too old to start a family, too old for that kind of commitment. There would be other women like Judy in Silverville. If he ever managed to get there.

He glanced at the clock in the dash. 2:00 a.m. He hadn't seen another car for over an hour and a half, and he suspected that no one but a fool would be out so late on a night like this. Not this early on a Monday morning. It began to snow harder, and his visibility shrunk to the point that the world around him was no more than a small dark room. A room with no toilet.

The wipers labored to push wet snow off the windshield, leaving an ever-diminishing hole for him to peer at the road. Earl Bob decided he might as well stop, clean the glass, and piss at the same time. He eased to a stop, not daring to pull to the side of the road since there was no telling where it started or ended. He left the engine running and the headlights on.

He pushed the door against the wind and felt wet slushy pellets splatter onto his face and hair as he wedged his beefy body out into the night. But when his slick-soled wingtips touched the snow, they slipped out from under him and sent Earl Bob into a graceless pitch forward onto his hands and knees.

"Son-of-a-bitch," Earl Bob muttered as he struggled to his feet and fumbled with the pants zipper. He stopped short as he noticed a swelling light over his shoulder. His eyes turned in the direction of the glow, which seemed to hover just above the snow-packed road with an eerie, bluish cast.

"Mother of God!" he gasped.

The glow quickly enveloped his entire body, tracing the silhouette of a small man with wet pants, and an empty bladder.

PART ONE

MAY

CHAPTER ONE

Grady

Grady pushed the plate away, leaned back against the chair, and glanced out through the window. Fresh snow clung to the high-mountain ridgeline on the east end of the valley.

"Damn, it's cold again," he said as much to himself as to his wife, Leona. He reached for a toothpick and began to poke the pockets between his worn teeth. After thirty-four years of marriage, talk of weather, water, and calves was something that always followed breakfast.

"We haven't lost calves to a late spring storm in a couple of years," Leona said as she tied an apron around her skinny waist and started to clear the dishes from the table, her spindly arms reaching easily over Grady's shoulder for his coffee cup.

"Just luck," he replied.

Even though he always welcomed the moisture, he hoped he wouldn't be working outside in a blizzard that afternoon.

With an unexcused belch, Grady rose from his chair and walked toward the bedroom to change into his work clothes. They differed little from the ones he wore to church at yesterday's Sunday service except for a few small tears and a few larger oil and grass stains. He pulled a shirt over lean shoulders and then pushed his feet into Levi pant legs. As he cinched the belt dangling from the loops, his mind already traveled forward to the day's job. Cleaning irrigation ditches wasn't exactly going to be pleasant with the wind and all. But with calving over, ditch repair was on the seasonal agenda. It was that time of year. It's what O'Grady families had been doing for four generations in this valley, a heritage that had begun when his great-great grand pappy Fergal had brought law and order to Silverville's 1870s boomtown days.

He padded on stocking feet to the "mud room," where he tugged on his old boots and lifted a battered felt hat off a hook.

"You comin' out?" Grady asked.

He walked back to the kitchen doorway, but before he took

another step, he paused. Leona would kill him if he walked on her clean linoleum floor trailing dried mud and manure.

"Soon as I finish up here," his wife replied.

Leona was the only ranch hand he hadn't fired on the place. By god, those young know-it-alls screwed up a lot. Not a one of them was a real cowboy. Just thought they were. Besides, Leona worked as hard as any man, and she didn't ask for Sundays off.

A bitter spring breeze hit his face as he headed out the door. By the time Grady tossed a few old shovels in the bed of his twenty-year-old flatbed pickup, Leona was coming out the door securing her salt-and-pepper hair with a dark purple scarf. They climbed into the cab and drove down a rutted gravel road toward the head gate that would soon feed water into the pasture's irrigation ditches. Both Grady's and Leona's eyes scanned the ground to evaluate the work that would occupy the coming weeks.

Grady's vision traveled easily over familiar structures – the dilapidated sheep barn his grandfather once used, sagging strands of wire that stretched across the creek, a twisted cottonwood tree that still held a rope he used to swing from as a boy. And, of course, the ragged mountain skyline of Buford's Folly, the home of Silverville's failed attempt to build a ski resort.

Always some fool project, and more than likely one Buford Price had dreamed up. Grady didn't so much mind the scars on the mountain; after all, felling timber was part of any mountain town. It was just that nobody ever stopped to think if there would always be enough snow to cover the ski trails Price and others had carved out of the slopes.

Other towns had survived the misfortunes of a fickle economy, and Silverville would, too. At least the ski resort had sounded like a respectable undertaking. Aspen, Telluride, Crested Butte – all had made a go at skiing. But when skiing didn't work, Price was quick to suggest this newest plan, this UFO scheme. Grady was sure it could only become Buford's latest failure.

But Buford's wasn't the only hare-brained idea. Beyond Grady, about a quarter mile ahead, loomed the outline of his new neighbor's nearly constructed home. Grady couldn't help but shake his head. Whatever possessed him to agree to sell That Woman a piece of his property?

"Goddamned crazy newcomers," he muttered to Leona.

"Done is done, Grady. Just let it be."

After all, that corner of the pasture was mostly sage and rocks. Seemed too good to be true when Chantale Getty-Schwartz offered him such a price for a worthless piece of ground. Hard telling where she came from. Someplace where folks fancied living in pyramids, he guessed, because that was exactly what the eyesore was going to be.

Of course, that was only the beginning.

He shouldn't have been surprised with this newest project. Instead of first putting in a well, the woman had contracted someone to grade and pave a helicopter pad that sat on Grady's side of her quarter section. "Gateway of the Gods' Ranch." Ranch. Who the hell would think of a name like that? The helicopter proved to be a real problem, too. Two cows had already tangled in barbed wire trying to run from the air-flogging noise of the rotors. A couple more had dropped dead calves. He couldn't prove it, but he knew down deep that the ruckus probably stopped their hearts.

She didn't know a lick about livestock. More than once he had drawn a bead on those two wild dogs she'd let run all over the place, even all over his place. Never did see an animal like them in his whole life. Irish Wolfhounds, she called them. Champion Irish Wolfhounds. If he'd had his way, they'd be dead Irish Wolfhounds. Not that he objected to dogs. Everyone needed to have a good cow dog to bark at coyotes, to help round up the stock.

Grady fished in his hip pocket for his can of Copenhagen. Just the thought of That Woman was enough to leave with him a dry mouth.

The truck lurched to a stop next to the head gate, and he and Leona stepped out of the cab. Grady reached for the shovels on his side, handed one to his wife, and started down to the ditch to clear debris.

As he pitched sticks and leaves from the gate, his mind just couldn't let go of That Woman. Why, the first week after she bought the place, she and a bunch of other kooks were out there in the middle of the night with sage torches, waving smoke on each other, beating on drums and singing. Scared him and Leona half to death. He was part way across the pasture with his shotgun before he realized it wasn't a gang of drunken trespassers.

He wondered what would happen once she finished the pyramid and moved in permanently. His hands worked harder and his heart beat faster.

At that moment, something above the ditch line caught the corner of Grady's eye. He looked up in time to see a shiny new SUV stop a hundred yards from the pyramid. He squinted against the wind as he watched Chantale Getty-Schwartz and a long-haired man he didn't recognize get out of the vehicle. At first, Grady stared mutely at the proceedings across the fence. Within seconds, his fingers began to throttle the neck of the shovel handle as he began to understand what was going on.

"Well, son-of-a-bitch!"

The two fools by the pyramid were lifting rocks out the back of the SUV and tossing them into the ditch above the head gate.

"Calm down, Grady," Leona cautioned. "They don't know."

"They're about to find out!"

Grady gripped his shovel, climbed out of the ditch, and stomped up the hill toward That Woman.

He hadn't walked that fast in years, and Leona had trouble keeping up. But his thoughts outpaced his stride.

This was exactly what he thought might happen with that stupid theme park idea – strange people moving in because now Silverville was a "special place," a place that attracted beings from other worlds. Well, they were right about that, anyway. Chantale Getty-Schwartz was not from any world that Grady knew.

"Keep your temper, Grady," Leona warned. "Give them a chance to explain."

Up ahead, the two people by the pyramid had already unloaded almost a quarter of a load of rocks into the ditch, chatting gaily, totally unaware of the storm about to arrive. Leona kept right on Grady's heels, but nothing she said made any difference at that point.

The fence between the two properties had no gate at the particular place where Grady intended to cross. It didn't stop him.

Years of crossing barbed wire, along with a surge of anger, helped him swing over the top strand with barely a nick in his pants. He didn't wait for Leona to get over the fence; she didn't follow.

"Hello, Mr. Graden," Chantale greeted him with a congenial wave as she bent over to position some of the rocks. To Grady, she looked like an overfed heifer in black stretch pants, sequined cowboy boots, and a fur jacket.

"O'Grady," he corrected her for the hundredth time. His whole body was so tensed with anger it hurt to talk. "What the hell are you doing?"

For a moment, Chantale looked back at him with confusion. She didn't have a clue. That Woman didn't have any idea what she was doing wrong.

"You don't own any water rights with this property," Grady managed to say between clenched teeth.

"I'm not messing with any water."

Her stupidity confounded him. He might as well be talking to a fence post.

"Then what are you doing with them rocks?" he demanded. The volume of Grady's voice increased.

"Oh, those. Why, we're preparing for a wonderful celebration," she replied with a smile over lipstick-smeared teeth. "We're planning on having a sweat, in the true Native American tradition, for the house warming. Of course, y'all are invited, Mr. Graden."

"But the rocks . . ."

"Why, Mr. Graden, you can't have a sweat without rocks," she replied. "And this here trench works beautifully as a fire pit. You see, first we'll build a lodge over the rocks, and then we'll heat and pour water over them to create enough steam to sweat. It's all very purifying and spiritual."

"You can't do that!"

"Don't be silly, Mr. Graden. This is my property, after all."

Grady didn't know what a "sweat" was, and he didn't give a damn.

"It may be your property, but my water flows through it!" By now, Grady was shouting. "Without water rights, you can't touch this ditch!"

"But there's no water in it." The indignant tone of her voice incensed Grady even more.

It was then that the stranger standing next to Chantale stepped forward and placed a hand on Grady's taut and shaking shoulder.

"No one really owns the gifts that the Great Spirit gives us all," cooed the man with long white hair. "The water that flows freely from Mother Earth –"

"Who the hell are you?" Grady sputtered.

"Oh, I'm terribly sorry," Chantale broke in. "This is Hans High Horse, my personal medicine man and spiritual guide. He'll be moving onto the property as soon as he can raise his teepee."

"What?" Grady asked incredulously, his hands gripping the shovel so hard his knuckles began to numb.

Hans High Horse, in a voice as smooth as the polished amber he wore, said, "I can see from your aura that you're upset. This is negative energy you must try to control before you –"

Without thinking, Grady raised his shovel, stepped forward and swung with all his might, striking Hans High Horse squarely between his pale, pink eyes.

Denton

"I'm always a little worried whether that coffee will wind up in my cup or my lap," Denton Fine remarked, smiling at Buford.

Together they watched Fawn move through the crowded tables at the coffee shop asking customers if they needed refills. Not everyone answered her immediately, since it wasn't always clear who she was talking to.

Buford turned back to his companion and leaned forward. "'S'pose it was all the drugs her folks took that made her eyes like that?"

Denton shrugged and looked at his watch. Still no sign of Jackson. If he didn't show up soon, Buford would have to greet him alone. Hard telling what his assistant might be encountering back at the Fine Funeral Home.

Outside, the streets were beginning to show midday activity.

Of each face that passed the restaurant window, Buford usually offered some interesting piece of information – some of it true, much of it probably not. Denton figured maybe half of the stories that circulated around Silverville started with Buford's off-hand remarks. After all, the guy had lived there most of his life, knew almost everybody, and kept his fingers stirring the pots of multiple business deals. Sometimes they worked, but not everyone agreed the deals were always a benefit to the town. No one could deny, however, the wheels in Buford's head were usually turning. It was Buford who had the initiative to organize the UFO Economic Development Committee. It was Buford who had single-handedly sought and secured investors to help fund the entire project. All as the result of what Denton's embalming assistant saw – or thought he saw – one night while riding his bicycle home to his cabin.

Denton should've figured he'd be dragged into this as soon as Buford started talking about it. He just didn't have the willpower to ever say no.

"More coffee?"

Denton looked up at their waitress, who stood beside the table with one eye on him and the other on Buford. They both mumbled yes to avoid the confusion and held up their cups to follow the wavering spout.

"Any idea what this guy Jackson looks like?" Denton asked after Fawn turned to another table, squeezing her scrawny butt between customers.

"Don't know. Never seen him. Only talked to him on the phone. But my guess is he's old enough to have prostate trouble. I don't give a shit what kind of trouble he has as long as he helps us pull off this project."

Denton nodded with nervous anticipation. A familiar old pain in his left hip crawled down his leg, making him shift around on the sticky vinyl chair. "Sounds to me like you found the right man for the job. Buford, I always figured you had cash for brains. This might just work."

"You goddamn right."

It seemed at that moment Buford's chest expanded a few inches, and Denton was sure his friend was reflecting on the well-planned scheme to bring tourist coins into the local coffers. One thing Denton did know was that old Buford would make out as well or better than anyone else in town. Some of that money might even make its way to the Fine Funeral Home. It would just take a little longer.

"This town is going to be on the map yet, my friend," Buford assured Denton. "And Jackson is going to help us get there."

If Jackson ever gets here, Denton thought to himself as he glanced again at his watch. This hotshot was supposed to pull into town forty-five minutes ago. The dead could wait; their bodies couldn't.

Buford turned his head toward the window. "There go those two –"

"I know what you're going to say, and I don't want to hear it."

"What are you squirming around for, Denton? You look like some old lady who's just wet her pants."

"Aw, nothing. Just that old injury bothering me again." Denton's eyes turned away from the window. He grimaced as he noticed his son bouncing along beside the two men who held hands as they walked down the sidewalk.

"Not that their lifestyle matters to me," Buford quickly added. "Business is business. I mean, what the hell, they scratch my back, I scratch theirs. What embarrasses the hell out me is that, after I sell a rifle to an out-of-state hunter, I have to send him to their lodge. What do you suppose folks think about a hunting lodge owned by a couple of limp wrists?"

Denton's shoulders collapsed as he thought about his own son's excuses to visit the lodge. He wondered if Buford realized the whole town knew the "limp wrists" were the financial backers for Price's Gun Paradise, and that Buford would not have been able to start the store if it hadn't have been for the two men Buford poked fun at.

Fawn again shuffled toward their table, this time looking at the floor with one eye and the cash register with the other. Guess there was an advantage to seeing the world the way she did. They waved her on by.

Denton glanced out the window at the curb. "How are we

going to know if it's Jackson?"

"I told him what I looked like," Buford answered.

Denton doubted it was an accurate description. Look for a pudgy man with unruly hair and fat fingers.

"I told him I would be wearing a red tie and sitting with a man who is always trying to measure people for a pine box." Buford laughed out loud at his own joke. Denton forced a weak smile.

Across the street, the town sheriff strutted his tall frame past the storefronts. He tipped his clean and brushed Stetson at each female passerby.

"Did you hear about Grady's run-in earlier this morning?" Buford asked.

Denton shook his head, figuring he was about to hear the story anyway.

"These days, Grady has taken to beating on albinos." Buford's eyes sparkled at the prospect of being the first to tell Denton the tale. "Seems the sheriff had to go out to the ranch to cool him down after he smacked some friend of his new neighbor's in the head with a shovel."

"Grady's always been a hothead," Denton said.

"Yeah, well this time Grady was just defending himself. Guess these weirdo neighbors were getting ready to hold a séance or something and Grady goes over to see what all the fuss is. This Indian – probably high on peyote or cactus buttons or something –"

"Wait a minute. I thought you said there was an albino."

"Yeah, he's an albino Indian. Go figure. Well, anyway, this Indian gives a bloodcurdling war cry and jumps Grady with a knife. But Grady's watching him carefully, and before the fellow can stab him, Grady smacks him across the head with a shovel."

"Kill him?"

"Naw, just knocks him out for a couple of minutes. But no one knows this when the call comes in. Grady's neighbor is hysterical and keeps shouting, 'He's dead! He's dead!' The sheriff figures he's got this big homicide on his hands. By the time he gets out to the ranch, this Indian is up and walking around, bleeding like a stuck pig. Grady is back over working the ditches, and the new neighbor woman is screaming and chanting. Seems she pasted sage leaves all over the albino's eyes. He's allergic to them and now can't see at all."

"Well, I'll be," Denton said, wondering how even more incredible Buford's version of the story would sound after several tellings. "Grady get arrested?"

"For what? The guy attacked him. When the sheriff went over to talk to Grady, he just kept mumbling about all the kooks moving into this valley. But Grady and all the others will sing another song once more 'kooks' get here and start spending their money."

Denton glanced at his watch. "I've got to get going."

"Now just wait, Denton. We've got to give Jackson a proper welcome. Hey, don't turn around, but guess who just walked in the door?"

"Jackson?"

"No, it's that guy who heads the Church of the Holy Snail."

"Church of the Holy Grail."

"Whatever. Now, I'm not saying this is true, but somebody told me they go out of state and steal children. They bring 'em here, brainwash 'em, and make 'em have sex with their sisters."

"For Pete's sake, Buford. I've held a service or two for that group, and they seem like normal folks to me."

"Well, all I can tell you is that I know for a fact there are some pretty unnatural-looking kids walking around that compound. And none of them go to school. They can't because they're retarded from inbreeding."

"I think they have their own school."

Denton was almost relieved when he saw his assistant, Howard, scurry across the street toward the cafe. The young man was slightly built, smallish, and wore a crew cut. He shuffled, swinging hands that poked out the sleeves of a red flannel shirt. Howard kept his eyes downcast as he walked, seeming content to watch the gangling strides of the plaid pants he wore, cuffs ending well above the ankles.

It couldn't be good news to bring Howard three blocks on foot from the funeral home, but to Denton it would be better than having to sit here and listen to stories about inbreeding.

Howard stepped up to the window and pressed his face against the glass with cupped hands to peer inside. Buford waved him in.

"Howard, my man," Buford boomed above the crowd. "Been watching the night sky lately?"

Howard began stammering, approaching the table with obvious embarrassment. A brief moment of anger flashed through Denton. As long as he and Buford had been friends, he was always a little uncomfortable with how Buford sometimes treated people. True, Howard was somewhat on the simple side – and Lord knew, he screwed up a lot – but Denton had never known him to lie, and he always put in a hard day's work.

Howard looked at Buford. "Hell-hello, Mr. Price."

"What is it?" Denton asked.

"I'm supposed to remind you about your doctor's appointment." Howard looked on, not knowing whether to sit or stand, his hands now pocketed.

"Thanks. I'm coming."

Denton struggled up and limped toward the cash register, Howard following so close behind he almost tripped his employer. They didn't even notice at first the late-model yellow Cadillac that rounded the corner and pulled up in front of the restaurant.

On the license plates were the letters UFO.

Billy

He had never before killed anyone. What bothered him was how little it bothered him.

It might have been the worst part of an already bad day. *Never get caught with your pants down,* his daddy always told him, but that's exactly what had happened. Billy just hoped LuAnne wasn't kicking herself too hard right now.

That poor kid. What a pathetic mess she was when he'd met her. The first day she walked into his life, she was hiding behind sunglasses and heavy make-up to disguise the black eyes and bruised cheeks. Somehow she kept smiling, insisting it didn't matter, that she didn't deserve any better. But Billy thought she did, and was more than willing to help her build her self-esteem. He had found a lot of married women all over the country needed his kind of support.

Maybe one of the things that drew him to LuAnne was how much her situation reminded him, in a sick sort of way, of his own relationship with his father. It didn't make sense, he knew now, but God, he still loved that man. Even between the regular beatings and cursing, his father had taught him a lot. At the time, his daddy had seemed so smart, always ready with the right turn of phrase for any occasion. Those words still rang in his head: *Never give a sucker an even break. Take the money and run. You can cheat a rich man as easy as a poor one. It's only a sin if you get caught. Don't look back.*

Yeah, don't look back.

He glanced in the rear view mirror, adjusting it for his height. No one was following – at least not that he could tell through the gray sheet of snow that blurred the highway behind him. He hadn't planned to stop in Placer City, nor had he planned to involve himself with a jealous cowboy's wife, but things just seemed to work out that way for Billy. Another town. Another buck. Another woman. Another alias.

He could almost see the smile that would brighten LuAnne's face when he told her how pretty she looked. It didn't take much. A flower plucked from a neighbor's garden, a little box of candy lifted from the local five-and-dime. He wished he could've bought her some finer things, but his last few "business deals" hadn't worked out the way he'd planned. *Win some, lose some.*

Billy was still waiting for The Big One, something that would've made his daddy proud. But his daddy was always looking for The Big One, too, and he only found it once. It must have been hard on his mother, living in dingy hotel rooms or skipping town in the middle of the night. It was all she had known with his father, and Billy figured she finally couldn't take the lifestyle anymore. One day she picked up his two-year-old brother and left, taking with her one of the only two framed photos of mother and sons. Daddy always hung the remaining photo on the wall of whatever cheap room they called home. Billy had just started first grade. Many a night while his daddy was out taking care of business, Billy sat before the picture she left behind, looking at the woman and two little boys. She gazed back at him with shining green eyes and a gentle smiling mouth that pushed dimples into the sides of her cheeks. With his fingers, he would trace the outline of her auburn hair and finely tapered neck. She was the most beautiful woman he'd ever seen.

In some ways, Billy missed that photo as much as he missed his old man. He was fourteen when he lost both the picture and his father in Nashville. Daddy had been putting together The Big One. For weeks, he had come home telling Billy about the suckers who believed in his scheme to tear down tenements and build a shopping complex. *There's one born every minute.* Billy had been working his own suckers in a pool hall down the street the night his father left. He would never forget walking into that room, the open drawers, the hangers strewn out the closet, the empty wall.

No note. No good-byes. No forwarding address. Daddy must have had to leave town fast. Now, twenty-nine years later, Billy still hoped his old man had left with a pocket full of money.

As he came down off Poverty Pass, the sun had just begun to lift above the mountain, flooding the trees with morning light. Billy was surprised, and relieved, to see bare grass. He still wasn't used to the sudden shifts in Colorado weather, and he longed for the predictable environment of the cities he'd known in the South.

Except for the past few hours, Billy had never driven a car this big, and certainly not on snow-packed roads. As the switch-backs began to straighten into the valley floor, he reached a free hand over to the briefcase in the passenger seat and pulled out a handful of papers. The words just blended together. He slowed the car's bulk and turned on a dirt road that led into a pasture. What he needed was a hot shower and a soft bed. But for now the best he could hope for was a few hours of sleep in the car.

He opened the door and threw his long legs toward the gravel. It had been a good twenty-four hours since he'd been to bed – to sleep anyway. He ran his fingers over the stubble on his face and pushed back a strand of bleached blond hair. Wrinkling his brow below a slightly receding hairline, Billy rubbed the sleep from green eyes as he glanced at himself in the rearview mirror. As tired as he looked, Billy knew he still had a face the ladies liked.

He stepped from the vehicle, into the morning and into the scent of wet sagebrush. Opening the back door, he plopped onto the bench seat and stretched across the interior. Just before he fell asleep, he wondered whose car it was. But within seconds, he was unconscious.

§   §   §

Hunger woke him before the sun reached mid sky. Slowly opening his eyes, he gazed out the car window at stringy wisps of clouds in the distance. With a start, he sat up disoriented, wondering where he was. And then he remembered.

God, had Billy been surprised to see a guy about to piss in the middle of the road during a midnight snow storm. Of course, there hadn't been time to veer away, and Billy could only watch the terror on the guy's face as the approaching car ran him over. It was weird, like a slow-motion movie. Billy could tell the Road Pisser was screaming as he hit him, but the howling wind voiced over any sounds that may have come from his lips. When Billy felt the bump, he knew it was all over. He also knew he had to think fast, but it was hard to even stop the car, his hands were shaking so hard.

For just a moment, Billy stood over the body, wondering if the poor guy had a family. Then he wondered if he had any money in his billfold. Billy rolled the man over and reached into his pants pocket. He hesitated, and then yanked the wallet free. It felt like genuine calf skin, and Billy stashed it in his own hip pocket.

Already, the snow had started to cover the body. Over the wind, Billy could barely hear the purr of the Cadillac's engine. For an instant, his eyes flashed back and forth between LuAnne's junked out Chevy Nova "loaner" and the Road Pisser's plush Caddy. It didn't take Billy long to decide which car he would leave in. Besides, *dead men tell no tales.*

He dragged the Pisser's bulky body over the ice toward the edge of the mountain road. Hard telling how far the ravine dropped off, but Billy guessed it might be deep enough to buy him time before anyone found the dead man. His hands had been so cold, he barely took time to apologize as he pushed the body over the ledge.

The Chevy Nova posed a different problem. He could push it over the ledge with the Pisser, but he hated to do that to LuAnne's car. After all, he didn't even ask her if he could borrow it. He decided to park the junker, then call and tell her where to pick it up. Billy made his way against the wind over to the Nova, turned off the ignition, and dropped the keys on the floorboard so LuAnne wouldn't have to break in. With any luck, the car would be gone before anyone made a connection with the body. He let the wind push him back toward the Caddy, climbed inside, and stepped on the gas to continue a slow crawl over the pass.

Now Billy Noble would go to his Maker a murderer. Would it really matter? Probably not.

What's done is done.

Billy yawned, hardly rested after his catnap. No, it hadn't been a good day, but he did have a thick wallet and a fancy car for a little while.

He reached into his back pocket and pulled out the billfold. It was time to find out who the poor sap in the snow bank was. He flipped it open and combed through several credit cards before he found the driver's license: Earl Bob Jackson. From Washington, D.C. – a long way from home. He looked deeper for any signs of family, but found no pictures. At least not of people. The Pisser must've been a lonely guy, if a rich one, judging by the hundred-dollar bills that lined his wallet. The briefcase would tell him more, but for right now, Billy was more interested in finding lunch and a motel.

He slipped back behind the wheel and continued down the road toward the next town. Within a half hour, Billy approached the outskirts of a small unremarkable community that boasted a modest collection of older homes. Here, a few kids played near the highway; there, a group of old men sat on a doorstep spitting on the sidewalk. In the distance, he saw a giant "S" marked in white stone on the side of a nearby hill. What he didn't see on that side of town was a restaurant of any kind, or even a McDonald's. He hoped this little rat hole at least had a motel. A few blocks in, Billy turned at a flashing light onto what he figured might be Main Street, spotted a local greasy spoon called the Lazy S Diner, and pulled the car next to the curb.

With his new wallet in his back pocket, he stepped out of the Caddy and headed toward the restaurant door. There, he met three men moving directly toward him. One had a visible limp, another kept his eyes on the sidewalk, and the third wore the most god-awful red tie he had ever seen.

Before he could step around them, the man with the tie grabbed his hand, shaking it vigorously.

"Mr. Jackson, are we ever glad to see you!"

CHAPTER TWO

Billy

In a state of confusion, Billy stood there watching the man in the terrible red tie pump his arm up and down.

"You *are* Jackson, aren't you?"

Billy's eyes jumped from one man to the next as his mind raced. The plump fellow with the red tie smiled up at him with anticipation, a gold tooth glinting in the morning sun. His companion with the limp stepped up beside him, wearing the same air of expectation. The third one stole shy glances at Billy. Clearly, "Jackson" was the man of the hour, but Jackson wasn't going to make this rendezvous.

"Yes, I'm Jackson. And you are?"

"Why I'm Buford Price," the man replied. "The man with the red tie."

Price thrust his necktie in Billy's face. Even in the wake of his exhaustion, Billy knew better than to hesitate — a skill Daddy had taught him at a tender age. *The early bird gets the worm.* He relaxed his grip and patted Price on the shoulder.

"Of course you are," he responded. If these guys thought he was the Pisser, Billy decided he had better play along — at least until he could figure out how the hell to make his exit without anyone becoming suspicious.

He turned toward the other two men, trying to buy some time.

The one with the limp spoke first, "I'm Denton Fine. Happy to —"

"Yes, this is our friendly neighborhood undertaker," Price broke in. "You can count on him to always get the last word!"

Price barked out a hearty chuckle, obviously enjoying a joke at his friend's expense. Billy noticed a slight look of irritation cross Fine's face before the "friendly undertaker" tried again to finish his welcome, offering a hand that Billy noticed was artistic, almost feminine in its delicate features.

"Happy to meet you. We're very pleased you agreed to come

out here. And this is Howard Beacon," Fine said, turning to the third man, who merely nodded a shy greeting.

"Yes!" Price interrupted again, and then continued with unnecessary bravado. "If it weren't for Howard, we wouldn't be having this little meeting."

Billy met the three men's gazes as an awkward silence threatened to overtake the "meeting." *Keep talking, just don't say anything incriminating.*

"So, are we meeting here on the sidewalk?" Billy ventured. The men stared back blankly. *Damn. Not good enough.* Then, all at once, they laughed.

"I suppose we could move into our office," Price announced, jerking his thumb back toward the greasy spoon.

The three locals turned and single-filed into the cafe. Billy wondered if they would accept Jackson just backing out now from whatever he was supposed to be doing. *I've decided I don't like your meeting. No, nothing personal, it's just that I can't work with limps and red ties. Unthinkable, but thanks anyway.*

He followed them through the door.

Inside, Price chose a table and motioned to the waitress for menus.

"Order what you will, Jackson," Price said. "It's on me."

Billy nodded and took a quick survey of the cafe. It was a little worse than the usual small-town eatery, offering an odd assortment of unmatched chairs and ugly vinyl booths. Three decorations hung on the walls: a clock with the words "Drink Coca Cola" under its hands, a poor rendition of a local landmark – a giant "S" created from rocks on a nearby hillside – slightly offset in its frame, and a yellow hand-drawn square of construction paper that warned, "No Shoes, No Shirt, No Service."

The several people left drinking their late morning coffee stared back at him from behind their cups as though they had seldom seen strangers in this local hangout. Some looked like cowboys and the rest were a few young mothers who had probably married right after high school and set out to increase the resident population.

What was it about this town that could have possibly drawn

Jackson in the first place?

"Jackson . . . Jackson?" It was Price again, waving a bloated hand in front of Billy's face. "I guess that road trip got to you, huh? Well, we'll keep this short and sweet. Then you can check into your hotel room. We've made reservations for you at one of Silverville's newest and finest — the Galactic Inn. Close to the site to make it convenient."

"Oh, yes. Thanks." What site? Was Jackson some sort of criminal investigator?

Fine sipped on his coffee; Beacon peered with admiration from behind thick glasses. It was obvious they were waiting for him to say more.

"Well, ah, so what's first on the agenda?" Billy asked them, turning to the waitress for the menu. He took a double take. For a couple of seconds, he studied her face, trying to determine whether or not she was somehow signaling Buford while she still looked at Billy. Maybe she knew who Jackson really was.

"Let me fill you in on the upcoming events that we've scheduled, Earl Bob. I can call you Earl Bob, can't I?" Buford didn't wait for an answer. "We've got a summer lineup I think you'll find interesting. Along with yourself, of course, there will be others here to give their testimonials to keep the believers coming."

Oh. Earl Bob Jackson was *Reverend* Jackson. It wasn't his forte, but Billy thought he could muster the role of evangelist. He knew how they talked, how they attacked the word God with unusual longevity and punch. "Ga-a-wd," wasn't it? Nevertheless, he'd say no thank you with a slight Southern Baptist brogue and get the hell out of there. This sounded like a little longer "job" than he cared to tackle — particularly under the circumstances.

Just as Billy opened his mouth to reply, Fine cleared his throat and nodded toward the menus.

"Howard, there's really no reason why you have to stay and listen to all this," Fine said. "Maybe one of us should be at The Home to receive people." The undertaker then said to Billy, "I'm sure you'll want to talk to Howard about The Sighting once you're rested."

Billy wondered what this "sighting" business was all about.

Did Jackson's gig include miracle working?

Without a word, Howard pushed back his chair and turned to go.

"Tell my wife to reschedule that doctor's appointment," Fine called after him.

When the waitress returned, all three men ordered and soon continued the business at hand.

"Tell me more about the sighting, Mr. Price," Billy asked.

"Please, skip the 'Mr.' stuff. This is western Colorado. Call me Buford and him Denton."

"Okay then, Buford. Tell me about Howard's sighting."

"It's the same story I told you on the phone. But you'll probably want to set up a time to talk to him and hear the story with your own ears. You can see how it affected him. He was never this quiet before he saw that saucer."

Billy nodded casually. Saucer! This Jackson must have had something to do with flying saucers. *There's one born every minute*, his daddy used to say.

"And you believe everything he said?" Billy pumped him.

"I don't care if Howard saw little green men or Jesus Christ himself. All that matters is that this town can make a profit on whatever Howard thought he saw. You can see what this town looks like, Earl Bob. It's in sore need of a shot in the arm. Folks around here are having to close their stores, mortgage their ranches."

Denton added, "To answer your question, I believe Howard believes it, and that's good enough for me."

Billy studied the expressions on their faces and decided they were for real. It was time to humor them until he found out where this was going.

"I know we've talked on the phone, but tell me what the plans are for today," Billy tested.

"Absolutely nothing for today," Buford replied. "We just wanted to make sure you got here safely and to brief you on the schedule for the theme park and everything else."

Their waitress arrived just then with three platters of eggs, biscuits, and gravy, all floating in grease. Billy didn't look up. She gave him the creeps. As unappetizing as the food looked, Billy was surprised at how good it tasted. He shoveled in a few scoops of runny egg and asked, "What's on the schedule?"

"You know, you're voice doesn't sound like it did on the phone," Buford remarked. "I would've taken you for an older man."

Billy shrugged and kept eating, hoping no answer would be answer enough. He'd been accused of many things, and was guilty of most, but he didn't want this conversation to lead to the man at the bottom of the ravine.

Buford continued, "My wife is printing up the list of upcoming events, which I'll give you, but broadly speaking, we've carried forward several of your suggestions already. We're still trying to arrange right-of-way to the actual spot of the sighting, but as I told you before, the Forest Service isn't cooperating like we'd hoped."

"What's the problem?" Billy asked, having no idea what Buford was talking about.

"Well, like we thought, they're making us jump through lots of hoops to get our hands on that property. So far, they're considering a land swap for a piece of city-owned river front, but I'm not holding my breath. If we can get it, we have plans to improve the area — maybe some concession stands, parking areas, you know what we're saying. Too bad The Sighting was three miles from Silverville. Course, we could tell folks it happened on the edge of town where we set up the theme park, but we took your advice and are trying to keep this as authentic as possible."

Little by little, the picture became clearer to Billy about what the town was doing. It still wasn't clear, however, what Earl Bob would be doing. That is, if Earl Bob had still been around to do it.

Buford again broke Billy's train of thought. "Of course, during the next month, there's lots to do. You'll need to meet everyone you'll be working with, see the theme park, the rides and whatnot. We also need some last-minute pointers for the museum."

"Of course," Billy reassured him.

"We've changed things around a little. The ribbon-cutting ceremony is now the night before the parade, and if you don't mind, we thought we would have you ride in the first saucer float as Grand Marshal."

Billy must have betrayed some surprise at this because Denton quickly spoke up. "Not only do we need your expertise, but we also need you to be as visible as possible."

"Excuse me?"

Buford and Denton exchanged doubtful looks. Almost under his breath, Denton said to Buford, "I told you he probably wouldn't go for this."

To Billy, Denton pointed out, "Mr. Jackson –"

"Earl Bob," Buford corrected.

"Earl Bob, a lot of people in this town have put up hard-earned money, as well as the investors Buford has lined up. We need both your credentials and your support to make this work. Surely you can understand that. If people think this is important enough for an expert like you to be here, they'll come, too."

Billy nearly choked at the thought of seeing himself on display before the town and God knows who else. *Get a hold of yourself, Billy. There won't be a display because you won't be here that long. You're going to eat this meal and skip out of town.*

Buford leaned toward the center of the table and motioned Billy to do the same. "You have to understand. Not everybody in town has been behind us in this project. Lela Schlopkohl, for one."

"The mayor," Denton clarified.

"Well, you know, she's older, more conservative," Buford confided in a lowered voice. "She was afraid Silverville would become known as a town full of crazies. Since she wouldn't endorse the project, there were several other business-owners who wouldn't either. That's why it's so important that everyone who comes on board shows the proper enthusiasm."

"What makes me so special?" Billy asked, trying to make his remark sound like a joke. It was just his luck if he had run down someone with a high enough profile to launch a missing-person inquiry.

Denton responded, "You're the kind of professional that lends a lot of credibility to the entire development project, what with your background and all."

Just who was this Jackson, anyway? Billy remembered the briefcase on the front seat of the Caddy and was more than anxious to find out what that background was.

It was then he remembered LuAnne's car. Damn! He should've called her by now. "Would you two excuse me for just a moment? I have to make a phone call."

Billy sauntered over to the pay phone, which hung near the bathrooms toward the back of the restaurant. He fished quarters from his back pocket and dropped them in the slot as he turned to watch Buford and Denton. About four inches separated their two faces as they huddled in serious conversation. He listened to the phone ring, wondering all the while if he had played his hand close enough to his chest.

Someone picked up on the other end but didn't speak.

"Hello? LuAnne?"

"Billy, is that you?" He could tell she had been crying.

"Yeah. Sorry I had to leave in such a hurry. You okay?"

"Been better. Where are you? Where's my car?"

"I don't have much time, honey. Listen carefully. I left your car just on the east side of Poverty Pass. The doors are unlocked and the keys are on the floor."

"Billy, where are you? Why is my car sitting there?"

"Just do me a favor and go get your car as soon as possible. I've hitched on west. You can do this, sweetheart. I can't explain everything right now. Is there someone who can help you go get it?"

"My sister can maybe get off work early."

"I'll call and check on you in a day or two."

"No! Don't call. At least for a while. My old man swears he's going to kill you if he ever finds out where you are."

"Leave that son-of-a-bitch, LuAnne."

"Don't say that, Billy."

"I've got to go. Will you be okay?"

"I can't talk anymore." LuAnne let out a sob and hung up.

Billy dropped the receiver back in the cradle and slumped against the wall. It wasn't that he loved her, or even planned to see her again. He just hated the thought of anyone laying a hand on LuAnne. If he'd had a little more time with her, he might have been able to see to it she left that good-for-nothing cowboy. That poor, sweet thing was probably feeling pretty alone and lost right now.

He took a deep breath and "Earl Bob" headed back to the table. "Everything okay in D.C.?" Buford asked.

"Tying up loose ends." Billy realized how tired he was. Right now, it didn't matter – not until he put a town or two more between him and Earl Bob's Colorado cronies. "Do you think we could wrap this up for now?"

As they stood, Buford pulled on his coat and started to pat his pockets. "Whoa! Wait just a minute there. We've got the first installment of your retainer – somewhere." Buford checked all of his pockets, at last spotting a folder whose contents had spilled on the floor. He stooped to collect the scattered papers and retrieved the checkbook with a wide smile. He handed Billy a check for $10,000.

It was all Billy could do to accept it calmly.

Buford was still smiling. "As agreed: Four more checks just like that one in the next four months, not including the bonus the city has offered at the end of the summer."

It didn't happen all at once, but as Buford spoke, each word brought Billy closer to the realization this could be The Big One. Instinctively, he pocketed the check as though he expected it.

"Why don't you go to the hotel, get some rest," Denton suggested. "Give yourself a chance to gather your bearings around here. We're having a little get-together tomorrow night at Buford's. Why don't my wife and I come by and pick you up at the hotel lobby? Would seven o'clock work for you?"

"Yeah, that's fine. So, where's the hotel?"

It was Buford who answered. "Straight up the street and north a little ways past the city limits. You'll see it."

"Okay, thanks. See you tomorrow."

Billy pushed the door open, went to the car, and started toward the Galactic Inn. On the way, he silently thanked Earl Bob for his good fortune.

§   §   §

Six hours later, Billy opened his eyes to an array of distant alien craft hovering above his bed. No, not distant, just tiny. The flotilla lay suspended amidst a universe full of gold and silver sparkling stars.

For a moment, he lay there staring above him. He turned his head to the side. The spacecraft continued down the wall in a display of stencils that stopped about a foot from the ceiling. The Galactic Inn, the best hotel in Silverville.

Staggering from the bed, he ran fingers through his hair and headed to the bathroom to splash cold water on his face. The drive to Silverville still hung like a heavy pall over his brain. He focused on the pseudo Jetsons' décor that filled the room. Saucer-like lamps hung near the bed, suspended on thin cords; eerie pictures of alien landscapes accented the walls, and floating ringed planets adorned the bed cover.

Billy, slow to shake the grogginess, flopped back down on the bed and tried to sort his thoughts. Okay. These local characters had mistaken him for the Pisser, who obviously had some kind of job to do for the city that involved UFOs. And they were willing to pay well for it.

Milk them for all they're worth. That's what Daddy would've done.

But would he have taken the risk of masquerading as a man he'd accidentally killed, a man ripening in a ravine less than a hundred miles away? Then Billy thought about the $10,000 check. Yes, Daddy might have.

As long as someone else was picking up the tab there was no point in being hasty. Maybe he'd just grab a sandwich for now and come back to rummage through Earl Bob's things.

Billy threw on his jacket and headed downstairs to the lobby. A friendly girl waved at him from behind the front desk, and he smiled back at her as he pushed through the front door. Turquoise and gold filled the western skyscape, offering last-minute rays that filtered across the parking lot. To the north, about a quarter of a mile, Billy could see the skeletal scaffolding of the theme park's rides and attractions, all surrounded by a newly constructed wooden fence. Even at this distance, he could make out the words on the garish park entrance: "ALIEN LANDING." In smaller letters below, he read, "They Have Arrived."

Shaking his head slowly, he hopped in the Caddy to look for a hamburger joint. He didn't have to drive far. The entire end of town was making ready for hordes of believers about to descend, offering at least four new-looking hotels and a variety of eateries with ridiculous names like "The Saucer Sub Shop," "Planetary Pizza," and "Hangar 18," which promised "out-of-this-world hamburgers." Most were still under construction, but "Hangar 18" looked like its doors were open.

He pulled through the drive-up.

"We don't have everything on the menu yet," a plucky young girl squeaked from the shiny new window.

"How about a burger and fries?" he asked.

"No fries, but I can get you a burger."

"Make it two."

After the waitress gave the cook his order, Billy asked her, "What do you think about this UFO park?"

"Got me a job."

"Do you know how long the project's been going on?"

She kept wiping the window counter and rolled her eyes. "Forever."

"No, really. How long?"

"Oh, I guess since last summer. Do you want onions with those burgers?"

"Sure. Who's behind it?"

"Behind what?"

"All this. The theme park, the museum, the new businesses, everything."

"I think the city's doing it, and some other people."

"So, it's all being done by locals?"

The girl rested her elbows on the window sill and began to twirl a strand of hair around her finger. "Mostly. And they're bringing in some guy from Washington, D.C."

"Yeah? What's that Washington guy going to do?"

"He knows all about aliens, or something. He's going to help with the museum, bring people in to talk, stuff like that."

"Ever heard of a guy named Earl Bob Jackson?"

"Nope. Am I supposed to?"

Billy grinned back at her and mimicked her casual tone. "Nope. Just wondering." She handed him the sack.

"That'll be $7.14." And she held out a hand.

"Are they really 'out-of-this-world'?'?"

She looked at him for a moment, then laughed. "Give me a break."

Toting his sack of burgers, Billy made his way back up the street to the Galactic Inn and parked the car. As he walked through the door, he expected to again wave at the friendly desk clerk, but he was instead startled to see the creepy waitress from that morning. She wasn't smiling, only staring back blankly – with one eye. The other was fixed on a newspaper spread over the desk before her.

Billy could feel the hair rise on the back of his neck. He couldn't shake the feeling she saw right through him, and decided it was time to put the old Noble charm to work.

"Hey, didn't I see you in the cafe this morning?"

With the same expressionless look, she nodded her head.

"Guess in a little town like this, it's hard to make a living," Billy commented.

The waitress-clerk said nothing.

"What's your name?" he asked.

"Fawn."

"Have you lived around here for very long?"

"Yes."

Before he could ask another question, Fawn terminated the conversation by directing both her eyes toward the newspaper. Billy stood around waiting for her to say more, but she didn't.

"Well, nice talking to you. Hope I see you around." He had a feeling he would.

Back in his room, Billy made himself comfortable on the bed and unwrapped the first burger while he leafed through the contents of the briefcase. The first thing that caught his eye was a day planner. He flipped it open and noticed the planner had notes dating back six months, from what looked to be the first phone call Earl Bob had with Buford, and ending with an entry just a week ago that read, "Give Judy back the answering machine." He set the planner aside for now and turned to a hefty stack of files squeezed into the briefcase.

The first one Billy pulled out was marked: "Mutilations." Inside, Earl Bob had gathered a collection of cases involving the unnatural deaths of dozens of animals. Most of the victims were cattle, by the looks of the photos, many left with macabre grins after their lips had been cut away. Some were missing genitals, and a whole series of photos showed a small herd of complete skeletons arranged across the ground.

Billy set his hamburger down.

Graphic case reports accompanied most of the photos, and Billy saw occasional comments, likely made by Earl Bob, scrawled in the margins such as "Prank," "Predators," and "Unexplained."

Other folders bore labels like "Civilian Sightings," "Encounters of the Fourth Kind," "Frontal Lobe Lability." Still others contained data about military involvement, implants, and famous hoaxes. Much of the documentation made for pretty dry reading, but once in a while a passage would catch his eye: "Case No. 68: Chupacabras. Puerto Rico. After a series of animal killings, in the mountain districts of Central Puerto Rico, there soon spread to the town of Canóvanas a creature inhabitants described as four feet tall with very powerful hind legs, spindly arms, and taloned claws. Its oval head encased red eyes, and quill-like appendages ran the length of its back. One local pharmaceutical night watchman reported three such creatures on the grounds . . ."

In another folder, he found himself unintentionally engrossed in a woman's account of an alien abduction that took place just several months previously: "I was led by the aliens past a human dressed in the uniform of a naval officer. They took me into a chamber where I was greeted by a child who looked part human and part alien. It pointed toward a glass cylinder with a woman inside, who I understood was held in suspension for future experiments. . . ." Entertaining, but not much help.

The slimmest file was marked "Classified" and didn't specify what kind of information was detailed inside. Billy skimmed headings with unenlightening descriptors like "JANAP 146(e)" and "C.E.R.V.I.S." These were filled with technical information and lists of names that meant nothing to Billy. He set the folder aside.

He stopped short when he saw a file of correspondence between Earl Bob and Buford. The first thing he noticed was a telephone log that contained entries from conversations made with Buford. Besides the log, Billy discovered a tentative list of scheduled speakers Earl Bob had evidently lined up for the summer. Earl Bob had already sketched out brief biographies of each, describing such claims to fame as "one of the Gulf Breeze Six" or "MUFON Field Investigator." What Billy couldn't tell, was if any of these people would be able to recognize Earl Bob on sight. But Billy did know he had his homework cut out for him if he was going to pull this off.

The second thing he noticed was a contract signed by both Buford and Earl Bob, spelling out the five installments of $10,000 each and a guaranteed bonus of no less than $20,000, depending on the gross sales of the theme park and museum receipts at the end of the year. In return, Earl Bob would act as consultant to the project, guide the museum in its UFO displays, schedule public lectures, arrange convocations by visiting experts, and generally provide credibility to the whole venture. The contract also included discretionary funds of an additional $30,000 to cover travel arrangements and fees for speakers.

This was exactly what he was looking for. Something to spell out for him the nature of his new "job." It was looking more and more like The Big One.

He carefully replaced everything in the briefcase and then remembered the second hamburger. Pulling it from the sack, he reached for Earl Bob's billfold. So far, Billy hadn't found a home phone number in any of the papers or the wallet. He stretched across the bed and snatched up the phone.

"Operator, could you give me the area code for Washington, D.C.?"

"One moment, please. . . The area code for Washington, D.C., is 202, sir."

"Thanks."

Gulping down the last of the second burger, he punched in the area code and the countrywide number for directory assistance. Evidently Earl Bob had kept a residence in D.C., since the operator on the other end gave him a phone number. He scrawled it on the pad by the phone. Might as well see who, if anybody, was waiting for Jackson at home in D.C.

He dialed the number, but after only three rings, an automated voice informed him the number "had been disconnected or was no longer in service." For the first time, he felt reasonably sure there would be no cavalry to come to Earl Bob's rescue – at least in the immediate future.

But one thing Billy hadn't yet taken the trouble to do was to look through Earl Bob's personal effects. It wasn't something he looked forward to doing. In a way, it made him feel like a grave robber. Business papers were one thing; toothpaste and underwear were altogether different.

He placed the garment bag on the bed and unzipped it. One by one, he peeled out a series of shirts, jackets and trousers. The side pockets held several pairs of shoes. Nothing he found told him anything more than that they didn't share the same taste in clothing. Or the same size.

Next, he turned to the oversized suitcase. Releasing the snaps, he flipped it open to an array of toiletries, socks, and boxer shorts. He lifted one bottle up to the light and read the label, chuckling. Old Earl Bob must have been older than he wanted to look, judging from the bottle of hair coloring he found. That's right. Buford had mentioned in the restaurant that morning he expected Earl Bob to be older. Billy clutched Earl Bob's wallet from his back pocket and looked again at the driver's license to find his date of birth. A quick calculation told him Earl Bob was closing in on fifty-four.

Going back to the suitcase, he rifled through miscellaneous articles until he found a lavender envelope simply addressed to "Earl Bob." He opened it and began to read a melodramatic narrative:

Dear Earl Bob,

As you have probably noticed, my answering machine is still at the apartment. I want it back along with everything else I was stupid enough to leave there. I'll never understand why you did this to me. I should've known better than to get involved with such a

selfish old fart like you. I hope your mysterious new job is as big a
flop as you are. NEVER EVER call me again!
--Judy

Well, it was short if it wasn't sweet. Guess Earl Bob was about as lucky with his women as he was with his pissing.

There was still one more little piece of paper jammed in the suitcase pocket. A yellowed newspaper clipping. Billy wondered if it would be as entertaining as Judy's fond farewell. He carefully opened its brittle fold and carried it closer to the lamp. The headline read, "Nashville youth suffers hit and run." The dateline was over twenty-five years ago. As faded as the print on the clipping was, he could still skim the story: "Today a Nashville youth is in critical condition at a local hospital after a near brush with death. Seventeen-year-old Denton Fine . . ."

Denton Fine! He read on.

"An unidentified driver struck young Mr. Fine near the courthouse, leaving the youth with a crushed pelvis and two broken legs. . . . He is a recent high school graduate who has frequently graced our pages with his many accomplishments as an amateur ice skater. . . . As of yet, the police have been unable to identify Mr. Fine's careless assailant, but no foul play is suspected."

Billy sank down on the bed with disbelief. Denton Fine. An ice skater? Could it be the same man? And what was Earl Bob doing carrying this tattered old clipping around for all these years? Maybe Earl Bob was a relative. No, of course not. Denton never indicated as much at the restaurant. The "careless assailant"? *What goes around, comes around.* Yet it seemed too much to be a coincidence; then again, the connection seemed too improbable to be anything else. Billy had to get to the bottom of this.

He couldn't afford to walk into something unexpected if he was going to be "Earl Bob." With the Pisser's documents, however, he might be able to play the game. Billy smiled to himself. He'd stay.

At least for a while.

CHAPTER THREE

Buford

Buford pulled a hand full of forks from his apron pocket and held them up to his wife.

"Skippy, I never can remember which fork goes where," he said. "Tell me again."

"Place the forks on the left side of the plate –"

"Yeah, yeah. That much I remember. What I don't know is which one of these goes where."

"Fish fork furthest left, then the meat and then the salad."

Buford looked thoughtfully at the individual pieces of flatware. "So is the salad fork the short one?"

"No. The fish fork." Skippy's voice trailed into the kitchen. Buford was grateful that her charm school etiquette seemed to overshadow the crude manners he usually brought to any social gathering.

"Tell you what," Buford bargained. "I'll pile the forks right here and you straighten them out."

For several minutes, each went about individual tasks without speaking, Buford attempting to set the table and Skippy keeping a watchful eye from the kitchen. She soon returned with a plate of hors d'oeuvres.

"I hope everyone likes tongue," she fretted as she carried the sliced meat on crackers out of Buford's reach. She arched one eyebrow and said, "Wait till everybody gets here."

As he dropped napkins on the plates, Buford silently rehearsed the points he wanted to make to Lela Schlopkohl. *As you can see, Lela, I've delivered everything I've promised the city. Revenue from new building, more jobs, more visibility for Silverville, and important people in government coming to support the project. Why we're even attracting people with money, like Chantale Getty-Schwartz.*

Buford extended a be-napkined hand to the imaginary Lela as if to say, "See, I'm delivering her money to you on a platter." He bowed deeply just as Skippy reentered the dining room.

"What are you doing?" she asked.

He laughed slyly as he straightened up, saying, "Just practicing. I want to make the right impression."

"Well, if you want to make the right impression, remember to take your apron off."

Her voice was unusually light as she reprimanded him. Buford couldn't recall seeing her this upbeat since the last party they threw. Skippy seemed always at her best at a formal gathering, and he watched as she glided gracefully into the hallway, stopping before a mirror to attach her earrings and check her hair. A mighty handsome woman, Skippy was. The years had been kind to her, considering her rocky past, leaving her face unlined and her auburn hair as dark and natural as the day they'd met. Her trim figure complemented the simple black dress she wore, but Skippy could make a pair of sweatpants look sexy. Buford admired her as much as any of his possessions. Perhaps even loved her some. He could always count on Skippy. From helping him choose the right suit to keeping his home office organized. Which reminded him …

"Have you seen a passbook laying around?"

"Which one? Buford, you've got to learn to pick up your toys. I can't keep track of everything you lose."

He scowled, feeling a twinge of alarm.

"It has a gray cover and if you see it, put it some place where I can find it."

"I don't remember ever seeing a gray passbook."

"Oh, it's just something for work," he lied.

The doorbell rang, and Skippy turned to greet her first guests. At the same time, Buford tossed the apron through the kitchen door and then dashed across the dining room to unlock the liquor cabinet. From the foyer, he heard her speak to the new arrivals. "Denton, Felicia, how nice to see you both. This must be Mr. Jackson."

"No, Earl Bob, please," Buford heard his hired consultant respond.

The voice from the hall struck him once again as very different from the phone conversations of the past six months. Maybe Buford was just feeling the pressure of the project bearing down upon him.

He *had* been overly critical the last week or so; he'd even caught himself snapping at Skippy. And after all, the man had driven up in a car with UFO license plates, and he had known where to meet him and Denton. He pushed the idea from his head and waltzed into the dining room all smiles.

"Welcome. Welcome. Let me take your wraps and Skippy, will you honor our guests with drinks?"

Just out of ear shot of Denton and Felicia, Buford overheard Skippy whisper to Earl Bob, "The price tag is still on the cuff of your blazer." She passed along the message deftly, hardly missing a beat. Buford detected an expression of gratitude flicker across Earl Bob's face as Skippy radiantly turned to say to the others, "Who would like something to drink?"

Seemed odd that Earl Bob would've bought a new jacket for this occasion. He should've already had a closet full of them from his job in Washington.

Skippy motioned for everyone to follow her into the living room. Earl Bob offered his arm to Felicia, and Denton shuffled along behind with Buford. Listening briefly to Earl Bob's polite questions about Felicia's involvement in the local theater, Buford entertained himself with his usual gouges about Denton's business.

"Did you plant your latest customer in the ground yet, Denton?"

Denton, not looking like he felt up to the regular banter, simply nodded and called out to Skippy, "Make mine a double. The usual."

"How about you, Earl Bob, what's your poison?" asked Skippy. She set out cocktail glasses for everyone except herself.

"He'll have a Salty Dog, my love," Buford offered. "That's what you told me on the phone that you drank, wasn't it, Earl Bob?"

He watched his guest closely for any signs of surprise.

"That'll be fine," Earl Bob replied. Buford couldn't tell for sure, but he thought he detected a slight hesitation. But then Earl Bob fixed his attention on Buford and gave him a thoroughly charming smile. "And I'm sure whatever drink your wife makes for me will be better than the tequila I had to put up with while chasing the Chupacabras in Puerto Rico."

Touché. Buford smiled to himself, wondering if he should

ignore his gut feeling. If this wasn't really Earl Bob, the guy played a damn good stand-in.

His mind groped for another trap to set. Buford blurted out, "By the way, Earl Bob, while you're in Silverville, it would look good for you to open up a checking account. Give us a chance to get back some of that high-dollar salary we're paying you." He moved over to his wife and slid an arm around her waist. "This is the little lady you'll need to talk to about that."

"That's a good idea. Guess I'll get to that sometime this week," Earl Bob replied with a thoughtful nod.

"In fact," Buford continued, "why don't you just leave your driver's license with her tonight, and by the time you stop at the bank tomorrow, she'll already have it set up for you."

Patting his back pocket with obvious dismay, Earl Bob frowned and said, "You know, I didn't think to bring it since Denton was driving tonight. You're the designated driver, aren't you, Denton?"

Denton raised his glass to toast him, but before he could speak, Skippy answered first. "Oh, I don't think that will be necessary, Earl Bob. This is a small town with a small-town bank. We all know who you are now. We only do that for people we're suspicious of."

The arm around her waist tensed as Buford added, "You're always so helpful, dear."

The second chime of the evening announced the arrival of Mayor Schlopkohl. Apparently only Buford heard the ring over the chatter of voices and the baroque chords of one of Mozart's Brandenburg concertos, something Skippy had chosen for the evening.

"Hello! Is anyone home?" a familiar woman's voice called through the front door.

Buford was already sprinting across the room to greet Lela. Immediately, he made an artificial fuss in the hallway about her gracing his home with her presence.

"Cut the crap, Buford," Lela retorted under her breath. She may have been short and squat, but she seemed to tower over Buford with her attitude. "I know you don't like me any better than

I like you. If it weren't for your lovely wife, I wouldn't for a minute consider coming here."

Buford wondered if she used the same blunt approach with her grandkids.

"Okay," Lela continued. "Let's meet this Washington hot shot."

Without further direction, Lela pushed past Buford and marched toward the sound of the voices. When he caught up with her, Skippy was already introducing the mayor to their "distinguished UFO specialist."

Clasping her extended hand in both of his, Earl Bob spoke with what sounded like obvious admiration, holding her attention with his mesmerizing green eyes. "This is such a pleasure. I've been waiting to meet you."

Buford stared with disbelief – the old girl was actually blushing! For once, Lela seemed speechless as she listened to Earl Bob. "I applaud you for having the courage to support such a bold project to bring prosperity to your town. You are truly a progressive woman."

A broad grin flooded her face as she stammered, "Why, thank you, Earl Bob, that's quite a compliment coming from someone like yourself. Buford told me you would be an asset to this project, and maybe for once he was right."

Earl Bob took her by the arm and guided her over to the couch. The leathery old snake was his total captive.

Denton sidled up to Buford and whispered, "Gee, he's good at this."

"Yeah, almost too good." For a moment, Buford heated up over Lela's quick surrender to Earl Bob's charm. For years, he had struggled to maintain even a speaking relationship with the old fish bait, she offering him nothing but caustic remarks each time he had tried to woo her. He recalled the day she had left him cooling his heels in her outer office for half a day. Another time, she had embarrassed him at a public meeting, telling him to "shut up and sit down" before a whole roomful of people.

"Buford, would you help me in the kitchen?" Skippy asked him as she passed by with the emptied hors d'oeuvres plate. He followed her to the kitchen, his head riveted to the cozy couple on the couch.

"Buford, where ever did you find this man?" Skippy remarked as she refilled the tray. "He is absolutely the most charming man I have ever met. Everybody in this town is going to fall in love with him."

Buford thought back to the halting conversations he'd had with Earl Bob on the phone. At the time, the man seemed like a near social misfit. He could recall having to pull answers to even simple questions from Earl Bob's reluctant lips. What really dumbfounded him was the instant rapport Earl Bob had established with Lela. When he left them on the couch, she was talking about the expected revenues from the theme park like she had supported the project from the very start. Earl Bob had her eating out of the palm of his hand.

Buford was still puzzling over the evening's turn of events when he heard the doorbell ring once again. "That should be the last of our guests," he told Skippy and walked to the hallway.

He wasn't quite prepared for the sight waiting for him at the front door. Chantale Getty-Schwartz stood before him in all her decadent splendor, her teased maroon hair falling over a white fur coat, hardly obscuring Buford's view of a neckline that plummeted to her belt. She was decked out in extravagant diamond jewelry, skin-tight designer jeans, and ostrich cowboy boots.

It wasn't a pretty sight.

Beside her stood a pale man. Four-inch fringe dangled from his buckskin jacket; silver conchos descended in a "Y" at the shoulder yokes, leading Buford's eyes to the five-pound turquoise belt buckle that clung to his black leather breeches. A string of raven feathers hung from the side of a red head band, the rest of his white hair gathered severely at the back of his head. He, too, wore ostrich cowboy boots. Despite the spectacle, what Buford noticed most were the bandages that covered the eyes of Chantale's escort. The man had tried to hide them with dark glasses, but the bandages overlapped the top of his shades, only half sticking to pink and blue flesh that swelled like a party balloon. Grady must've got him good.

"You must be Chantale," Buford said, staring at her breasts. It was a wonder they didn't fall right out of that skimpy little blouse. He had a feeling the stories he had heard about her might do her justice. "It's nice to finally meet you in person."

"And you must be Buford Prize," she responded, every line in her face accentuated by caked make-up.

"Price," he corrected. "Yes. Well, let's not just stand here in the door way. Come on in. It's always a pleasure to welcome another supporter to our project."

Chantale guided her blinded companion as she shimmied into the hallway, stopping to appraise the Price home. "What a cute little house you have here. I bet it was one of those squatter cabins from a long time ago. Was it difficult to remodel?"

"Why, no," Buford answered, somewhat taken back by the comment. "Skippy and I had it built ten years ago." It was a two-story Cape Cod he and Skippy had been immensely proud of, and it was a fluke that they even had it at all. Back before Buford had jumped into the ski resort venture, his land wheeling and dealing had taken yet another turn for the worse. He and Skippy had purchased a good-sized chunk of property for future development, but before anyone had the chance to build on it, word got out the ground was slowly moving.

"This land is unstable," an engineer had announced. "It's sitting on slumping ground, and only damn idiots would buy it or build on it." Unless they didn't mind their houses moving half an inch downhill each year.

By the time the whole escapade was over, Buford and Skippy were on the verge of bankruptcy – and right on the eve of building their new home. Thankfully, Skippy's maiden aunt had had the decency to die at about the same time, leaving the Prices with enough ready cash to recover from the land fiasco and still make the down payment on the house. Skippy had been ecstatic. Buford, relieved. They both considered it their "dream house."

Buford waved a careless hand in the air and lied, "Actually, I wanted to build something a little more elaborate, but Skippy just wouldn't hear of it. She insisted we live like other folks in this town."

"How sweet," Chantale drawled. "Oh, this is my protégé, Hans

High Horse. We had a little mishap two days ago, and he's temporarily handicapped, aren't you, Hans?"

"The Great Spirit gives us other ways to see than just eyes," Hans offered as his sightless head searched the room. He then strode forward and crashed into Skippy's antique China hutch, sending several saucers careening to the floor.

"You two come on in where the others are," Buford said, stepping over the broken porcelain. He escorted them to the living room. "Let me introduce you to everybody."

"Look everybody. Look who's here," Buford announced. "This is Chantale Getty-Schwartz and her progeny, Hans High Horse."

Skippy, always the gracious hostess, immediately stepped forward, making introductions for them all. After Denton's greeting, Buford noticed his old friend shooting him a questioning look. Denton made his way over to the host's position on the other side of the room.

"Aren't these the people who attacked Grady?" Denton asked in a lowered voice.

"Yep, they are." Buford waited for the next question.

"Why are they here?"

"Fifty-thousand dollars is why. That's how much I got in the mail today from her for the project. Would you have left her off the guest list?"

"No. Guess not."

Buford surveyed his guests with satisfaction. Except for the out-of-town investors, many of the key players to the project were standing in his living room. He watched as Earl Bob worked first Lela and, increasingly, Chantale, separating them from the herd with the same finesse as a fine cutting horse. Each woman responded even better than Buford could have hoped. Throughout the happy hour, he saw Earl Bob's gaze fall thoughtfully in the direction where he and Denton were standing. Occasionally, Earl Bob would venture a few steps toward them, but before he could make it over to their side of the room, one of the women would always corral him and bring him back to the herd.

"Did you know Earl Bob was such a ladies' man?" Denton

asked Buford with amusement.

"No, I did not. It's not the sort of thing that would've come up in our conversations."

"Frosting on the cake, isn't it?"

"Appears so," Buford replied, mulling it over in his head. As he finished speaking he overheard Skippy's conversation with Chantale and Hans High Horse.

"But why a pyramid?" Skippy asked her gaudy guest.

"Why, a pyramid draws all the positive energy from the universe and focuses the beams down on whoever is inside," Chantale explained.

Skippy politely nodded as though she understood, but Buford knew she didn't have a clue about the garbage Chantale was feeding her.

Chantale continued, "There's some other good stuff about pyramids, but I always forget what they are. You tell her, Hans."

Chantale clutched her companion at the shoulders and turned him toward Skippy, saying, "Hans, why are we building a pyramid house?"

"It is destined," he replied. "After all, only old souls can live comfortably in a pyramid and draw the warmth of the cosmos to them. Chantale and I are among the ancient ones."

Even after this declaration, Skippy still looked as though she understood this great white bullshitter. Buford continued to listen, amused.

"Yes," Hans went on. "Chantale was once a great queen of the Nile."

"I was Nefritis," Chantale interrupted. "I didn't even know that until Hans told me!"

"Nefertiti," Hans gently chided her. "I, of course, was her devoted high priest. And it was meant that we should be rejoined in a dwelling befitting our former status."

Fifteen minutes followed while Hans related his former and present lives, including a rather vague description of the obscure tribe of Mexican albino Indians he hailed from. Naturally, he was the last of his kind and the sole bearer of the legacy of his people, the Juanabees.

For once, Skippy seemed at a loss for words. Buford knew she was groping for the appropriate response.

"The two of you sound so . . . so spiritual," Skippy stammered. "Certainly, you belong together."

And in a padded cell, Buford thought.

When the hors d'oeuvres were gone and the guests warm with cocktails, Skippy announced it was time for dinner. She ushered everyone into the dining room and placed them as formal etiquette dictated: Earl Bob to her right at one end of the table, and Lela to Buford's right at the other end. The others she alternated male-female on the table sides. After everyone was arranged, Buford poured the wine and Skippy brought out the salads.

"Buford, would you say grace?" Skippy suggested to Buford's surprise, since an invocation was not in their normal routine, even for dinner parties. *Really putting on the dog, aren't we, Skippy? Well, it's your show.*

As Buford searched for appropriate words, Chantale, to his relief, raised a waving hand. "I know. I know. Why not have Hans say the blessing? After all, he is a holy man."

All eyes turned to Hans. He stood, trailing his waist-long ponytail through the butter dish, took a deep breath, outstretched his arms, and began. "Oh Wapa Wapa, oh Great One, look down upon these who hunger not only for sustenance, but also for your guidance. Grant that we below always walk on clear trails, feel the wind at our backs, change the things we can, accept the things we cannot, find the wisdom to know the difference, and . . . ," he paused to take another deep breath.

"Oh that was so wonderful! Hans has such original thoughts!" Chantale clasped her hands together with unabashed admiration. Hans, his face betraying as much confusion at the interruption as his bandages would allow, simply sat back down.

Buford took the opportunity to jump up from his chair, raised his wine glass, and blurted out, "Let's make a toast. To Lela for her undying support, to Chantale for her generous contribution, to Skippy for this fine meal, and to Earl Bob, for the many talents he brings to the project. May our endeavor bring pride to our community and money to our pockets."

Everyone chimed in with a multiple "Here, here!"

Skippy

"Skippy, what are you doing?" Felicia shouted. "Put that bottle down!"

Reluctantly, Skippy pulled the half-empty wine decanter from her lips and set it on the counter. It had been ten years since her last drink, and she still missed it.

"You're right, Felicia. I don't know what I was thinking."

Everyone had left the party in high spirits, and only Denton and Felicia had remained to help clean up. Felicia marched over and grabbed the bottle from her hand and poured the contents into the sink.

"You've done so well," Felicia continued. "Don't blow it now. You've been going to your AA meetings, right?"

Skippy groaned. "Twice a week."

"Do you have any more liquor in the house?"

"No."

Felicia looked unconvinced. "Are you telling me the truth?"

"Okay, okay, Buford locked the rest up in the cabinet."

Buford, always afraid she'd go back to her old ways, only brought liquor home for special occasions, but he made sure she couldn't get to it. Most of the time, Skippy handled her problem well, yet it seemed to get harder the older she got. She figured by the time she was thirty-eight, she'd have everything – a happy home, a loving husband, and a houseful of children. But she had none of these.

Felicia placed her hand on Skippy's shoulder. "Do we need to talk about something? I haven't seen you touch a bottle in years."

"I can barely do this anymore."

"You mean …"

"You know what I'm talking about. Living like this, pretending I'm the perfect wife, supporting Buford all the time."

"You seemed to enjoy yourself tonight."

"I did. But after everyone leaves, I'm left alone to face Buford."

"But you always seem let down after a party."

Skippy dropped her head over the sink and started to sob. How could Felicia have even said something so flippant? She knew better. She knew how unhappy Skippy was.

"Look," Felicia added, "I know this has been hard for you. I'm not sure I could live with Buford, either. I've said this before: Talk to an attorney and find out what your options are."

"I don't have any options." Or none she could share with her friend.

Truth was, she had thought a lot about leaving Buford. The first time was only a couple of years after they married, when her drinking started to escalate. But she'd been weak, and he kept supplying her with alcohol as a bribe to stay with him. By the time she'd entered rehab a few years later, she again tried to leave him. Her counselor suggested that she concentrate on the drinking problem first and then decide what more she wanted to change about her life. At Buford's reluctance, they started marriage counseling, which seemed to help at first. They even tried to have a child. When that didn't work, Skippy proposed they adopt, and of course, Buford would have no part of it, maybe because memories of his own childhood still haunted him. *An adopted kid can never live up to parents' expectations*, he'd said with hostility. Bitterly disappointed, she started making plans to escape. But then she'd done something she never thought she was capable of. When Buford learned about it, he'd held it over her so leaving was impossible.

She rinsed off the plates and glasses in the sink, handing them one by one to Felicia, who stacked them in the dishwasher.

"Those men should be in here helping us," Felicia muttered. "At home, Denton always helps me."

"Leave them alone. I'd just as soon keep Buford out of –" she wanted to say *my life*, but instead finished by adding – "the kitchen."

The two women untied their aprons, poured themselves some coffee, and sat down at the table.

"Are you going to be alright?"

"Yeah. I'll find a solution."

Perhaps she'd already found one, even if it was a plan she wasn't very proud of. She didn't consider herself to be dishonest, just desperate.

Felicia picked up a napkin and handed it to her. "Here, fix your make-up. Denton and I need to go home pretty soon."

Buford

"I think the evening went really well," Denton remarked to Buford as the two drew on long, twisted cigars.

Buford settled into a comfortable chair and rolled his stogie thoughtfully between his thumb and middle finger. "I believe it did. Lela has changed her tune and Chantale Getty-Schwartz is going to continue her backing." He didn't want to be the first to bring it up – how the evening turned in a more favorable direction than he had hoped. Surely Denton noticed the manipulative game going on.

But Denton didn't get into it. He said instead, "Yes, Chantale. She sure had a different version about her confrontation with Grady than you'd heard."

Buford burst out laughing and mimicked Chantale's words, "'*Graden* had murder in his eyes! He's a true bigot! His spiritual balance is in need of healing!' What a crackpot. I swear, Denton, when I first opened that door tonight, I thought I was face to face with a refugee from a millionaire's Salvation Army. Either that or a hooker from the Waldorf."

"And what would a hooker from the Waldorf look like?" Denton asked.

"I don't know, but I've always wanted to find out."

Denton looked toward the kitchen and asked whether or not they might help Skippy and Felicia clean up.

"Hell, no. Skippy would cut my head off if I tried to move in on her territory. She has her jobs and I have mine."

Buford sat in a reflective stupor for a few moments as he swirled the heavy, aromatic smoke around in his mouth. He chortled and said out loud to himself as much as to his friend, "That Hans High Horse is sure a piece of work. Do you think he's bedding Chantale?"

"Don't know. Guess it's none of our business. But if he is, it would be interesting to hear what they talk about in the dark. Do you suppose Skippy was offended that they wouldn't eat most of her food tonight?"

"Hell. Who would've known those two were vegetarians? Why would they have all those damn buffalo out there if they don't eat meat?"

"Didn't you hear Hans say the white one is his 'brother'?" Denton hooked his fingers like quote marks.

"Maybe they're related. They're both big, white, and ugly." Buford reached forward and slapped Denton's knee. "Anyway, tonight if they went home hungry, it was their own damn fault. Yeah, I bet Skippy was a little upset. She really prides herself on her cooking."

"Good thing she didn't serve up a cute little rabbit or –"

"A prairie dog!"

Denton joined him in a hearty laugh. Earlier that evening, Buford had had trouble keeping a straight face when Chantale related the story about *Mr. Graden's* heartless cruelty to the local rodent population. Evidently, old Grady had been trying to rid himself of the vermin that had taken over several acres of one pasture. Chantale had caught him out there shooting the heads off the critters as they peeked out of their holes. She probably thought they were some kind of real dog. *Those poor defenseless animals! Who could kill anything with such a darling face? It was a senseless act of barbarity*, she had told everyone at dinner. Grady had turned to her in the pasture and spat out, "Git!" (*Why, he talked to me like I was one of his starving dogs!*) Buford would sure like to be there when Grady got the news she was turning him in to the Humane Society.

What really surprised him was Lela's about-face to the project. She had ridiculed the idea from the start, pointing out a UFO theme park would make them a laughing stock all across the Western Slope of Colorado. Buford had tried for the past year to soften her, to talk her into encouraging the entire business community to get involved. Of course, some of the business leaders had already endorsed the project, but without Lela's conviction, others were slow to jump on the bandwagon.

Now, after one short evening with Earl Bob, Lela was gushing with enthusiasm. He couldn't decide whether it pissed him off or made him feel grateful.

"Denton, let me ask you a question. Do you think Earl Bob had anything to do with Lela's change of heart and Chantale's promise of more money?"

"Of course, I do. You saw for yourself how smooth he was with both of them. You did good. That guy is a real professional."

But professional what? It's true, Earl Bob had managed to field all questions everyone had asked him during dinner. He had impressed them with anecdotes of close encounters and crashed saucers, only occasionally denying the group information on the grounds it was "classified." He seemed to know all about the theme park plans and where they were going; he could quote part of his and Buford's previous conversations, almost as if he had them memorized. The words were right, but the voice and personality were not. And why was he quizzing Denton so thoroughly about his life before Silverville?

"He sure was interested in your past," Buford remarked casually.

"It's not that uncommon. Lots of people want to know what makes a person get into something like the funeral business."

"Yeah, I guess. Why didn't you tell him about your ice-skating days?"

"Didn't want to bore him, or anyone else, for that matter."

Buford paused, taking another drag on his cigar. "That reminds me. When are you having surgery? Hope you didn't plan it during the opening celebrations."

"It's going to have to wait for a while. Don't worry. I'll be around for the summer."

A few minutes later, Skippy and Felicia entered the room, their kitchen chores done.

"Whew, it's smoky in here," Felicia remarked. "Are you two boys about done bonding?"

"Just about," Denton answered. "That was a fine meal, Skippy. You really outdid yourself. Those new folks didn't know what they were missing."

"Oh, I know," Skippy replied. "Wasn't that too bad? I wish I'd had some idea that they wouldn't eat meat. Anyway, it was a nice evening, wasn't it?"

"Yes," Felicia said, with a questioning glance at Skippy, but then added, "We had wonderful food, interesting conversation, and charming company. I was telling Skippy in the kitchen that Earl Bob was the perfect choice for this job. Buford, I commend you."

Buford grunted a thanks.

"What a fascinating background he's had," she continued. "The hair just stood up on my neck while he was telling us those stories about those monsters in Puerto Rico."

Skippy jumped in, "And I thought he was quite intelligent, didn't you? I suspect he would have to be to have worked on such important projects for the government. I could've blushed when he told me that he had never had a more elegant evening, even in D.C."

"What a gentleman!" Felicia exclaimed. "I don't think I sat down or got up once tonight without that man holding the chair for me. I'm surprised he's not married with those looks and manners."

Denton smiled back fondly at his wife and said, "It's time to go home, Mother. Buford, what did you do with our coats?"

Buford pushed himself up from his chair. He was suddenly tired from the tension of the evening. Now, he just wanted to get rid of everybody and turn in. He helped Skippy see the Fines to the door and bade them goodnight, hardly aware of when they actually left.

Skippy turned her back on Buford and walked toward the stairs.

"I'll be up in a minute," he said absently. He sauntered back to the living room, making sure all the cigars were put out and the lights turned off. Standing in the middle of the dark room, Buford recalled that he'd never had the chance to talk with Earl Bob one-on-one, except, of course, on the phone. Maybe he would sit in on Earl Bob's interview with Howard on Friday to see how this stranger handled the meeting.

But it didn't really matter. Buford already knew what he had to do.

CHAPTER FOUR

Billy

"Of course, these panels aren't finished."

Billy listened to Mrs. Watson explain. Before him and Skippy stood a connected series of displays that reminded him of a stretched glass accordion propped on wooden legs. Some of the sections already held copies of documents that described the history of ufology. To Billy, most were not terribly convincing, depicting crude renderings of witness descriptions scrawled by amateur hands. An occasional newspaper clipping accompanied the drawings; overly enlarged photos turned alleged UFOs into blurs of light. There didn't seem to be an order in which Mrs. Watson had placed the "evidence," and it looked as though she had simply dropped the documents in the showcase as they came in.

As Mrs. Watson droned on to her two captives, Skippy whispered to Billy, "She's really gotten into this." Skippy shot him a subtle smile, apparently amused at the zealous curator. Mrs. Watson didn't appear to notice when they lagged behind.

"I think this must be the monologue she intends to offer visitors to the museum," Skippy confided to Billy.

The old woman shuffled into the next room and continued talking.

"S'pose we should keep up with her?" Billy asked.

Skippy laughed. "I don't think she'll notice."

Billy found her laughter disarming. For two days now, she had taken him under wing, introduced him to her town. There was nothing coy about Skippy's personality. It was an opportunity Billy had rarely encountered – the opportunity to make a friend – but the vulnerability made him a little uncomfortable.

Everyone he had met greeted him with warm words of welcome. Since he had arrived, Billy had met dozens of townspeople, many who had invited him to dinner and some who had offered a home to stay in. One woman even hinted that she would be glad to introduce him to "a nice girl." Billy politely declined that offer. True, the people in this town were nice enough. Sickeningly sweet, was more like it, and it was getting a little claustrophobic.

Catching Mrs. Watson was easy – she was still pointing out the highlights of the museum's exhibits. They trailed her into a darkened room that featured well-lit paintings on opposite walls, one spacecraft and the other a terrified man. The whole effect was intended to give museum visitors the feeling they were caught in the middle of Howard's infamous sighting from almost two years ago. Mrs. Watson pushed a button on the wall that started the sound track of what must have been an old B-grade science fiction movie. She slowly turned to face them with heightened drama, and began to speak.

"Just imagine the fear poor Howard Beacon, a respected Silverville citizen, must have felt when the alien craft swooped down before his bicycle and blocked his path. How long he stood there in awe, no one will know. Not even Howard. He completely lost any track of time or of any events that may have taken place between him and the unearthly visitors."

Billy nudged Skippy and asked softly, "Was he abducted?"

"I don't know. I haven't heard this part of the story before. Let me know after you talk to Howard."

Mrs. Watson continued, pointing her finger at the little heads in the craft's portholes, "Witness the hideous faces Howard might have seen that fateful night. And no one knows for sure when they will return."

Apparently finished with her speech, the museum curator interrupted the background music by again pushing the button, and she moved on to the next room.

"This is the screening room where we keep a collection of UFO documentaries," Mrs. Watson explained with a sweep of her hand toward a shelf of videos. "If you wish, you can select a title and view it here."

"Another time, Mrs. Watson," Billy suggested. "For now, I think I'll just take a look at what you've got." He and Skippy walked over to the shelf and began browsing. Among the "documentaries" their guide had to offer were *The Day the Earth*

Stood Still and *Earth vs. The Flying Saucers.*

All at once, the eerie music from the previous room began to blare, and Mrs. Watson bustled away in that direction.

"Technical difficulties?" Billy asked Skippy.

"Evidently. There must be a few bugs to work out." They turned over a few more video titles before Skippy questioned, "These aren't exactly 'documentaries,' are they?"

Billy held up a video box in front of Skippy. "Seems to me I saw this one at the Saturday matinee about twenty-five years ago. Do you suppose she serves popcorn in here, too?"

"Shhh. Here she comes."

Mrs. Watson motioned them to follow her into the souvenir shop, the last stop on the tour. Inside, boxes of rocks from the "Silverville Landing Site" – $3.50 each – rocket pencils, alien-head refrigerator magnets, and other curios all waited to be purchased by future museum customers. The old woman dawdled over each item, detailing more information than Billy cared to hear about, her cataracted eyes glistening with enthusiasm.

"You're doing a fine job, Mrs. Watson," Skippy assured her. "Earl Bob, what else do you think we should add to these displays?"

Billy pretended to mull over the museum's inventory of wonders. "Give me a few days to go through the files I brought. Just off hand, I think we might reorganize the entrance to focus more on Howard's experience. That way we'll hook the visitors right off the bat, catch their imagination before we start telling them the history of UFOs." At least this was one game Billy really knew – how to sucker people in. "I'll draft out some suggestions, if you think it might help."

"We're counting on your suggestions!" Skippy exclaimed. "Mrs. Watson, we appreciate you taking the time and trouble to give us such a wonderful guided tour. Perhaps Earl Bob will want to get with you early next week to rethink how we present some of this material."

The smile faded from Mrs. Watson's face as though she could hardly fathom the need for any improvements, an expression of disappointment Skippy no doubt recognized.

"Of course, we'll need your guidance in making changes,"

Skippy quickly added. "Earl Bob will be depending on you to see that everything is done properly."

Billy noticed a change of attitude on the old girl's face that might as well have said, "Okay, you young pups, let's not forget who was here first."

Twenty minutes later, Skippy and Billy joked over lunch about the last scene with Mrs. Watson.

"I can see you know just how to handle your curator," Billy complimented her.

"Your curator."

They both laughed.

"Earl Bob, I'm sure she'll warm up to you like everybody else in this town. It might just take a little longer. You are, after all, moving in on her territory. Keep in mind, Mrs. Watson is a volunteer who has already put quite a few hours into the museum. She takes it pretty seriously."

"I noticed."

"She lives alone, and it's all she has. I suspect it's given her a new lease on life."

"We'll get along just fine," Billy promised.

"So, tell me, besides the 'documentaries,' what did you really think of the museum?"

What do I really think? Really? He lied, "I think it shows a fair amount of research and a lot of involvement from the community."

"No, please, tell me what you think."

"Well, the souvenirs are pretty tacky and the first-grade drawings of saucer men need to go."

His remark didn't seem to offend her at all. Instead, she agreed, teasing, "And the Star Trek mobiles, they definitely should stay, shouldn't they?"

"Yes. Those and the alien ashtrays," Billy countered. "Where did you find some of that stuff?"

"Hey, don't you go ridiculing Mrs. Watson's hard detective work. You'd be surprised what you can order off the Internet. The ashtrays, on the other hand, are one-of-a-kind. Local craftspeople."

The conversation lagged as they finished their lunch. The pause gave him the courage to ask a question that had been plaguing him these past days. Now might be the right time to ask her about Denton Fine.

"You and Buford are pretty good friends with the Fines, aren't you?"

"We've known them for years. In fact, Denton is probably Buford's closest friend. Why do you ask?"

"Just wondering. I noticed Denton's got a pretty bad limp. Was he injured, or what?"

"Gosh, he's had that since he was a kid. I don't even notice it any more. Felicia told me he plans on having that hip replaced, but they're scratching for the money to pay for it. Guess their insurance refuses to cover an old injury."

"How'd it happen?" Billy asked as nonchalantly as he could muster.

"An accident. While Denton was in high school, he and Felicia were ice-skating partners, and I think they were pretty good. I know the two used to compete all over the country, and at one point, they were Olympic hopefuls."

"Did he take a spill on the ice?"

"No, it was more tragic than that. Denton was about seventeen when some careless driver ran him down at a crosswalk."

Even though Billy half expected some such version of the incident, the story still caught him off guard. Skippy must have misinterpreted his reaction as sympathy, because she started to share her own concern.

"Oh, I know. It's really a shame. It changed Denton's life."

"This didn't happen in Silverville, did it?"

"No. As a matter of fact, it was down south, in Tennessee."

"Nashville?" he blurted out.

"Why, yes, how did you guess?"

"It's the first town that came to mind." Before she could ask him any more questions, Billy continued, "Did they ever catch the guy?"

"No, it was a hit-and-run. Denton wound up in the hospital for three months with a crushed pelvis and the man who hit him was never found. It completely ruined Denton's skating career, and Felicia could have gone on to compete without him, but they were sweethearts, too. She stuck by him all the way. She's such a dear person."

Skippy stole a glance at her watch. "I've got to be going. Let me buy your lunch, Earl Bob."

"Certainly not. The most I will allow you to do is leave Fawn the tip."

"This has been fun, hasn't it?" she asked. "And the first time I get another day off from work, we'll do it again."

"Yes." Billy winked. "I'm glad you asked me on a date when I stopped at the bank. Do you suppose Buford will be jealous or people will talk?"

Skippy laughed. "I hope so!"

They parted company at the door and Skippy drove off in her BMW. Billy dropped two quarters in the newspaper vending machine, tucked the paper under his arm, and started off at a brisk walk back toward the Galactic Inn. The question of Denton's accident still lingered in his mind.

The driver was never caught.

It just didn't add up. Did Earl Bob know he would find Denton in Silverville? Nothing in Earl Bob's papers indicated that. Denton Fine's name never came up in the correspondence log with Buford nor was Denton's name mentioned in the planner.

Maybe, just maybe, it was pure coincidence. If it was, Earl Bob could have traveled to Silverville and unknowingly come face to face with his victim of thirty years before.

It would've been something to see.

§   §   §

Howard. The poor schmuck. His trembling hands sent such ripples through the coffee in his mug that Billy thought he would drop it.

"Just relax, Howard. I'm a nice a fellow. I won't bite you." Billy flashed his best reassuring smile across the kitchen table. "Start at the top and tell me what happened."

"I still think we should wait till Mr. Price gets here," Howard said timidly.

"He's heard it all before, hasn't he?"

Howard nodded and gazed out the window above a sink filled with dirty dishes. He rarely looked Billy square in the face, his behavior like that of a guilty man. But Billy suspected the guy didn't know how to lie.

Right over that hill, Mr. Jackson. That's where I first saw those lights."

"Okay, back up a little. First tell me what night this was and what you were doing out on the road."

Howard winced and took a deep breath. "It was the winter before last. And it was late at night."

While Billy scribbled notes as though he were really investigating, Howard leaped from his chair and retrieved a clipping of a story from a UFO magazine.

"Look here, Mr. Jackson. This article says alien visitors have underground towns right here in Colorado."

Billy had already been in Howard's two-room cabin for twenty minutes, trying to get the account everyone thought he should hear. But Howard couldn't seem to focus for long on a single question Billy asked. So far, Billy had heard about Howard's magazines, his new bicycle pump, and the new puppies down the street from the funeral home.

He listened patiently and then tried again. "Back to your experience, Howard. Where had you been when you saw the lights in the woods?"

"I was coming home from helping Mr. Fine. It was late, maybe after midnight. It was cold, but there wasn't much snow on the ground."

"Is that when the craft swooped down in front of you?"

Howard paused and looked confused. "Why no. That never happened. I saw lights, red ones, through the trees. I pulled my bicycle over to get off and see what was going on. I thought maybe there was a fire or something."

Maybe Howard had had a few too many drinks that night. "Did you stop anywhere for a beer after you left work?"

"No, sir! I know what you're thinking, but I don't do that, Mr. Jackson. I don't smoke, I don't drink, I don't do nothing," Howard stammered in slow and deliberate words. In his face was the desperate need to be believed.

Jesus, somebody should do something for this guy. Maybe he needed a shrink, maybe he needed to get out more. He sure as hell needed some friends, but Billy wasn't going to be one of them. *You can't help the hopeless,* his daddy would have said. But what would Daddy have thought of him sitting here in the woods talking seriously to a crackpot about aliens and flying saucers?

While Howard took off on another tangent, this time about the broken window in the back room, Buford walked in the front door without even knocking and ambled over to the table. "How's it going, Earl Bob. You getting the scoop?"

"Yeah, we're doing fine. Just taking a break 'til you got here."

"Howard, did you tell him yet about those little aliens you saw?" Buford asked.

Howard looked up, uncomfortable, as though he had tried to convince Buford before. "I didn't see any aliens, Mr. Price. Just the light and the flying saucer in the woods."

"You would have, Howard my boy, if it hadn't been so damn dark."

Billy sighed and said to Buford, "Let him tell his own story." He turned back to Howard, looked directly into his face, and said as clearly and distinctly as he could, "Let's go over this again. You left work; it was late; you saw the lights. Then what?"

"Then I walked up the hill toward the lights. Like I said, I thought it was a fire. I came to a clearing a little ways from the road, and that's when I saw it."

"What did you see?" Billy asked.

"The flying saucer. It was big, and it looked like a giant triangle."

Buford started to interrupt, but Billy raised a hand to silence him. Howard seemed on a roll and Billy didn't want anything to stop him.

"The lights were so bright it hurt my eyes. I stood and watched it for a few minutes. It was just floating there, above the ground, making this humming sound."

"The rays paralyzed him," Buford suggested.

"Couldn't you move?" Billy asked, trying to ignore the remark. He'd had just about enough of Buford's interruptions.

"No, that's not it. I just didn't want to move," Howard continued. "I stayed until it starting floating up. Then just like that –" Howard snapped his fingers "– the saucer was gone. It was beautiful — it was a miracle, the lights, the humming. And they wanted me to see them. They wanted me there."

"How many of them were there?" Buford broke in again.

"I told you, I didn't see anybody."

"How do you know they didn't abduct you when you passed out?" Buford insisted.

"I didn't pass out."

Billy tried to redirect the questioning. "Howard, if you didn't see anybody, how do you know they wanted you there?"

"Do you believe in 'meaningful coincidence'?"

Like shit happens? "I'm not sure I understand you."

"I've got a book that talks about it." Howard jumped up again and headed for the bedroom.

As soon as he was out of the room, Buford started to laugh. "He doesn't know what he's talking about. Poor Howard wouldn't know a ripe tomato from a pimple on his ass."

Billy snapped at him. "Since you seem to know so much about this story, why I am talking to Howard?"

Without skipping a beat, Buford fired back, "Because you're the UFO specialist." He paused, narrowed his eyes, and added, "Aren't you?"

Billy glared back at him, biting his tongue. *Not cool, Billy. Don't blow this.* "I can't do my job if you're going to interfere."

Buford stared right back, not flinching. "Seems to me the only job you've had so far is charming the socks off everybody around here."

If Buford was baiting him, Billy had to be careful.

"Look, if you're mad because I took Skippy to lunch, just say so."

Buford leaned back in his chair and laughed maliciously. "This isn't about lunch and you know it."

Howard returned, flipping through the pages of the book he

carried in his hands. "I don't understand too much, but this book explains it. 'Meaningful coincidence.'" He repeated the words as if they were a magic phrase. "I can't find the page that talks about it."

Billy struggled to pick up where he had left off with Howard. "Just tell me in your own words."

"Well, the flying saucer didn't have to be there the night I was riding my bike home, and I didn't have to be coming home the night the flying saucer was there. But it was and I was. It was meant to be and everything changed."

"I think that's pretty goddamned obvious," Buford said.

Billy asked Howard, "How did things change?"

Howard leaned forward and clasped his hands to his chest. "I was chosen, Mr. Jackson. I was picked to give the world a message."

"Yeah, tell him the message," Buford said.

Howard dropped his head and said softly, "I can't remember."

Billy sat back in the chair, stroked his chin, and gazed across the table at his interviewee. Almost before Howard's final words, Buford slapped his knee and laughed like he had heard the punch line of his favorite joke.

The ringing phone startled Billy out of his reverie. Howard got up and answered it.

"Hello . . . Yes, I can . . . Okay . . . Be right there."

Howard headed toward the door and then stopped and said to the two men seated at the table, "You two can stay here and visit if you want to, but I have to go to work. Mr. Fine needs help."

"Who died?" Buford asked.

"Don't know."

As Howard closed the door, Billy stood and said to the man across from him, "Look, it seems we have some things to talk over, but this isn't the time or the place."

"Don't be in such a hurry." Buford settled back in the chair and rocked it off the front legs. His voice was steady now, composed. And somehow more confident. "I think this is the time and the place."

His next words silenced Billy, making him sink back into his own chair.

"Sit down, Earl Bob – or whatever your real name is. You're not going anywhere."

CHAPTER FIVE

Grady

Grady stepped out of the pickup, reaching behind to pat the Copenhagen in his back pocket. If there was one thing he hated, it was coming to town without his chew. He paused in front of Price's Gun Paradise and stuffed a pinch between his lip and gum, letting the spearmint flavor ooze between his teeth.

"Mornin', Grady," he heard over his shoulder.

"Mornin', Carl." He didn't have to turn around to reply.

"You cooled off yet over that spat with your neighbor?" the sheriff asked.

"I'm working on it."

"You're lucky they didn't press charges."

Grady didn't respond.

"So, got business in Buford's, too?" the tall, lanky lawman drawled.

"Yup." Grady walked toward the door. That was as much as Carl needed to know.

Grady glanced at the display windows, covered with signs and posters announcing the upcoming grand opening of Alien Landing. With two days to go, the town was already swarming with too many unfamiliar faces – faces with earrings in their noses. Half-naked women with safety pins in their navels. It was a goddamned circus, and Grady'd had just about enough.

He pushed past a young fellow with short orange hair and a tattooed skull and crossbones on a sleeveless arm. The young man muttered a barely audible "excuse me," to which Grady merely spat a long stream of brown tobacco juice in the vicinity of the newcomer's shoe. Grady then wiped the back of his hand across his mouth as he glared at the man, daring him to object.

"Can I help you?" Carl quickly asked, jumping between the two. "Are you lost?"

The young stranger looked up at the sheriff, who towered a full foot above him. "Ah, no, thanks. Just looking around."

Gently grasping Grady's arm, the sheriff maneuvered him into the store. When they were well inside, Carl grinned and asked, "Kinda tough on the visitors, aren't you?"

"Not if they stay out of my way," Grady replied, walking toward the glass-topped counter right below a rack of assorted rifles and shotguns. For a few moments, his eyes scanned the display, seeing not what he'd come into the store for, but instead spotting a collection of ridiculous ashtrays painted with the words "They Have Arrived."

"Who's arrived? What kind of foolishness is this?" Grady demanded of nobody in particular.

Through the door behind the counter, a pimply youth who appeared no more than seventeen scrambled up to the display. To Grady, he seemed too young to be selling guns, or even ashtrays.

"C-can I help you with something?" the boy asked with apprehension.

Why, his voice wasn't any deeper than a young girl's, and his hands were as soft and pink as a baby's butt. Buford should have been arrested for making a boy do a man's job. Chances were, he wouldn't even know a .30-06 from a .22.

"If you're looking for the cartridges, they've been moved into the back room," the youngster explained. "Let me go find them for –"

"Don't bother," Grady snapped. "I know how to get there." Before the clerk could object, Grady made his way around the ashtray display and into the back room.

"Ah, sir, you can't go back there," the clerk called out after him.

"Let him go," Grady heard Carl say. "His uncle owned this store long before you were even a bulge in your daddy's pants."

Grady fumbled around in the dimly-lit stockroom, trying to find the right kind of cartridges. He'd be needing a hot load, something that could drop his target at 200, maybe 300 yards. He felt, as much as heard, the loose board creak below his boot. The sound almost made him smile. At least some things didn't change. It was probably sixty or more years ago that that loose board hid a Buck knife Grady had stolen from his uncle. *Yup, they named these knives after me,* Uncle Buck used to tell him. And for a long time, Grady had believed it. He also believed his father would have beat the living tar out of him had he known his son stole from the family's general store.

But if Grady hadn't, he'd have probably died a long time ago. That knife literally had saved his life a few weeks later, on one of the last wild horse round-ups in the valley. Golly, he sure had begged his dad to go on that ride, but not many boys his age were allowed. That old red horse he'd ridden that day had always been a dependable mount until, that is, the gelding saw about fifty head of mustangs break out of the barricade the men had corralled them in. No one figured that horse could buck like he did, least of all Grady. Before the rider knew it, the ground had slapped young Grady on the back, his lariat tangling around his foot and dragging him behind his horse. Dodging hooves and rocks, Grady had managed to fish the knife from his pocket to cut the rope. Old Red trotted on back to camp on his own after he figured out he couldn't keep up with the herd. Grady had limped in a couple hours later, and his dad never asked what happened. Grady never told him, either, especially about the cave.

He could have done without that adventure.

Those were good times, if hard. Since Uncle Buck had owned it, the building had served as a grocery, a shoe store, an ice-cream parlor, and now, a gun shop. All those changes, and the loose board was still there. Grady shook his head as he picked up the box of cartridges and headed back toward the front room.

He just caught the tail end of a conversation between the young clerk and a man who must have come into the store while Grady was looking for the cartridges.

"We don't carry anything like that," the boy was saying.

"But you carry halters and saddles," the customer insisted, as his jowls quivered with each word. "What kind of a western store is this?"

"It's a gun shop, sir. Some of the equipment you see is for outfitters and hunters. If you want old horse shoes, you'll have to talk to a horse shoer."

Grady couldn't help but interrupt. "What are you goin' to do with them old horse shoes, shoe an old horse?"

Before Grady could get an answer, the hefty customer swung around and discharged a bright flash in Grady's eyes. For a moment, Grady was blinded, forever frozen in surprise on the film of the tourist's camera.

"Hey!" Grady shouted. "What the hell you do that for?"

"Are you a real cowboy?" the man asked, staring at the old rancher's worn boots and hat. "Do you have any old horse shoes to sell?"

"No, goddammit, I ain't got any shoes to sell." Grady rubbed his eyes with his thumb and forefinger.

"Well, if you think of somebody who might have some, or any other old western junk, give me a call." The tourist fished a scrap of paper out of his shirt pocket and scribbled a phone number on it. "I'll be in town for the next week."

He shoved the paper into Grady's hand and walked out the door, mumbling about small-town hicks.

"What you s'pose that fella needed horse shoes for?" Grady asked Carl, who had been watching the whole episode.

"Some folks collect all that old stuff you throw away," Carl explained. "Maybe he wanted to hang them on his wall."

"You mean for luck?"

"For decoration."

Grady thought about it for a few minutes and wondered if that guy would come to the ranch and clean out one of his old sheds to get some "western junk." And pay Grady to boot.

"What's happening around here, Carl? Is everyone going crazy?"

He watched the sheriff sigh and shrug his shoulders. "Seems like it. You wouldn't believe the kind of complaints I've been getting lately. Know those new folks who just built that house twelve miles east of town?"

"I've seen 'em around."

"They called me a couple nights ago yelling about some guy who was out shooting coyotes near their property while they were out on a walk."

"Didn't like getting shot at, huh?"

"No. That didn't even come up. They were mad about the hunter flattening the sagebrush with his pickup."

Carl was on a roll. Next he told Grady about another newcomer who was using his water to sprinkle a new nine-hole golf course. "He built the course up near Baldy Ridge. You know the place – not enough pasture to feed a grasshopper in the whole area. So he sinks a well in the only spring for miles around to water golf balls!"

It was sure a damn shame things had come to this. Saving sagebrush and wasting water. Grady's world was changing before his eyes, and he began to feel desperation gnaw at his guts with the thought of it all.

Carl must have felt it, too, because he asked Grady, "You ever seen such chaos in Silverville before?"

As far back as Grady could remember, Silverville had always been a sensible town. Folks behaved the way they were supposed to. Well, except for the nonsense about the Jingle Jangle Ghost haunting the old livery on Main. Sounded like spurs, some said, but more likely some fool dropped a handful of nickels on the outside stairs and got the rumor started.

And, of course, he did recall his father telling him about the town lynching back around 1910 when an Italian railroad worker had gotten into a fight with the company foreman over money. The Italian ended the fight by shooting the foreman dead. The sheriff had to talk the killer into giving himself up, promising him a fair trial. But by nightfall, the foreman's friends stormed the jail, hog-tied the Italian, and dragged him through town to the hanging tree. Some folks said he was already dead by the time they strung him up; one guy claimed to have found one of the Italian's ears cut off in the street. Kept it in a jar for years.

The morning after the hanging, the body was gone. It showed up a week later when people started to complain about the stench coming from the roof of an abandoned assay office. Everybody figured the body had been tossed up there for mischief, maybe to spite all the foreigners who had come to town to work on the narrow gauge railroad.

Come to think of it, this town never did like newcomers.

Grady finally answered. "Not in a long time, Carl." And maybe it was time for a little more vigilante justice.

The pimply boy still stood behind the counter. "Is that going to be all, sir?"

Shaken from the thoughts of the past, Grady walked over to the cash register, pulled two bills from his wallet, and dropped them on the counter. He watched the clerk fumble with the coins, the boy obviously unaware of how to make change.

"Let's see now, that's $17.89 out of twenty dollars. That would make uh, a dollar, no two dollars, and . . ."

"Just give me two dollars," Grady said. "That's close enough."

With his box of cartridges under his arm, Grady started toward the door, Carl right at his heels. Once outside, Grady asked the sheriff, "I thought you had business in there, too."

"I was just looking for Buford. You seen him anywhere?"

"Yup, he's coming down the street right now."

Carl turned to watch Buford's approach. "Always in a hurry these days, isn't he?"

"Takes a lot of time to poke your nose in everybody else's business." Grady opened the door to his pickup and stepped inside. Through the windshield, he could see Buford stop in the middle of a crosswalk to speak to Mayor Schlopkohl. The two stood there, Buford's mouth going a mile a minute, Lela listening with her hands on her hips. Then, she threw her arms in the air, spun around, and stomped away, leaving Buford all alone on the street.

Grady burst out laughing and said to Carl through his open pickup window, "There's one woman who's never bought what he's selling."

"Aw, he's not that bad."

"Not until you get to know him."

"Least he doesn't sit on his hands like a lot of other folks do around here."

"Maybe, but he's sure an odd one," Grady remarked. "Just like his mama."

"Mrs. Price?"

"No, she ain't his real mama. The Prices adopted Buford when he was just a little tyke."

Carl looked puzzled. "Guess I don't know this story."

"You probably don't."

Grady didn't offer to fill Carl in, and the sheriff didn't press for details. Wasn't much to tell anyway. All Grady knew was the Episcopal Church took Buford in, and the boy was passed from family to family until the Prices finally gave him a home. Good folks they were for putting up with that ornery little devil. Grady always felt sorry for them.

Starting the pickup, he jammed the stick shift into reverse and backed into the street as he saw Buford approach the front door of Gun Paradise. Grady didn't want to stick around and listen to Buford's boastful shenanigans. He waved good-bye to Carl and slowly drove down Main Street, headed toward home. He reached over and rattled the box of cartridges on the bench seat beside him. Too bad he had to buy a whole box; it would only take one shot.

There was no hurry; he had already made his decision. He had made it the day he first saw that big white bastard inside his pasture.

PART TWO

JUNE

CHAPTER SIX

Denton

Denton felt relieved the day was nearly over. His hip had begun acting up even before the ribbon-cutting ceremony had started at eleven o'clock that morning. He'd listened patiently as Buford stood at the podium, performing before the captive audience that crowded around the theme park entrance.

Buford had begun, "It's been my pleasure, as your humble servant, to help bring this project together for the benefit of Silverville, our great country, and our vast universe . . . to welcome visitors from past and present, from near and very far." By the time he had "humbly" delivered everything he wanted to say, there had been almost no time at all for Earl Bob and Lela to speak. To a grateful crowd, Earl Bob took only five minutes to thank the community for its vision; Lela took less time than that to merely thank everyone for coming, and not very enthusiastically, at that.

The barbecue didn't begin until one o'clock, and the parade not until four. As a member of the theme park committee, Denton not only had to take part in the orchestration of all the activities, but he had also volunteered to judge the children's alien costume contest – the last event of the day's festivities.

He almost wished now he hadn't been so quick to offer.

"Mr. Fine," a little voice said. He felt a tug on his jacket and looked down to see a small blonde girl almost drowning in a silver costume with spring-loaded antennae.

"Mr. Fine, if I win that twenty-five dollars, I'm going to give it to my pastor so he can feed all the hungry children in Africa," she squeaked.

Behind her, fifteen other little faces looked up expectantly, all waiting to begin their turns to parade their costumes down the sidewalk.

Denton raised the microphone to his mouth. "Can I have your attention, please. The children's costume judging is about to begin. Will the parents please be ready to claim their little aliens after they finish showing their costumes?"

As soon as he spoke, the chatter of the children died down. While they walked down the makeshift runway, some tried to look fierce, others started to cry. One little boy announced loudly he had wet his pants, and sure enough, his costume sported alternating dark and light streaks down the legs.

All the children joined in a hopeful circle that surrounded Denton at the end of the contest. He glanced over his notes and scores on the clipboard. To his dismay, most of the costumes he had rated bore a mark of "10."

Just as he debated which lucky little alien would win the twenty-five dollars, Buford ambled over to the judging station and whispered in Denton's ear, "Make us proud, Denton. There's at least three or four contestants with parents who might still be persuaded to contribute to the project."

Denton looked again at the scores of the sixteen children, then made the mistake of looking up in time to see one little tike take a deep breath of anticipation and clasp two tiny hands together. They were all cute, and it was obvious they all expected to win. The sweat trickled down Denton's forehead and he pulled a handkerchief from his pocket to dab his face.

"The winner of the children's costume contest is . . ." Denton began, clearing his throat. "The winner is . . . everybody!"

A cheer rose up from the crowd, and sixteen miniature aliens leaped up and down with excitement. Denton shot a sheepish look at Buford, who looked back with an expression full of horror.

Denton licked dry lips and continued, "All the children and their parents may pick up their checks tomorrow at noon at Price's Gun Paradise."

Even though he knew there was no escape, Denton made a half-hearted effort to cut his way through the crowd to avoid Buford's wrath. Buford was at his side in only three or four strides. His face was smiling to the proud parents, but Buford's firm grasp of Denton's shoulder told another story.

"We need to talk," Buford said between clenched teeth. "We don't have four-hundred dollars budgeted for this."

Trying to avoid Buford's glare, Denton replied, "I know that.

But how could I disappoint sixteen kids? Don't worry. I'll make up the difference out of my own pocket."

Buford walked along in silence. Finally, he blurted out, "Hell, you don't have that kind of money to throw around, especially with your operation coming up." He sighed. "We'll just have to siphon the money off somewhere else."

Denton stared down at his shoes while Buford talked. "Look, the Gun Paradise will cover all the checks tomorrow, and maybe I can get the committee to reimburse me later. That reminds me. I seem to have misplaced a passbook. You haven't seen it, have you? It's gray."

"Sorry, no." Denton shook his head, but his mind stayed on the contest he'd just judged. "Hey, thanks, Buford. I just didn't know what else to do."

Buford raised his hand and ended the conversation, saying, "Forget it. I've got to get to the hospital." He walked off to join Lela Schlopkohl and Earl Bob waiting in a nearby car.

Denton wandered toward the parking lot. Giving away four-hundred dollars had been one more fiasco in a day full of unexpected chaos. He climbed into his old Chevy Impala and drove the eight blocks to Fine Funeral Home.

Felicia was just coming out of their living quarters to meet him in the reception room. She pecked him on the cheek and asked, "Who won the contest?"

"It was a tie."

"Between who?" she asked.

"Everybody."

"What? You mean you split the prize money between all the children?"

"Not exactly," Denton answered. "They each won twenty-five dollars. It was a last-minute decision."

"Well, I bet that made Buford's day."

"I offered to make up the difference –"

"Denton Fine!" she interrupted. "What were you thinking? We can't afford that."

Denton gently pressed his forefinger against her lips. "Buford wouldn't let me. He's covering the prize money out of the gun shop."

"He is? Boy, sometimes that guy really pulls through, doesn't he?" she said, tilting her head slightly and smiling. "You, on the other hand, need watching."

"Did anyone come in while I was gone?" Denton asked in order to change the subject.

"No, it was surprisingly quiet. I could have locked the doors and come along this afternoon and no one would have noticed."

"Yes, but you never know."

"It did give me a chance to get supper ready early. Hungry?"

"Famished. Judging aliens makes a person work up a real appetite."

Together, they walked through the reception room and into the family's living room. Denton plopped down in an overstuffed chair and pulled off his shoes.

"Go ahead and sit down at the table, Denton," Felicia told him. "I'll be right in with the casserole."

§   §   §

"Where's Duke?" Denton asked, helping himself to another homemade biscuit.

"He'll be along pretty soon. He must be working late."

At the lodge, of course. Denton struggled to push the bolus of biscuit down his suddenly dry throat and said nothing.

Felicia continued, "He didn't know we were eating early tonight. Tell me about the day."

"It was really eventful. We learned a lot about what not to do next year."

"Uh-oh, what happened?"

"For starters, the trips out to the landing site weren't coordinated very well. About half-way through Buford's ribbon-cutting speech, they announced the first tour, and a few people escaped in the van. By the time Lela spoke, the crowd was getting pretty restless."

Felicia laughed. "That's not so serious."

"Well, it gets worse. We probably should have waited to open up the theme park until after the barbecue because not too many waited around to eat."

"Too bad. All that food going to waste."

"Not all of it went to waste," Denton explained. "Fawn's dog got into a meringue pie during the ceremony and scared the wits out everybody."

"You mean Portia?"

"Yeah. She came tearing around the tables with meringue dripping all over her face and someone started shouting, 'rabid dog!' People were climbing over each other trying to get away, which gave Portia the opportunity to jump on the picnic tables and help herself."

"Then it was a good thing most people went on to the theme park."

"Except two of the rides broke down immediately, which just made the lines to the other ones that much longer."

The phone rang, and Denton got up to answer. It was Buford reporting from the hospital on the accident that day. Evidently a van step collapsed just as a man boarded to visit the landing site. He'd been diagnosed with only minor injuries. The conversation was brief, and Denton returned to the table.

"Who was it?" Felicia asked.

"Just Buford." Denton didn't bother to explain when he noticed his answer seemed enough to satisfy his wife. Besides, she'd hear all about it from Skippy, anyway.

Felicia had just started to clear the table when Duke sashayed into the room. He pulled out his chair and slid gracefully into the seat.

"Hi, Felicia. Hi, Denton," he greeted his parents. "Anything left to eat?"

"Hi, Son," Denton answered. Duke had started calling them by their given names when he was four, and refused to call them Mom and Dad. It was the first inkling they'd had that Duke was a little different.

Felicia set the casserole back on the table. "I bet you're exhausted," she said. "Are the rooms full out there?"

"Slightly," he replied with a sixteen-year-old's edge of

sarcasm. "We're booked solid for the next two weeks."

Duke filled his plate with food and began to eat in silence. To Denton, it was obvious that something preoccupied his son. As always, Duke's eyebrows arched and flattened, and his head nodded from time to time as the boy rehearsed something they would no doubt be talking about in a few minutes. Denton knew the pattern well.

"Got something on your mind?"

"Well, actually, Denton, I do," Duke confessed. "I met someone today at the lodge. His name is Cecil, and he made the most profound impression on me."

Denton and Felicia simultaneously drew in sharp breaths and stared at Duke. They both knew it would happen someday. Duke would fall in love and announce that he had found the right man.

"I know now what I want to do with the rest of my life."

Denton braced himself for Duke's next words, but said only, "Oh?"

"First, let me tell you a little bit about Cecil."

"We want to hear all about him, Dear." Felicia's voice sounded supportive.

"He's a medical student from California, twenty-two, and a real hunk. And brilliant – lots of world experience. I talked with him for hours, and heard all about the school he goes to, his classes, and everything. And I've decided . . ."

Here it comes, Denton thought.

". . . to go to med school. I want to be a doctor."

For a few seconds, no one spoke.

"Well, what do you think?" Duke asked. "I've already taken most of the right classes. I could start contacting some colleges and get some more information." He looked at his father. "It's what you wanted to do, wasn't it?"

Denton relaxed a little and took a deep breath. "Why yes, I did."

"I think it's an excellent plan," Felicia broke in. "Do you have any idea what kind of medicine you want to go into?"

"Not really," Duke said. "I want to talk to Cecil some more and see what he suggests. Do you think we could have him over for dinner tomorrow night?"

"Well . . . yes," Denton answered slowly.

"Why don't you talk to him and see if he can come," Felicia suggested.

All the while he had been talking, Duke had stirred his casserole and Jell-O into a small mountain of red glop. He had hardly eaten anything. "I'm going to see him tonight at the theme park. I'll ask him then."

He rose from the table and headed for his room. As he walked away, he turned toward his parents and said, "Thanks. This is really important to me."

Denton stared absently at a reflection in his water glass, only slowly becoming aware Felicia had moved around the table and sat down beside him.

"It's weird, isn't it?" she asked.

Denton nodded. Naturally, he would do whatever he could for his son, whatever he could to help make the boy's plans come true. He didn't want Duke to feel the disappointment of broken dreams like he had.

"Denton?" Felicia tapped gently on his head. "Are you in there?"

"I'm okay. Just brings back lots of old memories." He suspected she knew exactly what those old memories were. It wasn't that he complained about what life had dealt him. After all, he had managed to provide for his family despite all the bumps. And he had settled for a profession that had still let him serve others, just not the way he had originally planned.

"I don't remember ever telling Duke I'd wanted to go to medical school," Denton remarked.

"I did. He knows the whole story."

"Oh."

He hadn't thought about the "whole story" in years. It was better not to dwell on the past. But Duke's announcement flooded his mind with painful recollections. First, the accident had ruined his chances of continuing any kind of a career as a professional ice skater. As an eighteen-year-old, it had taken a tremendous amount of regrouping to find an alternative direction for his life. He had found that direction, ironically, through the many hours he had spent in the hospital.

"Your life isn't over," his doctor had told him. "You're a smart young man. You can make it through medical school."

His parents had been thrilled at the idea, and his father had immediately set up a fund for his education. Denton spent the first two years of pre-med studying every night until dawn, working as an orderly on weekends, and almost ignoring Felicia – all to assure his acceptance into med school.

Then came the second blow. Denton could still see the anguish on his father's face when he told his son there was no more money for school. An investment plan had gone awry when the organizer of a downtown Nashville shopping mall project had skipped town with most of his father's money.

"Felicia, do you know what it's like to be young, full of promise, and then have the world come crashing down on you?"

"Remember, I was there."

"How will we help him? We're talking tens of thousands of dollars." Denton dropped his head into his hands.

"I don't know where the money will come from."

It had been a slow year, even for Silverville. To make matters worse, there had been some unexpected expenses. The old hearse had to be replaced and new federal health codes demanded that he renovate the embalming room. Now, his doctors told him if he didn't replace that hip soon, he'd be in a wheel chair within the next five years.

"We can't let Duke settle for second best, like I did," Denton said. "We have to find a way."

"Oh, Denton. Duke may change his mind by tomorrow. You know how kids are."

Yes, Denton knew. They were full of enthusiasm, full of high expectations for life. And even if Duke did change his mind tomorrow about med school, he'd still want to go to college somewhere for something. For the past few years, Denton had tried to push this worry from his mind, always hoping he and Felicia could catch up with their expenses. It just never seemed to happen.

"I'll have to put off the operation," Denton declared.

"Denton! You can't. You know what the doctor told you. Besides, what good can you do anybody if you end up in a wheel chair?"

He slowly rose from his seat and started toward his office. "That's a good question."

CHAPTER SEVEN

Billy

Just as Billy seated himself on a back-row chair, the sun broke through the trees, casting a final golden spotlight on the podium. The gentle slope around The Landing Site offered a natural amphitheater to the spectators who gathered to hear Howard relate his experience. For most of the afternoon, Billy had helped Howard rehearse what was left of the original lecture.

"I'm not too good at talking to lots of people," Howard had told him. "Now Mr. Price wants me to lie about what happened."

And Buford had supplied plenty of lies in the re-written script.

"Sometimes you just have to tell people what they want to hear," Billy coaxed. "Believe me, Buford knows what he's doing."

It was a line of bullshit, of course, the kind Billy had given folks for the past month serving as Buford's "yes" man.

He'd reached out and patted Howard on the shoulder. "I'll be there tonight. If you stumble, I'll ask you a question from the audience to help get you back on track."

Howard looked doubtful.

"We can do this, Buddy." Billy encouraged him with a thumbs-up gesture, but the truth was, Billy was also a little nervous to see if Howard could pull off the lecture. Luckily, Buford wouldn't be there tonight, still having his hands full from picking up the pieces of yesterday's grand opening mishaps.

Billy started counting heads in the seats before him. A good two-hundred people turned out for what was to be the first of several lectures – so many people that the city had resorted to school buses to shuttle the spectators to the site. Many had already seen the location that afternoon from the vantage point of Up, Up and Away, Bob Hardin's hot air balloon rides. Unlike the noisy cacophony that often accompanied large gatherings, this group seemed to file into the rows of folding chairs with an almost reverent awe. Not even babies cried.

Sheep. A crowd full of sheep, and Billy was powerless to lead them down any path but Buford's.

Someone in the back of the podium fired up the gasoline generator that would provide sound and, later, light for the "special effects." A mechanical squawk blasted from one of the speakers, followed by the same irritating sound-track from Mrs. Watson's favorite B-grade sci-fi movie. With no coordination, the music stopped as abruptly as it began when Howard stepped up to the podium.

Even with the thirty feet separating Howard from the crowd, he looked more uncomfortable than usual to Billy. The man's eyes nervously scanned the people in front of him, his fingers spasmodically clenching the edges of the lectern. Billy silently stood until Howard spotted him and repeated the thumbs-up gesture.

Howard opened his mouth to speak, but nothing came out. Instead, he appeared to be mesmerized by the throng of attentive saucer heads. For a full minute he stared at the crowd, and then he must have remembered his notes and turned his head downward.

"I want – I want to tell you all what happened to me," he stuttered. It wasn't the way Howard was supposed to begin, but at least he got the words out.

"There was a light. Right here. I stopped. There was a craft. And aliens, I guess." The words came out in rapid fire. "And I watched it and then it left. Any questions?"

Billy couldn't believe it. He and Howard had rehearsed the whole thirty-minute speech at least four times that day.

A woman in the crowd raised her hand. "What did the aliens look like?"

Howard looked perplexed. "The, ah, what?"

From behind Billy, a voice boomed through the fading light. "Why, they looked just like you and me, Ma'am."

It was Buford, in all his obnoxious glory. The weight of his bulging stomach pulled him down the hill toward the podium.

Billy's jaw tightened at the sound of Buford's voice.

"The person sitting next to you could be one of them, and you'd never know it," Buford continued.

"But don't they have large heads and oval eyes?" the woman

insisted.

By then, Buford had reached the stage-struck speaker. "They can – if they want to," Buford said with an air of mysterious authority. "Have you ever talked to one?"

The woman opened her mouth to answer, but Buford talked right over her.

"Well, this young man talks to them all the time." Buford swung his arm around Howard's shaking shoulders. "He gets telepathic messages from them every day, don't you, Howard? But let's not put the cart before the horse."

Billy cringed at Buford's last remark. It was the sort of thing Daddy used to say.

Buford leaned over, whispered something in Howard's ear and sent him scurrying beyond the podium's floodlights. It was clear that Howard had been dismissed.

Even from this distance, Billy could see Buford's sagging jowls vibrate with each fantastic assertion he offered the crowd. In Billy's mind, those flabby features grew until they were all he could see. How satisfying it would be to sink his fingers into one of those bulldog handles and wrap it around Buford's neck. Instead, he reached into his pants pocket for a roll of antacids. Billy popped a couple into his mouth and sat back to listen to the ever-growing tale of terror about the night Howard happened upon the UFO.

". . . and that's when Howard laid eyes on a scene most of us only see in nightmares." Buford's voice echoed through the microphone, the calculated pacing of his words adding a macabre element to the story. He then offered what Billy thought must have been a dramatic pause. All at once the lights cut out from the podium and a whole new set flooded a small area to the right of the audience.

The solitary figure of Howard seemed to wince in surprise at the sudden burst of the spotlights upon him. He stood like a man frozen in time, recorded on film after the flash of a camera, and uncertain what to do amid the oohs and aahs of the crowd.

"With the utmost caution, Howard crept stealthily toward the craft until he could almost touch it," Buford began. A second spotlight beamed toward the crowd's left, illuminating a smooth, foil-covered disc constructed of wood and wire.

"Yes, ladies and gentlemen," Buford continued, "it was, perhaps, the most significant day in Howard Beacon's life – maybe all of our lives – when he came face to face with these travelers from outer space."

Buford was stealing Howard's thunder. According to the plan, Howard was to use the special effects to tell his story. Billy rummaged around his pocket for another antacid.

As instructed, Howard had already moved to various predetermined points in the amphitheater by the time Buford finally reached the part of the story where he always inserted aliens. Howard should've been humiliated. Instead, it looked to Billy like he was a little relieved to no longer be speaking at the podium.

"When the aliens waved their farewells to Howard, the ship may have left, but the story isn't over," Buford explained with a great air of suspense. The crowd looked captivated, and they waited for Buford's next words. He took full advantage of the dramatic moment and poured himself a glass of water.

"No, the story isn't over yet," Buford insisted. "They left Howard with a message. A message to tell the whole world. A message that will change the course of humanity."

Someone in the crowd gasped. A child cried out.

Buford's command of his audience struck Billy as nothing less than masterful. The only other time Billy had seen that kind of skilled control and deceit was once when he had watched his own father smooth-talk an entire roomful of gullible investors into backing a non-existent shopping mall project. The guy had natural talent, no matter how much Billy hated to admit it.

The same curious woman who had questioned Buford before, spoke up, "Tell us. What is the message?"

Billy cringed. *The poor son-of-a-bitch can't remember, Madame. He's one brick short of a load. He's juggling with two oranges. His light switch is set on dim.*

Buford leaned forward on the podium and focused on the woman. "The answer to that will not be revealed until Labor Day. It was the travelers' instructions to wait until then." Buford then straightened his back and addressed the whole audience. "But we've got some great celebrations planned for that day, too, so y'all come back and visit us again at the end of the summer."

Audible disappointment rumbled through the crowd at this last announcement. The podium lights dimmed, and escorts with little theater flashlights began directing people back up the hill to the buses and cars. Despite the lack of light, Billy made his way toward the front of the amphitheater to look for Howard. He nearly ran into Buford on the way.

"There's my man," Buford's voice boomed loud enough to be heard among the people passing nearby. He started to slap Billy on the shoulder. "A good showing for the first lecture."

Billy ducked away from Buford's hand. "Yes, a good showing," he agreed. "What did you do with Howard?"

"I suspect he high-tailed it home as quick as he could," Buford answered. Then he lowered his voice, "I thought you two were going to rehearse that speech this afternoon."

"We did, for two hours. I guess Howard just panicked."

"That poor guy couldn't piss in a pot without instructions. What an asshole."

"You're the asshole, Buford. And you've made this all too complicated. Something was bound to go wrong. Something still might."

Buford frowned. Then he pushed his bulldog jowls within inches of Billy's face.

"Don't you forget who's calling the shots here, *Earl Bob,*" Buford warned. "We got a deal, and don't make me remind you again."

Billy jammed his hands into his pockets, swung around on his heels, and headed up the hill. Howard was probably already home. Buford may have saved today, but it was Billy's responsibility to see that Howard didn't break down under the weight of Buford's expectations.

Billy started the ignition of the Cadillac and turned the vehicle in the direction of Howard's cabin. Yes, he and Buford had a "deal," but not one Billy had any say in. Buford had sealed that agreement on the day Billy had first interviewed Howard in his home. And it was the last day Billy had been in control of his own scam.

"Sit down, Earl Bob, or whatever your real name is. You're not going anywhere." He could still hear Buford's commanding tone. The moment had caught Billy uncharacteristically red-handed. The truth was, he hadn't planned to leave, having already decided to work the town until it was no longer profitable – or safe. The last thing he expected was being the pawn in someone else's game.

"So, whatever happened to the real Earl Bob?" Buford had asked that day. "Did you bump him off and steal his car?" Buford's guess had been so close to the truth that Billy found himself too stunned to come back with a quick explanation.

He'd had no idea Buford would be smarter than he looked. Billy didn't have his ducks in a row, that's what Daddy would have told him, and now he would have to pay the price – Buford Price.

Before Billy could respond, a slow smile spread over Buford's face. "That's it, isn't it? Well, I don't give a goddamn who you are or where you came from. I don't even care what you did with the real Earl Bob. I've worked too long to pull this project off, and you're going to help me finish it.

"From now on, you are, and will be Earl Bob, and you will do exactly what I tell you. Unless you prefer to spend the rest of your life in jail."

Despite the turn of events, Buford hadn't treated him altogether unfairly. He had promised Billy a cut from the profits, and Buford helped shield him several times from contacts Earl Bob had known. There were advantages to working with an insider. But all the while, that same insider held the threat of exposure if Billy didn't cooperate. Buford had only guessed at Earl Bob's fate, having no idea that the Pisser's body lie rotting only a hundred miles away.

That was one part of Billy's past he was reluctant to share with anyone, and he had no desire to add a murder conviction to his rap sheet.

Billy stepped on the accelerator a little harder than he should have up the rutted road to Howard's cabin. The bumps rattled the Caddy and jarred his already upset stomach. Even if Buford was a natural panhandler, he still had no idea what he was doing and it made Billy nervous. For the past month, he had skillfully swept up the mess behind Buford, helping him pull off a job better handled by an experienced hand.

He turned the car into Howard's driveway and saw that Howard's bike was gone. Billy backed out and headed downhill toward Silverville. As he passed the landing site turnoff, he noticed the cars of the crew still parked in the lot. Driving on, he saw no one else until he reached the valley floor.

Then, without warning, the sheriff's oncoming four-wheel drive spun around a curve and narrowly missed the Cadillac. Lights blazing and sirens full blast, the vehicle sped past Billy and careened down the gravel road that led to Grady O'Grady's place. Billy wondered briefly what all the commotion was about, but at that moment, he had his own problems to attend to.

Howard

Howard slid off his bicycle, laid it on the ground, and walked to the entrance gate, all the while keeping his eyes fixed on the glowing letters that spelled out "Alien Landing – They Have Arrived." He'd pushed from his mind the events at the real landing site earlier that evening. Howard didn't want anything to interfere with the warm feeling that grew in his chest each time he walked through these gates. Lights sparkled around him, happy people laughed, music drifted down the corridors of wondrous exhibits and booths. It was all here because of him, because of what he had seen, and he felt a sense of responsibility to it all.

He leaned through the turnstile, waving at the man behind the counter.

"Back again, Howard?" the ticket collector asked him.

Howard just smiled and kept on walking down the main causeway. He didn't need a ticket. Mr. Price had seen to that.

Like his other two visits since the park had opened, Howard first stopped at the "Uranus Yogurt Company" for a double scoop of vanilla, no nuts. Next, he wandered over to the glass-blowing booth to watch a woman create yet another tiny starship. Howard carefully studied a tent wall lined with pretty trinkets. Someday soon, he was going to buy one for Mrs. Fine to pay her back for all the meals she'd cooked for him. He'd know the one when he saw it.

"Hi, Howard."

He turned around to see a four-foot-tall "extraterrestrial" dressed in a gray cape and plastic disguise that covered the creature's head. He could just make out through the two large almond-shaped eye holes that it was his barber's youngest daughter.

"Would you like an 'I believe' button?" she asked.

Howard fished around in his pocket and found at least four other buttons just like the one she offered, but he opened his hand for another one anyway.

"Sure."

He took the souvenir from the palm of her six-fingered glove and continued deeper into the park. Butterflies began to flutter in his stomach just before he reached the outdoor stage. Every time he had visited, someone who knew a lot more about the universe than he did was speaking there. Mr. Jackson had arranged for all the guest speakers although Howard had never seen him come and listen to any of them. Howard sat down on a back bench to hear a storyteller explain how groups of stars got their names. Behind her, on a wall, a large poster showed clusters of stars that were supposed to be a bear, a lion, and a scorpion. Howard didn't get it. He could never see any animals in the night sky. But he liked the woman up on the stage. She had a kind voice, and she made people laugh. Howard licked at the last of his yogurt and promised himself that he would try harder to find those animals in the sky.

The audience clapped when the storyteller finished, and Howard stood when everyone else did. He then turned to his right to make his way over toward the museum's planetarium, which was connected to the south end of the theme park. On the way, he had to walk past a row of fortune tellers and palm readers. Mr. Fine told him not to stop at those places and waste his money, but he couldn't help staring at the colorful clothes that most of them wore. The closest fortune teller leaned over a crystal ball and ran her hands over the glass until she suddenly stopped and threw her arms up.

"What? What?" asked the man sitting across from her as he jumped in his seat.

"Something important is about to happen in your life," she told the man. "It will change everything for you. You will become an important man."

Just like what happened to me, Howard thought as he strolled toward the museum, but a big wad of gum had attached itself to his shoe and almost pulled it off when he stepped away. Hopping on one foot, Howard removed the soiled shoe and tried to pluck the pink strands off the sole. Then he noticed the round hole in the heel of his sock and quickly replaced his shoe.

Just before he walked through the museum's gate, a group of teenagers stampeded past him. One turned his head toward Howard as they raced by, shouting, "Hey, Space Boy! Take us to your leader!"

He heard the others laugh and Howard just smiled. If those boys meant Mr. Jackson, he would have to remember to tell him they wanted to talk to him.

A stream of people was filing out of the planetarium just as Howard stepped up to the ticket booth. The man behind the counter looked up and said, "The show just got over. There won't be another one for forty-five minutes."

Howard nodded, not sure what to do. The last two times, he had been able to walk right into the planetarium and watch. He stood there for a few minutes and then turned uncertainly toward the exhibit wing. He barely got through the door when Mrs. Watson called from across the room.

"There's Howard Beacon now!" she announced to her small crowd of sightseers. Howard started to back out of the room, but Mrs. Watson bustled over, grabbed his arm, and led him into the middle of her audience.

"What a special treat this evening," she said loudly, all the while beaming at Howard. "Would you like to tell these folks about your experience yourself?"

"No, thank you," he answered, looking at the floor with embarrassment. At that moment, Howard found a small, flattened paper cup sticking to his shoe. He must not have gotten all the gum off, and he balanced on one foot as he peeled the cup from his sole.

"Do you have a trash can in here, Mrs. Watson?" Howard

asked as he held up the cup and trailing gum strands for her to see. That's when he noticed everyone was looking at him. He stepped forward and offered it to her. Mrs. Watson didn't seem to understand what he wanted, but she slowly reached up and took the cup. Howard backed out of the room.

Once safely away from the crowd, he took his time to enjoy all the pictures of flying saucers and drawings of aliens. Everything looked identical to the displays in the museum. Eventually, he found himself in the room painted with a spacecraft on one side and a frightened man on the other. Howard still couldn't understand why Mr. Price had insisted that the picture of him look scared. Howard hadn't been scared that night. Why, seeing that flying saucer was probably the most important thing that had ever happened to him – that and the message he received. Sometimes, he almost thought he could remember what it was, but it was never in words that made any sense. He just wouldn't worry about it right now. Mr. Price said he'd probably remember it by Labor Day.

After walking through several more rooms, Howard decided not to wait for the planetarium show; it was time to go to the rides. He walked out the door, past the fortune tellers and stage area, and over to the section of the park that held the rides. It was his favorite part of the theme park. Everywhere, people were screaming, but he knew they weren't really afraid. The bright lights and bright colors always made him happy, and he liked the different music played on each ride.

He stopped at the Bumper Saucers first. Howard watched as people in little round saucer cars raced around a flat floor trying to hit each other. One little boy bumped into car after car, yelling, "I'm going to run you down!" But Howard knew it was just in fun. No one at a theme park could really get hurt.

Lots of rides seemed a little scary to Howard, like the one that reminded him of a giant octopus, but with swirling seats. And the Space Bullet – he didn't think he would ever try that one.

"Excuse me, aren't you Howard?" a voice from behind him asked. Howard turned around to see a man dressed all in black. He had seen the man around for several weeks, and knew his name was Brother Martin. Once Howard had overheard Mr. Price telling Mr.

Fine that this man was a leader of some sort of church, but Howard had never seen where the church was. Mr. Fine had said this preacher seemed to think Howard's sighting was a sign from God.

"Yes, sir, I'm Howard."

"Our family of believers would like to invite you to our next meeting. We hope you'll come," Brother Martin said.

Mr. Price called him a pedophile even though Mr. Fine didn't think he was. Howard didn't know what that meant, but he knew it was bad.

"I might have to work that day," Howard replied.

"But I haven't even told what day the meeting will be on. We can hold a special gathering some night when you can come. We'd like to talk to you about your experience and the message you received."

Howard kicked at the gravel under his feet and stammered, "Oh, well, that's a secret, and I can't tell anyone yet."

"We believe that, in these End Times, a higher power holds the future of humanity in its hands." Brother Martin's voice started sounding like the preachers Howard had heard on the radio. "From time to time, a messenger is chosen to lead us back to the path of righteousness. Don't turn away from the signs He has given you. You must take up the staff and go forth into the dark valley of sinners, urging them to return to the truth and the light."

Howard listened politely, then said, "Okay," and turned and fled.

Pushing deep into the crowds, he stopped and closed his eyes, trying to make out the different tunes going on at the same time. To his right, he heard a woman scolding a crying child; straight ahead, a barking voice encouraged people to go on one of the rides. "It will thrill. It will spill. Show the young ladies how brave you gents are!"

Howard let the sounds fill his head, wishing it would never end. Somewhere, not far away, he could just make out a low hum. Children screamed gaily as they raced past him, leaving the smell of cotton candy in the air. A bottle shattered on the ground and someone said a bad word.

Above it all, he heard the hum grow louder and figured the sound must be coming from an airplane. With eyes still closed, he listened as an old woman complained about her sore feet, a man's voice replying, "Now, Mama, we've driven all this way . . ." But Howard couldn't hear the rest of what the man said because of the hum. Within seconds the hum turned into a loud screech, and Howard clutched his ears with his hands. He opened his eyes in time to see stunned people looking toward the sky.

He followed their gaze, half expecting to see a low-flying airplane, but what he saw made him gasp in terror.

"No, it's not supposed to happen this way!" Howard shouted, but he couldn't hear his own words over the screams of the crowd around him.

Grady

Grady threw his saddle on Ole Moss's back. The sorrel cocked an evil eye in her rider's direction and flattened her ears. Ole Moss always threatened to cow-kick or bite, but she seldom carried through. Grady had long learned to ignore the horse's sour attitude. For twenty-two years, he and Ole' Moss had been partners, handling everything from separating calves to mending fences in the high country.

After he tightened the cinch, Grady reached behind him, grabbed the rifle, and slid it into the scabbard lashed to the saddle with latigos. Ole Moss didn't flinch. She was used to a gun hanging from the saddle, and he had dropped elk from the horse's back for almost as many hunting seasons as he had owned her. He'd first laid eyes on her at a sale ring in a town the other side of the pass. Far too young to be taken from her mama, she was a bit spindly for even the kill buyers to take notice. He paid thirty-five dollars and wondered on the drive home why he had wasted the money. For two years, she was nothing but a hay-burner – and a cantankerous one at that. He'd once seen her touch her nose to a hotwire fence as a yearling. But instead of running away like most horses, Moss had attacked that fence with a vengeance, striking it with her front feet until she tore the whole thing down. As a two-year-old, she'd run off a pack of coyotes in a pasture full of calving heifers. Those varmints had their eyes on a newborn close to the fence, but Moss bared her teeth and charged right into the thieving coyotes until they dodged, tails tucked, back under the wire. Not that she was trying to protect the calves; she just didn't like strangers in her pasture.

At that point, Grady figured thirty-five dollars hadn't been too much to spend.

He bitted her up and climbed onto her back. He turned to the ranch dogs and shouted at them to stay home as he and Ole Moss headed off across the field in the direction of his new neighbor's property. Leona didn't know where he was going, and he hadn't told her. With any luck, he'd be back before she pulled bread out of the oven.

A lot of the ranchers in the valley didn't like riding mares. Too much attitude seemed to make it harder for a mare to keep her mind on her work. But something about Moss had made him want to give her a try. He almost changed his mind when he started breaking her. The first time he put her in the round pen to throw a saddle on her back, she turned on Grady and chased him clear over the fence. Several weeks later, when he got close enough to actually get on her, she bucked like her tail was heated kerosene. Every cold winter day, his hip reminded him of the falls he'd taken those first few years riding Ole Moss. Still, she never spooked at wild game or gun shots, and she worked harder than any gelding on the place. She was a handful, that was for sure, but she was as brave a horse as he'd ever ridden. Ole Moss was going to be perfect for the job they had to do today.

Within fifteen minutes, he saw the unfinished pyramid looming before him. That Woman's damn dogs must have seen him coming first because they came tearing down her driveway and into Grady's field, barking ferociously as they circled his horse's legs. Maybe Ole Moss didn't take kindly to the commotion. In a flash, she cocked a hind leg and caught one of the mutts across the side of the head. By the time Grady heard the yelp and looked, the dog was lying motionless beside the road. Grady just snorted and kept right on going.

At the same time, That Woman came running out of the pyramid, screaming and waving her arms. Hans High Horse followed close behind.

"Mr. Graden! Mr. Graden! My dog, my dog!"

Grady ignored her as he approached the fence. He swung down off his horse and unlooped the wire that kept the gate shut leading into the pasture that lay next to her land. As he fumbled with the loop, he could hear their voices getting closer.

"Do you have no regard for the sacredness of life?" It was High Horse who spoke.

Slowly, Grady turned around to face them. That Woman was kneeling beside the fallen dog as the albino strode over to Ole Moss's side. Grady watched as the mare pinned her ears and sidled her rear end around in the direction of Hans.

"Wouldn't do that, if I were you," Grady said calmly, shooting a stream of tobacco juice in the dirt.

The Juanabee Indian jumped to the side before Moss could nail him. "Your horse, Mr. O'Grady, he tells me of his injured spirit, of his desire to be free."

Ole Moss again started to back toward the albino but stopped at Grady's quick jerk on the reins. "My horse is telling you to get the hell away from her."

At that point, the second dog came lunging forward to reach Grady and High Horse. That Woman clutched his rhinestone collar, leaving the dog gasping for air.

"He's dead. You've killed poor Skywalker!" she shrieked.

Grady put a foot in the stirrup and threw his leg over the saddle. "Yep."

He turned Ole Moss through the gate, adding, "Ain't done either."

"What do you mean, Mr. Graden?" That Woman asked, sobbing.

Grady pulled Ole Moss up and spun around to face them. "I told you once to keep that white son-of-a-bitch on your own property. Now that buffalo has broken into my cow pasture."

"But he's lonely!" she pleaded.

"It's breeding season, you damn fools."

Grady reined Ole Moss back toward his cow pasture and squeezed his horse into a slow lope.

"What are you going to do?" That Woman called after him.

Grady didn't bother to answer. As he topped the hill, he saw the two running toward their SUV. But if they planned to get the sheriff, it would be too late.

In front of him a herd of fifty red and white heifers dotted the slope, a large white buffalo pestering a few of the cattle near the edge of the main group. Before Grady's blood pressure could even start to rise, that white bastard mounted one of the heifers. If Grady didn't do something to stop it, he'd have a pasture full of little white beefalo by spring.

Ole Moss shot out like a pistol as Grady dug his heels into her sides. The two raced over prairie dog mounds and sagebrush, the horse's feet barely touching the ground – until she saw the buffalo. Without any signal from Grady, the mare took it upon herself to plant her hind legs in the dirt and slide to a stop. He collapsed forward as the saddle horn punched the breath from his chest. Bouncing in front of the saddle, his cheek slapped hard against the crest of her neck. Ole Moss kept her eyes pasted on the buffalo, paying no attention to the rider who balanced precariously behind her ears. Snorting as she probably picked up the scent of the huge white beast, she spun on her forelegs three-hundred-sixty degrees to get another look at the new critter in her cow pasture. Grady took the opportunity to slip backwards into the saddle.

"What the hell are you —?" Before Grady could finish, Ole Moss bolted to the side and started to buck as she veered away in the opposite direction of the buffalo. Grady tried to rein her in, but she jerked free of the leather and tucked her head between her front legs just before she let go with another series of pitches. This time Grady thought he was ready. But when Ole Moss's back legs shot forward in a mighty buck, she managed to catch the right stirrup with her hoof and yanked it off the saddle. Grady reached for the horn with both hands and hung on like he was wringing the neck of a Thanksgiving turkey.

Within less than a minute, Ole' Moss must have figured she had bucked enough and came to a complete stop.

"What the hell's gotten into you?" Grady rasped. "You're not afraid of nothing."

The old mare quivered beneath Grady's saddle, and sweat

lathered her neck and shoulders. He didn't feel too steady himself, but he reached down to give his horse a pat.

"You're okay, old girl. I ain't never seen a buffalo in our pasture before neither."

He gave his horse a few moments to cool down and twisted his head around to look for his stirrup. He didn't see it and decided to keep going anyway. Slowly turning the horse again toward the buffalo, Grady urged her forward. She stepped without hesitation for the first few strides, but she must have caught wind of that white bull again because she started dancing sideways and wringing her tail. Grady kept enough leg on her to move Ole Moss closer.

When they were within thirty yards, the buffalo turned in their direction and evaluated the intruders with one piercing pink eye. Grady halted the mare. She stood still. With a careful, deliberate motion, he slid the rifle from the scabbard and drew a bead on his target. Grady held his breath and slowly squeezed on the trigger.

That's when he heard the rattling behind him.

"Wait, Mr. Graden!"

Grady lowered his rifle and turned his head to see That Woman and High Horse approaching on foot directly behind him, their vehicle parked at the top of the hill.

"Here, Tatanka," she cooed, shaking a small can of feed.

At the same time, a snort coming from the buffalo pulled Grady's attention back toward his quarry. The animal lowered his head and pawed the ground, throwing plumes of dirt onto his massive, shaggy hump.

Grady recognized the threatening behavior. "Get back to your truck! He's gonna charge!"

"No, he won't," she called out. And then she changed the pitch of her voice and continued, "Come on, Tatanka. We have something yummy for you."

The buffalo didn't wait for them to argue. He bunched up his muscles and sprang forward, barreling like a runaway eighteen-wheeler toward them all. Ole Moss wheeled around and started to run. Before she had a chance to gather any speed, Grady grabbed the left rein, snubbed the horse's nose to his left knee, and dallied the rein securely around the saddle horn. The action sent Ole

Moss into a tight spin as he leaned into the only stirrup he had left.

Grady tried to aim the rifle at the charging bull and fired off a shot. He missed and the bull ran right past him, cutting a path straight toward That Woman and High Horse. Grady knew he couldn't dawdle with his second shot. The world was spinning around him. At each two-second revolution, Grady caught consecutive snapshots of his new neighbors, like interrupted images in an old-time nickelodeon – That Woman frozen with her jaw hanging in surprise and High Horse hightailing toward the SUV on the hill. Time seem to slow down for Grady as he again lifted the gun's butt to his right shoulder. One spin, two spins. If his aim wasn't true, he could hit Chantale or High Horse. But if he didn't fire quickly, the buffalo would trample one or both of them. No doubt you'd shoot a critter that size in the same spot as an elk, right behind the shoulder. But the angle of the receding buffalo made it harder to get a clean shot. A graze would only make the animal more dangerous. He couldn't make a mistake.

At the next spin, Grady tried to slow the barrel by twisting his body against the motion of the horse. He fired.

Almost instantaneously, the beast's front legs collapsed, catapulting his mass into a forward tumble. A thick cloud of dust covered the scene before him, and he couldn't see Chantale at all. Ole Moss began winding down. Grady unwrapped the rein from the saddle horn and tried to convince the mare to lope toward the settling haze. The best he could get out of her was a slow trot.

As they approached, Chantale's standing form started to emerge from the sandy cloud. The buffalo lay dead only two yards from her feet.

"My poor buffalo," she mouthed, almost inaudible. She stood over the animal with tears streaming down her face.

"He was about to run you down, ma'am," Grady responded, but his voice was as dry as the ground around them. He looked down at the buffalo's size. It was the closest he'd ever been to one. Several years ago, he'd guided a group of elk hunters from the Midwest. One of the fellows had told him a story about a buffalo round-up he'd been to in South Dakota. Rough stuff it must have been because the man recounted how all the riders on horseback carried revolvers with loads of bird shot to keep the animals at a distance. Even at that, one of the damn things had turned on a rider and gored his horse. The hunter had told Grady that buffalo were unpredictable and often foul-tempered.

"He was only coming for the grain," Chantale whined.

"Not likely. These animals ain't pets. You can't treat 'em as such."

By that time, High Horse came panting up beside them. He took one look at the dead buffalo and started singing some fool song, staring at the sky as he uplifted his arms. Ole Moss stretched her nose out and sniffed at the dead animal. She blew out a long snort, seemingly satisfied that it wouldn't jump up and get her.

Chantale looked up at Grady and said, "You're a murderer, Mr. Graden. You've killed two of my animals today."

She no longer cried. Instead, she stared dry-eyed at Grady with a look of resignation.

If his day hadn't been bad enough already, Grady began to feel guilty, maybe even a little sorry for the way things had turned out. He pulled a handkerchief from his back pocket and wiped the dirt from his eyes. "If it'll help, I'll go get the tractor and drag that animal to my kill pit."

The din of High Horse's singing had gotten louder, and Chantale looked questioningly at Grady. "What?"

Grady repeated his offer loud enough for the albino to hear also. High Horse interrupted his caterwauling and stomped over to Grady.

"Once again, the White Man has taken our buffalo from us. These are our brothers, children of Mother Earth, spirits that accompany us on our journey to a higher plane. Too long have we suffered such indignities at the hands of people who lust for our blood. No, Mr. O'Grady, this magnificent creature will not be dumped in a pit littered with the bones of your other unfortunate animals."

Grady stared at them for a full minute, trying to figure out why they turned down his offer to dispose of the carcass.

He shrugged and said, "Suit yourself. But I want it out of here by nightfall."

Grady meant it. Dead critters attracted predators.

He reined Ole Moss toward the hill and headed back home. Over his shoulder he could hear That Woman's voice calling after him.

"You've not heard the last of this, Mr. Graden."

Ole Moss picked up her pace and flicked her tail. Even she seemed sick of those people.

CHAPTER EIGHT

Buford

The city council meeting hadn't begun. Buford looked around at the people who stood in the hall within the municipal building. A few had already taken seats in the council chambers, but most lingered outside the door, drinking coffee and quietly voicing their own concerns about the recent turn of events in Silverville. Not that they could characterize that turn in so many words. It was more like a series of waves crashing against their well-laid plans.

Buford glanced at tonight's agenda. A few short phrases summed up the plethora of issues the council would have to address. Two lines glared ominously at Buford from topics on the roster he held in his hand: *Ride Accident Lawsuit* and *Hells Angels*. Both issues made him sweat.

Also on the list he saw the council planned to discuss the controversial "Big Box." That alone would have brought Buford to the meeting. The last thing community businesses needed was competition from a gigantic discount store. Up and down Main Street, he'd heard the murmurs and complaints about what such a store would mean to Silverville. Everybody knew those big chains used sweatshop labor and they paid their employees dirt. And what if the store carried guns and ammunition that far undercut the merchandise at Price's Gun Paradise?

Of course, his first priority tonight would be damage control concerning the theme park and the larger economic project he had envisioned.

"Looks like pretty serious stuff tonight, huh."

Buford jumped at the voice. He looked up to see Denton standing beside him. Although Buford felt uncomfortable with the issues that would surface during the meeting, he shrugged as though he were unconcerned. "I'm not worried about the ride accident. Earl Bob can take care of it."

In fact, Buford had already instructed Earl Bob to work on that little problem.

A flash of confusion crossed Denton's face. "Earl Bob? That's sort of a stretch for a consultant, isn't it? Seems like you have him doing lots of things that aren't part of his job description."

"Think about it, Denton. You know how he handles women."

As if on cue, the crowd in the hall parted to allow a woman in a neck brace hobble towards the meeting room, banging her crutches on the door jamb as she entered. A man in a dark, expensive suit followed her. No doubt her attorney.

Buford turned back to Denton. "How's Howard holding up?"

"Not very well. I can't talk him into going back to the theme park."

"He's got to be more visible. Howard is a key player in this project, and people want to talk to him."

Denton shook his head and looked doubtful. "If you had seen a car fly off the arm of the Saturn Ring ride and crash just in front you, you might be shaken up, too."

"Well the woman didn't die, for Pete's sake."

"Thank heaven for small favors. But Howard helped pry her out of the car, and he held her hand until the ambulance arrived." Denton paused thoughtfully and then asked, "Do you know what the investigator found out?"

"The guy's being pretty close-mouthed so far. Lots of people heard a hum right before it happened."

"Maybe a cable unwinding?" Denton's words sounded more like an observation than a question.

"We can only hope. If that's the case, we'll sic that woman's attorney on the manufacturer and get the two of them off the city's back."

Buford heard the mayor bring the meeting to order with a loud rap of her gavel, and he and Denton stepped into the room to take a seat in the back. Tonight's issues drew a larger crowd than usual, and latecomers would have to stand along the walls. Glancing at the people sitting in front of them, Buford noticed Earl Bob had already taken a chair near the injured tourist. Their consultant must have slipped in when he and Denton were talking in the hallway.

As the meeting commenced, Buford watched Earl Bob lean over to the man beside him, whispering a few words and patting his neighbor on the back. Both men chuckled quietly at some private joke. He elbowed Denton in the side and pointed at Earl Bob.

"Look at that. The guy's a regular Prince Charming."

Denton gave Buford a funny look but said nothing.

From behind the council table facing the crowd, Mayor Schlopkohl blathered her opening remarks, but Buford didn't pay any attention to what she said. He was thinking instead about last Thursday. The way he had managed to stretch Earl Bob's job description. At first, Earl Bob had wanted nothing to do with negotiating the land deal, but it was easy for Buford to convince him. All he'd had to do was add a little innuendo to the conversation, reminding Earl Bob he needed Buford's protection if the man didn't want to be turned in for fraud – and maybe worse. But the truth was, he needed Earl Bob more than Earl Bob needed him. Whoever that con artist was, he had a finesse that had always eluded Buford. Earl Bob could sell manure to a stockyard whereas Buford was more likely to walk away with it smeared on his shoes. So far, he'd been able to convince Earl Bob that Buford held all the cards. When the expansion for the theme park had stalled, Buford had sent his trusty consultant to the reluctant landowner to make the deal. After one short meeting, Earl Bob walked out with a contract in his hand.

Buford was proud of the way he had talked Earl Bob into mediating the settlement between the landowner and the economic council. In his head, he could hear Earl Bob's protests. *I don't want to do this. I'm no land wheeler and dealer.* But Buford had quickly countered, jabbing his finger at the consultant's chest. *You will do it, Mr. Jackson. Just get used to being versatile.*

"Buford Price, what are you doing back there?"

Mayor Schlopkohl's voice slapped him back to the meeting. Buford realized that everybody was staring at him.

"Is there something wrong with your finger?" she asked sharply.

Buford looked at his finger, which was still pointing toward an imaginary Earl Bob.

"Uh, nothing, Mayor," he offered weakly.

He dropped the offending finger to his lap, covered it with his other hand, and ducked his head. Nevertheless, he felt Mayor Schlopkohl's glare on him for a full five seconds before she returned her attention to the meeting.

Buford studied the agenda and tried to match the current discussion with the appropriate item. Easements, zoning, property line disputes – Buford had trouble focusing on the more mundane issues of city council. He turned his eyes toward Mayor Schlopkohl as though he was giving her his undivided attention, but he didn't give a rip about other people's problems. Patiently, he waited to hear some mention of the Big Box issue, which would signal him to concentrate on the meeting again. He didn't have to wait long.

When the chain store took center stage, the council introduced a representative for Shop-Mart, who set up a flip chart and explained how the store would enhance the economic prosperity of the community. She maintained that a Shop-Mart would add to the city's sales revenues, pointing to graphs on her chart. She also insisted the store would encourage people to buy locally.

"In a pig's eye," Buford leaned over and whispered to Denton. "If I don't take Skippy out of town to shop at least once a month, she'll start climbing the walls."

When the Shop-Mart rep finished her presentation, she asked if there were any questions. Buford raised his hand.

"Is the store going to sell sporting goods?"

"Can you be more specific?" she asked.

"Guns and ammo."

She shook her head, saying, "Our store policy is not to sell firearms."

Buford relaxed back into his seat. Maybe having a large chain store in town wouldn't be such a bad idea. If it brought the town more revenue, how could it hurt?

Several other people raised their hands to voice concerns. Most worried about small businesses' loss of sales to the big discount center. It was all getting boring to Buford. Those downtown store owners were being petty whiners who couldn't see the bigger picture. One of them asked why Shop-Mart had ignored Silverville until now.

The rep smiled, saying, "You can thank Mr. Price and his hard work with the economic council. His vision has put Silverville on the map. Your new UFO theme for the city is starting to attract nationwide attention. It's the type of environment that demands a super store."

Buford puffed up as she gave credit where credit was due. But then he noticed quite a few people in the audience had started to scowl at him. He saw one man four rows up mouth the word, "asshole." The mayor announced to the crowd that the discussion would remain on the table. Although the discount store had a contract on a tract of land, Shop-Mart wouldn't be able to break ground for another two years. The city still had plenty of time to hold forums to explore apprehensions from the townsfolk.

As the rep put away her flip chart and packed up her briefcase, Buford turned his eyes toward the injured woman and the man sitting beside her. They huddled whispering, and Buford figured they were planning their tactics. The accident was the next item on the agenda.

Lela, looking expectantly at the city's attorney, said, "The ball is in your court on this one, Ralph."

Ralph Baldwin had served Silverville for only three years, but he had lived in the community for much longer. When he first arrived from Massachusetts twelve years ago, he'd hung a fancy shingle on a fancy new building. But no one trusted his northeastern accent, and he damn near starved that first year. Buford liked the fellow all right, although he'd never seen him win a case. The city had hired him for a song. He took the job because he seemed reluctant to return to his home state, and he liked to fish. At least that's what Buford had heard.

Clearing his throat, Baldwin stood and droned in a monotone voice to the council. "A suit has been filed alleging the city's theme park is unsafe, and . . ." he paused and slipped on glasses perched precariously near the tip of his nose and glanced down at a document, "let's see now, yes, that our fair community has taken inadequate precautions to assure the welfare of those who visit the park."

He peered up over his glasses as if to assure himself everyone was listening, and added, "Mayor Schlopkohl, the plaintiff and her attorney are here this evening, not to plead their case, but to follow the measures the city might take to eliminate future accidents."

"How much is the suit?" someone called out.

Since Buford already knew and had told so many people, he was surprised anyone asked.

"A million dollars," Baldwin reported to the assembly.

Although the council sat grim-faced at the amount, a ripple of gasps spread through the crowd as the city attorney continued, "The suit requests fifty-thousand dollars for medical expenses, and four-hundred fifty-thousand for mental anguish."

"For a broken leg?" Buford blurted out before he could stop himself. He'd heard the figure but not the breakdown.

"And an additional half million dollars," Baldwin continued, "the city must raise to upgrade the rides and have them periodically inspected for safety."

A woman near the front asked if the city didn't have insurance for this kind of thing, to which Baldwin responded, "Of course. But it only covers the accident, not a fund designed to augment facilities already in place. It's a discussion of such plans that are before the council tonight."

He sat back down.

"We could propose a mill levy to cover upgrades to the rides," the mayor offered.

A murmur arose from the crowd as they reacted to the idea of increasing taxes. Buford frowned and looked over at Denton.

"I don't get it. Why would the council even suggest that? This thing hasn't even gone to court yet."

"I suspect the city wants to go on record as being diligent about this," Denton answered. "Might make the judge more lenient on us if we've taken a step to fix this even before it goes to court."

Lela rapped her gavel to restore order in the room, and then said, "Whether a mill levy will be needed or not, I propose the council approve funds for initial upgrades and inspections. Let it be known that the city's first priority is to provide a safe environment for its visitors. Do I hear a motion?"

Within minutes, the council members approved the measure although Buford could see in their faces they probably felt they had no choice. At this, the man from the fourth row turned around and faced Buford, again mouthing the word, "asshole." Buford tried to shrug it off. The town had to learn to expect some growing pains if they wanted Silverville to prosper. Besides, a mill levy would go to the voters for approval, and by the time citizens cast their ballots, they'd realize how much they'd gained from the theme park.

When it was clear the topic would go no further during the meeting, the accident victim and her lawyer stood and then worked their way toward the door. Buford caught Earl Bob's eye and motioned with his head in their direction as they left the chambers. Earl Bob nodded and followed them into the hall at a discrete distance.

Buford looked down at the agenda and saw one topic left. One that would surely interest everyone. The Hells Angels.

As Schlopkohl announced the final item, three men who'd been standing near the side windows began to move toward the front of the room.

"As you all may have heard," the mayor began, "the Hells Angels are planning to make a stop in Silverville this July on their way to their annual rally. To shed light on what we can expect, we have three gentlemen from the town of Sagebrush, Colorado."

One by one, the mayor introduced them. "Let me welcome the Sagebrush city manager, the town's chief of police, and that county's sheriff. We've asked them all here to share their own experiences when this gang traveled through their town.

"Chief Freeport, would you care to speak first?"

Buford had trouble seeing the man the mayor had introduced as someone who could inspire law and order. Freeport couldn't have stood more than five feet, five inches, and he was as wide as he was tall. At his center of gravity rested a large square belt buckle, of which only the bottom half was visible. The top portion remained hidden under a layer of belly fat that threatened the snaps of the man's white cowboy shirt. When the police chief began to speak, his voice reminded Buford of a girl's.

"We're happy to share with you folks what happened in our town," he squeaked, "when the Hell's Angels came through last summer. I can tell you this, we weren't ready for the trouble they caused. For one thing, we had anticipated roughly one-hundred to two-hundred Angels passing through, and we didn't expect them to stop. We saw instead up to six-hundred, and they decided to camp in the area for a few days."

A hush had fallen over the audience in the council chambers to the point you could almost hear the sweat drop from the speaker's forehead.

"As you can imagine, that many Angels had quite an impact on a town of three-thousand. Besides the fact that people were afraid to leave their homes, our bars were packed every night, our streets were crowded with bikes, and business as usual seemed to come to a standstill. There were fights, lots of them. Mostly amongst themselves, but they busted up one drinking establishment and scared the regulars out of the other one.

"Our dispatch line was ringing constantly, and with only two officers on duty per shift, we just couldn't be every place at once. One of them shot a dog, and a group of them drove through the park's flower bed. We never could find out who was responsible, but it could have been any of them. Make no mistake, these people are the scum of the earth."

No one spoke when the Sagebrush chief of police had finished, but a good many spooked faces turned to look at Carl as though they expected him to protect them then and there. Carl didn't return the looks with much confidence. He only coughed a couple of times and shifted his feet.

Mayor Schlopkohl then invited the Sagebrush city manager to speak.

"Good evening, folks," he said, stepping forward. He smiled and a silver tooth flashed under the fluorescent lights at the same time as his over-polished wingtip shoes. His snappy suit showed barely a wrinkle even though the party had driven a hundred and fifty miles that hot afternoon. "I'm Tom Hodges, city manager of Sagebrush. As Chief Freeport mentioned, three law enforcement officers at a time couldn't manage the disruption the Angels created in our town. Even though Silverville has about the same pool of police officers, I can't stress enough the importance of beefing up the force you have on hand. You might even consider contracting out of town for more officers and security people."

"How much man power do you think we'll need?" asked a council member.

"I think the best person to answer that question might be Sheriff McCullough," Hodges replied, and he turned to the third Sagebrush representative. "Ed, what kind of numbers would you recommend for Silverville?"

McCullough was slow to answer, as though he were making calculations in his head. The sheriff stroked the strings falling from his bolo tie as he said, "At least eight per shift, and if you can muster it, twelve."

Someone from the audience called out, "Won't that be pretty pricey?"

McCullough shrugged. "You might check into getting national guard units. It's probably what we should have done."

All the discussion of the need to maintain law and order made Buford nervous. This wasn't good PR for Silverville. Undesirables shouldn't even be allowed to step foot into town and he spoke up and said so.

But the city attorney responded to Buford's complaint. "It's a free country, Mr. Price. You can't stop people from coming and going just because you don't like how they look."

"But these people cause trouble. Don't forget I own a gun store. Maybe the city should hire an officer just to stand guard in my store."

"*You* can hire an officer for Gun Paradise," the mayor corrected him. "The city is responsible for the welfare of the entire community."

"Hey look, if we let this sort of riffraff into town, who knows what other kinds of trash will follow."

The man who earlier had mouthed obscenities at Buford jumped into the conversation. "You should have thought about that before you started this damn UFO crap."

Several other people started to shout in agreement, and Schlopkohl again slammed her gavel on the table.

"What can individuals do to protect themselves?" an audience member asked.

Chief Freeport was quick to address the question. "Mind your own business and keep your daughters off the streets."

Mayor Schlopkohl looked aghast at the implication. "Why? Were there any sexual assaults?"

"Well, no," Freeport confessed, "but you've seen those movies. You know what they're capable of."

The mayor nodded thoughtfully and glanced down the row of council members seated at the table to see if anyone had anything to add. No one offered to speak. "Let it be duly noted that the council has taken the recommendations from the Sagebrush representatives, and we will move forward in our investigation of hiring additional law enforcement officers.

"Do we have any other business to discuss?" Hearing none, she wrapped her gavel and adjourned the meeting.

As everyone stood and prepared to leave, Buford noticed an uncharacteristic hush over those who'd been present. Instead of the usual din of noise, people seemed lost in their thoughts, hardly aware of their neighbors as they exited the room. Buford imagined that every person pondered the issues that affected each one personally. Buford did the same. What did it matter if a Big Box came to Silverville? It certainly would be no skin off his nose, particularly since they didn't plan to sell guns. Besides, those good folks who visited Silverville needed more places to shop. The town needed to show the world it wasn't some little backwater dive that couldn't survive in the twenty-first century, he rationalized.

As for the ride accident, the town had to expect a few bumps in the road toward success. The city would show good intentions by upgrading the rides, and Earl Bob might even talk the injured tourist into dropping her suit. The judge would surely come down easy on Silverville since the city had only the best intentions for the theme park.

Of more concern was the charge that Silverville's recent notoriety had begun to draw a more unsavory element. This one stumped Buford. How could the town continue to attract the right kind of paying customers if they had to contend with the likes of bike-riding rabble-rousers and rapists? It wasn't the Silverville he had envisioned.

Buford noticed Denton easing himself slowly out of his folding chair. The undertaker returned his look, smiling apologetically.

"Your hip bothering you?"

"It was a long meeting, wasn't it," Denton said as he stood on unsteady legs.

As they headed toward the door, Buford guided their steps past Carl. A small crowd surrounded the sheriff, a crowd that appeared to be demanding answers about their concerns regarding the Hell's Angels. Buford tugged on Denton's sleeve to join the throng gathering around Carl.

"You've got a question for Carl, too?"

"Yeah," Buford replied, "but not about the bikers."

They waited until the crowd thinned and the last person finally walked away.

Carl looked haggard as he turned to face his two friends. "If you've got questions about the bikers, you can stop right there. I'm still trying to figure out what to do myself."

"No," Buford said. "It's something else. There's a rumor around town that Grady shot that albino and now he's in jail."

Carl swore, "Sweet Jesus! How do these stories get started? No, that's not what happened. Grady killed Chantale's white buffalo because it was in his heifer pasture. To make matters worse, the damn old fool killed her dog, too."

Buford winced. All he needed was to have her pack up her money and leave town.

"No reason to put Grady in jail," Carl continued. "The buffalo was trespassing, and the dog attacked Grady's horse. In fact, it could be Grady's the one who has a case. That bull might have bred all those heifers. Grady said when he put his own bull in the pasture, he didn't see no romance."

Everything seemed to be going to hell in a handbag. Buford shook his head, wondering how he was going to be able to hold it all together.

What else could go wrong?

CHAPTER NINE

Billy

Billy scanned the city park. She was the one who suggested they change their usual weekly meeting at the Lazy S to discuss progress at the museum. But so far, Skippy was nowhere in sight. The ten acres of grass before him provided the city with two tennis courts, a small complex of baseball diamonds, assorted playground equipment, and a vast picnic area. Here and there, people sat at outdoor tables or on park benches; a young boy stood on the edge of the pond's bank, fishing pole gripped in his tiny fists. Billy had heard that in the winter, when the pond froze over, the townsfolk used it as a local skating rink. Free, of course, and compliments of the city.

He walked to the nearest empty picnic table and swung one leg over to straddle the seat. He glanced at his watch. Four-thirty. Skippy would probably just be getting off work and would be there soon.

Smelling the aroma of grilling hamburgers, Billy watched as a young family prepared a late-afternoon cookout. He recognized the faces of the adults although he didn't know their names. At a line of picnic tables, he saw many familiar faces. Most, when he met them on the street, greeted him with a polite smile or wave, behavior he was unaccustomed to because he'd never stayed anywhere long enough to acquaint himself with a whole community. A quick hustle, and he'd always been gone. Even more amazing, most of these people seemed friendly and appeared to respect the work the City had hired him to do. Never had Billy experienced this type of esteem. These poor suckers were desperate to bring money into the community even if it did mean dealing with a stranger and a crackpot like Buford.

Of course, not all the faces looked familiar, and he suspected those he didn't know were tourists. It was easy to pick them out. For one thing, out-of-towners slowly strolled the city streets, gawking in shop windows and holding hands. They wore the typical uniform of vacationers – Hawaiian shirts and garish shorts that showed blue-white skin unaccustomed to mountain sunshine. Every now and then, one would try to "fit in" by wearing a hat they presumed was cowboy attire. Instead, the headgear was usually some unidentifiable brimmed affair, perhaps better worn in Australia or Mexico. In any case, the sandals or spiked heels would give them away.

He looked down at his own new pair of Justin boots and wondered if he hadn't unconsciously purchased them so he, too, could fit in.

A black BMW sedan rounded the corner, slowing to pass the row of RVs parked along the curb. Skippy's silhouette in the car window outlined her delicate features and perfectly coiffed hair. She was unlike any woman he had ever known. Gracious and elegant, Skippy always seemed to command respect – but somehow without ever asking for it. Billy had over the past month seen quite a bit of her, not exactly on a social basis but mostly because of the work they'd done on the museum. He felt it was just enough time to shift from a strictly formal relationship to the beginnings of a friendship. And he'd grown to admire her sincerity. For a woman with so much class, she never acted self-absorbed and she showed the same kindness to everyone, regardless of their station in life.

How had she ever ended up with a man like Buford?

Buford no doubt wondered that himself. He seemed to treat her more like a trophy than a wife. Even that car – Buford had probably bought for appearance's sake. Billy had noticed when things would start going south for Buford, he'd bring out Skippy, as if to say, *No matter what you think of me, I'm good enough to have this wonderful woman at my side.*

The BMW nosed in just past the string of Jurassic-sized vehicles and parked. Skippy popped the door open and gracefully slid from her seat. Smoothing her skirt and pushing her auburn hair behind her ears, she surveyed the park until her eyes landed on Billy. She lanced him with a brilliant smile and headed his direction.

When she reached the picnic table, she seated herself opposite him.

"Isn't this much nicer than the coffee shop?" Skippy asked.

"No argument there."

Earlier in the day he'd called, telling her he had a favor to ask. The favor he had in mind resulted from a deal he'd cut with the woman injured on the theme park ride. It had taken some finagling, but Billy had talked the tourist into dropping the mental anguish part of her lawsuit – on one condition, that the city organize a safety board to field complaints and take suggestions about the theme park.

"What's up, Earl Bob? What did you want to talk to me about?" Skippy peeled off her sunglasses and placed them atop her head.

"I need a chair person."

She laughed. "Am I the only one you know around here?"

He felt a sheepish grin spread across his face. "Well, the only one with enough finesse to do it right."

"Okay, what committee? You know, Mr. Jackson, I'm already on a lot of committees."

Skippy's involvement in the community was considerable. He knew full well she served on the museum board of directors. She was also on the boards for the Friends of the Library and the hospital. There might have been more because he'd heard Buford say Skippy attended one meeting or another at least four times a week.

"It's for the new theme park safety board. I'd take on the job myself, but Buford keeps me hopping. Besides, the position needs somebody who's diplomatic and can round up the right people to serve on the committee."

Skippy appeared to mull it over in her mind. For a couple of minutes, she said nothing, and Billy wondered if she was trying to figure out a nice way to turn him down.

Finally she spoke. "I'm going to have to think about this."

He didn't want to push too hard, but he needed to get his board together. The injured woman demanded Silverville act without delay. Before his meeting with the tourist had ended, Billy had softened her to the point sympathy for the struggling city outweighed her need to extract revenge. She did, however, want to see evidence that this new board was on track, so Billy didn't have much time to wait for Skippy's answer.

"At least let me know soon if you come to a decision."

"Okay, I've just thought about it, and no. I just don't have time." She changed the subject, chatting about the museum and the upcoming UFO lectures Billy had arranged. Mention of the lecture topic sent a spasm through his gut. So far, Billy had managed to schedule his speakers via emails and written letters, avoiding at all cost any personal conversations though the telephone. When Billy had gone through the Pisser's proposed list of guest lecturers, he couldn't discern if any of them were personal acquaintances of Earl Bob's. Billy knew he had to proceed with caution in making the contacts. Luckily, Buford, in his zeal to present Earl Bob as the bona fide consultant, had engineered excuses for Billy's absence from the earlier presentations – just in case somebody might recognize the scam. But even Buford agreed Billy couldn't stay away from the lecturers every time. In the end, the two of them evolved a plan to have Buford meet the visiting specialist in advance and tease out whether he or she had ever met Earl Bob in person.

The third guest speaker of the series was due in the next day, and Skippy mentioned she was looking forward to the theme.

"The first two lectures seemed a bit too sensationalized for my taste," she said.

"I take it you didn't attend?"

She rolled her eyes and grinned. "I heard you didn't go either."

"Well, I got wrapped up in something else. Besides, I've heard all that stuff before," Billy lied.

She gave him an odd look, and then asked, "But you're going to the SETI presentation tomorrow night, right?"

Billy had never heard of the Search for Extraterrestrial Intelligence project until a month ago, when he'd found the contact information among the Pisser's notes.

"I don't know. I need to find out from Buford if I have anything else to do." Actually, Billy had to wait to see if Buford could find out if the SETI specialist knew Earl Bob.

"I'll make sure Buford doesn't give you some other job so you can go. In fact, you can come with me. I think the topic sounds interesting."

He briefly looked away as he said, "We'll have to see."

She tilted her head and stared at him questioningly.

"You're the Washington consultant. I would have thought Buford would take his cue from you, but it seems the other way around. Or am I mistaken?"

Billy laughed, hoping it would be enough to dismiss the issue.

"I heard you were out soliciting support from local business owners who haven't contributed to the project," Skippy said.

"Well, Buford needed some help with –"

"Denton is right," she interrupted softly. "He said Buford was sending you in all sorts of directions that have nothing to do with your consulting job. What kind of agreement do you two have to let him push you around like that?"

"See, that's why you would've been the perfect chair," he joked. "You seem to take on everybody's problems."

"Do you consider this a problem?"

Her question startled him. Was his struggle that apparent? Perhaps he had let Buford become too overriding when it came to situations the local entrepreneur couldn't manage himself. If Denton and Skippy suspected something odd, then other people might as well. But how would he fare if Buford pulled the rug out from under him?

Picnickers sauntered by, and neither Billy nor Skippy spoke until the people passed out of hearing range.

She reached her arms across the table, and for a moment Billy thought she was going to take his hand.

"You're a wonderful person, Earl Bob. People in Silverville respond to you, and you're helping us make this project a reality. But you're not really a UFO consultant, are you?"

Her words shook Billy. Had Buford told her the truth, or somehow said too much? Billy doubted it. The man didn't strike him as someone who willingly shared secrets – not even with his wife. That would mean Buford would lose the power to call the shots, and Billy knew from personal experience what a control freak he was working with. No, Skippy had to have guessed something of Billy's secret by some other means. Not that Billy felt he had much choice in the matter, but her question was a reminder he was working with an amateur.

Skippy continued to look at him, obviously waiting to see how he would respond.

Probably best with caution, he decided. "What do you mean?"

"Buford knew he couldn't pull off the UFO promotion on his own. He'd been looking for someone outside our community from the start, someone who could provide the credibility he lacked."

She broke eye contact with Billy for just a second, almost as though she felt uncertain how much she should say. "Oh, Buford is a great promoter, but, well, he's had his share of schemes that didn't work out. He told me he had to find some way to inspire confidence in the project. It was shortly after that he began talking about the new contact he'd made. The contact with you."

Billy studied her carefully. For a professional con man, he was surprised at how hard he found it to lie to Skippy – at least, now that he'd gotten to know her.

"That's right, Skippy, he contacted me." That was true enough. Only, the contact was outside the diner when he'd first arrived in town.

"Yes, but – oh, excuse me, Earl Bob, maybe I'm getting too snoopy, but I feel I can ask this because we've become friends. It just seems odd, the way Buford pushes you around. Like he's holding something over your head. And the way you've been avoiding the lecturers. It just doesn't make sense to me. Unless Buford is forcing you into some kind of charade." She paused and then added, "Is he?"

Billy realized that he'd arrived at a critical moment. Even more important was how Skippy would react to any kernel of truth. If he told her the real story, she might go to the police and he'd have to hightail it out of town. But even with Buford's manipulations, Billy wasn't ready to bail out of what could become The Big One.

At the back of his mind another thought began to take shape as well. One of loss. At no time in Billy's adult life could he remember developing any type of a lasting friendship. Lovers, yes, but not friends. After he lost the anchor of his mother's influence, life had cast him adrift in a sea of hustlers and easy marks. Skippy was the first person he'd met who seemed grounded and stable. A knot in his stomach rose to his throat and he couldn't speak.

Children behind them chattered happily as they played catch. The sky had folded into the rich azure blue of late afternoon. A breeze began to drift lightly across the park, carrying the scent of freshly cut grass.

"It's okay," she said. "I know what Buford is like. I've seen him do this kind of thing to other people before."

The truth – or at least some version of it – began to trickle from his lips. She didn't interrupt as he confessed that he'd stumbled onto the town, that he and Buford had made a pact, and that he now felt trapped by a secret he couldn't tell her. When he finished, Skippy sat without stirring.

At first, she said nothing at all.

Denton

Denton joined the assembly gathered beside Chantale's unfinished pyramid. Considering it was a funeral for a buffalo, she had managed to pull together a pretty large crowd. Buford had seen to that – at least for some of them. The rest, Denton figured, showed up because they expected the sumptuous spread laid out on the picnic tables before them. Champagne would flow freely, too.

Thank goodness, Chantale hadn't asked him, the only undertaker in town, to embalm her cherished "Tatanka" when she'd called him for advice about the service. The bull's great white hulk rested on a sturdy wooden platform raised two feet above the ground and covered with twisted sage bundles. Expensive flower arrangements surrounded the animal, allowing no more than glimpses of the shaggy pale hide. The whole display stood a short walking distance from the gathered mourners. Luckily, the two-day-old carcass was downwind.

Several people hung around the tables of food as though they were hoping to be the first ones in line when the time came for Chantale to signal the feast. Denton knew the order of events for how this was going to work. Although he had never officiated over an animal funeral, he had once sold a baby coffin to a grieving family who had lost their dog. To Chantale, he simply suggested a sequence of rituals commonly observed in human funerals.

She hadn't followed them all.

That morning, she and Hans High Horse had conducted what the Juanabee Indian had called a traditional sweat. Denton turned that invitation down, explaining that his hip wouldn't allow him to sit for the ceremony. However, Felicia learned from Skippy that Buford attended, and it didn't go well for him. When the steam from the moistened hot rocks filled the cavity of the sweat lodge, Buford began gasping for breath. Within minutes, he was crying like a baby. He collapsed on his side and started sucking at the duck-canvas flooring for air, but High Horse wouldn't let him out of the lodge, saying it would taint the "medicine." Evidently, Buford passed out because the albino had to drag him outside when it was over. It was amazing how good Buford looked this afternoon after the two-hour ordeal.

Chantale had also hired the Bad Booze Boys, a local country-western band, and she'd had a dance area cleared next to the teepee. Denton had heard these musicians before, and he didn't think too many people would be able to dance to their tunes. For one thing, the lead singer appeared perpetually drunk. Even now, he staggered through the crowd, spilling beer on anyone who happened on his path. His glory days were well in the past. A beer belly inflated the singer's gut and strained against the silver concho buttons of his black leather vest. Obviously unable to cinch tight his matching leather pants, he seemed unaware of his backside cleavage shining in the afternoon sun. He made occasional passes at some of the women, but most made polite excuses that left him standing by himself.

Buford appeared out of the crowd and strolled toward Denton. His face looked redder than usual. A steam burn?

"I can't stand that goddamned noise," Buford complained, looking toward High Horse. The Indian sat cross-legged beside his teepee and banged on a drum while he chanted. "What's with this 'hey-he-high-ho' stuff? It's giving me a headache."

Denton ignored his question. "How are you after this

morning?"

"This morning? You mean the sweat?" He shrugged it off. "A piece of cake. I thought that Indian would faint and I'd have to drag him outside. Guess albinos can't take all that heat."

"Un-huh." Denton changed the subject. "Is Skippy going to be here?"

"Of course. She should be showing up any minute now, at least I hope so. She didn't want to come."

Denton gave Buford a questioning look without saying anything, and Buford continued. "She's been in a mood the last two days. PMS or something. But she'll be here. Oh, there's her car driving up now."

They watched her BMW drive into the make-shift parking lot in the pasture below the teepee and maneuver next to Earl Bob's Cadillac. But instead of emerging from the sedan, she sat there for a full thirty seconds before putting her car in reverse and backing out of the line of cars.

"What's she doing?" Buford asked, shaking his head.

She pulled the car to the other end of the string of vehicles, parked, and got out. Skippy walked to the edge of the crowd and stopped, looking around.

Denton decided she was looking for Buford and said, "Maybe you should wave."

Buford flung his arm up until Skippy caught sight of him. She waved back but headed in the direction of a group of women clustered near one of the picnic tables.

"That's my girl," Buford said, "mixing and mingling."

"Does everybody have to be useful to you?"

"Never hurts."

Big talk, coming from a man who anonymously contributed the trophies for the mutton busting at the rodeo every year. Denton knew Buford wasn't as uncaring as he sometimes pretended to be. Too bad a lot of folks in town didn't know that.

"Maybe I better go mix and mingle, too, before you find no use for me either," Denton said, and he ambled over closer to the crowd, which began to form a line in front of the tables laden with food.

While he scanned the gathering, looking around for Felicia,

Denton saw Earl Bob wave at Skippy and walk toward her. At the same time, Skippy turned in the opposite direction. Earl Bob paused and Denton thought he saw a look of consternation on the consultant's face. Skippy had clearly seen Earl Bob, yet she appeared to avoid him. The whole scene struck Denton as odd. But then, Buford did say that Skippy had been acting temperamental lately.

Perhaps she was feeling overwhelmed with her involvement in the museum. Felicia had mentioned that Mrs. Watson had been calling Skippy about the panhandlers hanging around the museum entrance. Skippy told Felicia she was reluctant to have Carl oust them because she feared they were homeless people who had drifted in with the throngs of visitors. She even confessed to having dropped a dollar into one of their cups. When Buford heard about that, she said he hit the roof. His solution was to give "those bums" a one-way bus ticket over to Sagebrush. Yes, Denton could see why Skippy might be in a mood these days. He just hoped the stress wouldn't push her off the deep end.

For ten years, she'd teetered precariously close to the edge of alcoholism, a life she tried so hard to avoid. It must have been hell for Skippy to wake up behind the steering wheel, not knowing how she'd driven into some strange alley. Or to have whole days missing from her memory. Felicia once told him Skippy had called her from a hotel room in a neighboring casino town, crying that she had no idea how she'd gotten there. Surprisingly, only Buford, the Fines, and her counselor were aware of her problem. No easy feat in a town the size of Silverville.

Clouds began to gather over the mountains, and a slight breeze blew against Denton's back. He hoped Chantale's affair was done before an afternoon storm swept in.

The squelch of a microphone startled him. Chantale stood at a podium resting atop a boxed platform placed between the picnic tables and the buffalo's funeral pyre.

"I'd like to thank y'all for coming to this celebration of my beloved Tatanka's life. Hans will offer a blessing to send our loved one on his way to the Plains of Everlasting Happiness. Afterwards, we'll commend his spirit to a Higher Power through the purification of flames. I invite you to stay for lunch, champagne, and dancing when the ceremony's over."

Someone in the crowd called out, "Right on!"

Chantale scowled at the interruption, stepping down from the podium as Hans took her place. The Juanabee Indian stretched his arms toward the sky and stood perfectly still for over a minute. Just as Denton decided the blessing was silent, Hans began to speak.

"Oh Wapa Wapa, oh Great One from whom all things flow and toward whom all things return at their appointed time." As he spoke, he opened his arms in a gesture that seemed meant to gather the crowd into his embrace. "Look down on us, your children. See our heavy hearts. See our pain and grief at the loss of one so dear to all of us."

High Horse's tremulous voice was so convincing, Denton half expected to see a gathering of actual mourners. In fact, he couldn't help but wonder if the Indian had missed his calling. He ranked up there with the preachers at any of the funerals Denton had witnessed.

High Horse continued, "Prepare to receive one who is noble of spirit and wise beyond his station in life. As he walked the long and winding road, he took a sad song and made it better. He taught us the stuff that dreams are made of. But now, somewhere over the rainbow, skies are blue for Tatanka. Oh Wapa Wapa, please give Tatanka a home where he may roam, where the skies are not cloudy all day. . ."

Denton's mind wandered as High Horse droned on. After fifteen minutes, the Indian stepped down from the podium. He marched over to the funeral pyre, lifted a torch, and lit the structure on fire. He began anew the chanting Buford had complained about earlier, pausing to face each of the cardinal points of the compass before setting fire to the pyre from all four sides. The tinder and wood beneath the buffalo's platform sparked and crackled. Within seconds, Tatanka was engulfed in flames. A torrent of dark smoke snaked away and down into the valley below Chantale's property.

A half hour later, the fire had made little progress in diminishing the bulk of the animal's carcass. People standing at a distance began to show signs of restlessness, and Denton speculated it might take all night to reduce the buffalo to ashes – certainly, longer than the gathered mourners would be willing to wait for their food. He decided to explain that little detail to Chantale and edged his way closer toward her.

She stood gazing into the fire, rivulets of mascara running down her cheeks. It was a familiar scenario for Denton's type of business, and he donned his best professional persona as he stepped up to speak to her.

"You've started Tatanka on his, um, journey," Denton said, gently touching her elbow. "Perhaps this is the time for the commemorative meal."

Chantale turned to him, grief lining her face. For a few moments she said nothing, then stuttered, "Oh, oh, of course. I'll do that now."

She faced the crowd behind her and announced it was time for the feast to begin.

Denton, stomach growling, slid into the line right behind Carl. "Afternoon, Sheriff."

The lanky lawman eased himself around and gave Denton a nod. "I've been meaning to remind you, we're counting on you to work the sound booth at the rodeo next month."

Denton swallowed hard and smiled. For seven years the job had been his, and now he couldn't seem to get rid of it. Initially, the rodeo board had asked him to buy a sponsorship sign, but Denton didn't feel comfortable having the name of Fine Funeral Home hanging in the arena as cowboys risked life and limb before a crowd of spectators. He'd offered to make a donation without publicity. The board gladly took his money and still asked him to help out. It wasn't that Denton minded working the sound booth. After all, the system wasn't so different from the one at the funeral home. But no one told him that once you took on a rodeo job, it was yours until you died.

Carl continued, "Looks like we're going to need all the help we can muster if those Hell's Angels come through about that time."

Denton nodded. The talk around town for the past few days had been about little else. Two of the local motels reported that bookings from the bikers overlapped the dates for the July rodeo.

That made the timing particularly bad because Silverville would fill up with cowboys and bikers on the same weekend – a potentially explosive mix. Denton could see local vigilantes butting heads with hardened gangs wearing leather and chains. He shuddered at the thought.

The closer Denton moved to the silverware, the more he began looking for Felicia. Just as he spotted her, he picked up two plates and waved them above his head to catch her attention. While he waited for her, Denton surveyed the fare before him. Heaping bowls of caviar were sandwiched between sweetbreads and crackers. Plates of fruit, vegetables, and cheese lay upon the tables, followed by trays of lobster medallions and fantail shrimp. But where was the real meat? Denton searched the tables until he noticed a platter full of round burgers perched inconspicuously right before him.

"Those are probably veggie-burgers, Denton," Felicia said as she came up next to him. "I doubt Chantale would serve beef, let alone buffalo."

From behind him, a waiter in a white chef's hat carried a large ice sculpture of Tatanka, carefully placing it on a separate pedestal. The man reached into nearby buckets and retrieved bottles of champagne, which he uncorked with ceremonious flair. Everyone in the vicinity held out glasses to be filled.

As the guests loaded plates with food, the wind began to whip the linen table cloths. A pile of napkins caught in a gust and soared overhead like a flock of paper birds.

"What is that smell?" Felicia asked, wrinkling her nose.

At the same time she spoke, a billow of smoke pushed into his face, stinging his eyes. He looked up from his plate to see an ash-filled cloud from the burning buffalo blowing straight through the tents covering the food and mourner-guests. The wind had shifted direction, bringing with it the stench of Tatanka's burning hair and hide.

For an instant, nobody moved. Then the crowd scattered away from the direct path of the smoke blanketing the picnic tables. Most still held onto their plates; several tried to wolf down food as they retreated. Denton couldn't imagine how anyone still had enough appetite to eat, considering the smell that now permeated the entire grounds. Obviously, some people couldn't. They had abandoned their plates on the grass and were heading toward the parking area.

Through the haze, the shadowy figures of Chantale, Hans, and Carl tried to stomp out the sparks that leaped from the pyre. A ring of fire spread in the grass and away from the burning buffalo – the beginnings of a prairie fire that stomping feet had little chance to quell.

"Come on, Felicia." Denton grabbed his wife by the arm and maneuvered her toward the parked vehicles.

As they opened the doors to their car, Denton glanced over his shoulder to see the top of one of the tents ablaze. The picnic tables where everyone had stood would be next.

He started the car and steered it toward the driveway. But with so many vehicles jammed near the exit, he had to wait his turn to get out. The wind continued to carry the flames up the hill and away from the cars so there was no immediate danger. By the time they had reached the gravel road leading to the highway, they met two of Silverville's three fire trucks arriving at the scene.

At least Chantale's pyramid would be spared before the flames reached further up hill.

Billy

The mid-afternoon sun struggled to filter through the grease-coated windows of the Lazy S Diner. Except for a group of cowboys sitting around a large corner table, most of the folks taking their coffee breaks had emptied out of the place. The Coca-Cola clock on the wall read four-twenty.

It was unusual for her to be this late for their weekly meetings. But the way they had ended their last conversation had also been unusual. Billy wondered if Skippy would show up at all. She certainly hadn't seemed interested in talking to him when he'd seen her at Chantale's. She barely gave him a look before she melted into the crowd.

"If you want lemon meringue pie, you'd better order it now," Fawn said as she stopped at his booth to refill his coffee cup. "There's only one slice left."

Damn, was he becoming that predictable? Every Thursday he and Skippy had met that month, Billy had fallen into the routine of eating pie.

"Yeah, sure."

Odd as Fawn was, Billy no longer felt as uncomfortable around her. And he had grown to like her dog, which always accompanied her when she worked the desk at his hotel. He'd once heard that people and their dogs looked alike. It wasn't entirely true of Fawn and Portia. Red freckles splattered the mid-sized, overweight mutt, characteristics Fawn didn't share with her pet. Still, the dog had the uncanny talent of being able to twist its radar ears in independent directions – a trait similar to Fawn's independent eyes.

The door to the diner pushed open and in stepped Grady. The old rancher looked around and gave Billy a perfunctory nod. Of course, he would. Courtesy was standard in these small western towns, Billy had noticed since he'd made his way west of the Mississippi. Even more so to strangers than to troublesome locals like Buford. Grady moved toward the table of cowboys and sat down. Seeing the old rancher at the restaurant on Thursday was another predictable ritual. Billy had overheard enough from the corner table to know the group gathered every week to discuss the upcoming rodeo.

Fawn arrived with his pie, set squarely on a familiar blue flower-stenciled plate – a pattern he'd come to know well. Billy's life had begun to fill with Silverville patterns. In some ways it almost seemed natural now, and a sharp contrast from the sporadic lifestyle he'd always known. There was an advantage, however, to being stuck in this two-bit cow town. Every day he learned something new he could use to turn his situation into The Big One.

He pushed his fork into the slice of pie, but his mind replayed the confession he'd made to Skippy in the park. Why couldn't he have kept his mouth shut? He should have resisted the weak moment he confirmed her suspicion that he was an imposter, even if he had skipped the part about running over the Pisser.

"So who are you really?" she'd asked. "How did you end up pandering to Buford?"

"My real name is Billy Noble, not that it matters."

"Noble? I know that name." Confusion laced her voice, but Billy kept right on talking.

"And no, I'm not a real UFO consultant. But it's not what you think. I didn't come here to pull a scam on Silverville."

At that point, he'd expected her to get up and leave. Although she didn't.

"But you have. That's exactly what you're doing."

"Yes and no. It depends on how you look at it."   It was true he and Buford had deceived the community. But playing the role of Earl Bob served a greater purpose. Without him, the town wouldn't have had the inspiration or the self-confidence to move forward with their economic strategy. The argument was Buford's justification, but it was one that had begun to make sense. Billy had surprised himself by coming up with proposals that had actually been popular.

However, when he told Skippy how he looked at it, she didn't seem to share his appraisal of the situation.

She shook her head, saying, "This is turning out to be another one of Buford's schemes."

"But this one could work."

"Maybe." She paused. "How did you get mixed up in all this anyway?"

"I didn't seem to have much choice."

She took a deep breath and then said, "He's got something on you." She said it as though it was a statement of the facts.

"Yeah, he has." Billy shrugged but kept his head down as he admitted his fix.

She sat quietly for a moment, and then said, "I'm sorry, Earl Bob – I mean, Billy."

"Probably better to keep calling me Earl Bob. No one – not even Buford – knows my real name."

She said under her breath as much to herself as to Billy, "That figures. I doubt Buford would even care what your real name is." Tears filled her eyes. "Damn that Buford."

She had spoken with such animosity in her voice that Billy had been taken aback.

Today, as he sat waiting for her to arrive at the diner, he was still perplexed at her reaction. Billy looked at the empty plate and didn't remember eating the lemon meringue pie. The hands on the Coca-Cola clock now displayed four-thirty.

"She's not coming," he murmured to himself, feeling a pang of regret pinch his gut. Skippy must hate him for being an imposter.

He sensed someone standing behind him, but before Billy could shift sideways in the booth, he heard Fawn saying, "She's right outside the door."

"Excuse me?"

"Skippy. She's right outside."

He shot a grateful glance at Fawn, slid out of the booth, and walked over to the door. Skippy stood on the other side of the plate glass, her hand resting on the knob. She looked like she didn't know whether to come inside or not.

He pulled the door open. "Skippy, are you coming in?"

She looked up. "I don't know. Should I?"

"You're here."

She smiled without conviction and said, "Yes."

He guided her back to the booth. Fawn already had an extra cup of coffee waiting for her.

"I almost didn't come," she started.

"Because I'm an imposter."

"What?" Her eyebrows raised in surprise and she leaned forward. "That's not at all what was stopping me."

A large outbreak erupted from the corner full of cowboys. Grady threw his head back and slapped his knee. The others joined him in raucous laughter, the words "Chantale" and "grassfire" punctuating the guffaws.

Billy leaned closer across the booth to hear Skippy's words over the fracas. "What then? What was stopping you?"

"What I said."

What she said? Billy was so certain his own confession had caused her to avoid him that it hadn't even occurred to him it could be anything else.

"You mean what you told me about Buford?"

She nodded. "It was totally out of line. I shouldn't have dumped my problems on you. And I was so embarrassed I didn't know if I could face you."

What she'd said that day in the park revealed a darker side to what Billy had assumed was a congenial marriage. Yet somehow, none of it surprised him, knowing Buford as he had these few short months. After quietly listening to how her husband had blackmailed Billy, Skippy loosed a torrent of anger about Buford. Although the man never physically abused her, Skippy found it hard to meet his expectations. He was the big shot about town, at least in his mind, and she was supposed to play a role in that public image. She had always complied. Buford never denigrated her, but he insisted on defining her personality. Love didn't fit into their relationship, only functionality.

She supported his various ventures but hated the way he used other people to realize his goals, she'd explained. Even though he'd wine and dine his business partners, he'd take their money and laugh behind their backs. She tempered her discontentment with knowing that Buford could, at times, show remarkable generosity to chosen people in the community. But it still wasn't enough for a happy marriage.

Divorce was out of the question. Buford had blackmailed her, too.

In the corner, the cowboys continued their loud joking about the buffalo funeral, but Billy kept his voice low anyway. "Are you going to tell me what Buford is holding over you?"

Skippy shook her head. "No, I can't. I've already told you more than I've told anyone else. Not even Felicia knows about the blackmail."

Clearly, she was unwilling to tell him more. At least for the moment. Nevertheless, he felt relief that she wasn't avoiding him because of his own role in Buford's scheme.

"Why are you smiling?" Skippy asked. "Do you think this is funny?"

He had no idea he was smiling. "Oh gosh, Skippy, no. I was just thinking," he covered, "that I'd finished off the last piece of pie and wondered what you were going to order."

She smiled back. "You men are so shallow. A lady spills her guts to you and all you think about is food."

Skippy

I've got to keep focused on what I'm doing. That had been Skippy's mantra since the whole theme park scheme began. Playing the perfect wife had become critical now, and she couldn't afford to reveal to just anyone how disgusted she really was with her marriage and with Buford. But then, "Earl Bob" wasn't just anyone.

As she drove toward her two-story, Cape Cod home, she had to admit how attractive she found this UFO specialist – impostor or not. Yes, she was slightly embarrassed about confessing her discontent, but more so, angry at herself for having such a loose tongue. Her feelings were probably safe with Earl Bob. After all, he had also confessed to her, even telling her his real name.

Noble. Billy Noble.

Was that last name a lie, too? There must be lots of Nobles on the planet. The mere sound of it brought back a cascade of bittersweet memories. Seven years ago, another man named Noble had passed through town, and he had also become intertwined in the affairs of Buford and Skippy. Surely, the name was a coincidence, but an unsettling one.

Sam Noble came to Silverville with a grand plan to develop a ski resort. The idea played right into Buford's hands since he was already looking for a get-rich-quick investment opportunity. Buford didn't like Noble, thought he might be an old con artist, but he gladly took part in the proposal to develop a new ski area north of town. Skippy, on the other hand, had become charmed by this dapper Southern gentleman. Or maybe she was a sucker for hard-luck cases.

"Honey, you're a vision for these sore old eyes," she'd remembered him once saying. "That pretty auburn hair of yours makes me think of another special little gal I used to know but haven't seen for years."

His eyes misted as he spoke. She'd always felt that he carried scars from some debilitating relationship. And it gave her a sense of shared camaraderie. They'd both lost loves – his from a physical separation and hers from an emotional one.

As the deal took shape, Noble approached multiple outside investors with his slick, fast talk, making the idea seem as lucrative as other Colorado ski resorts. Silverville would become a popular winter destination like Aspen or Telluride. Buford's job was to serve as local contractor and to get the ball rolling.

They'd bankrolled the investors' money in the Savings and Loan where Skippy worked, and she'd helped them set up the accounts. In a complex flurry of financial transactions to pay for excavations and publicity, the account balances fluctuated wildly in the first few heady weeks. Buford would come home in the evenings bragging about the dollars pouring in, even giving her the figures. What bothered her was the remark he'd made one night about how the old guy wasn't as smart as he. The next day, she examined the accounts and found a discrepancy between debits, credits, and the figures Buford had given her about his part of the take. It wasn't long before she discovered Buford had set up an extra subcontractor account above and beyond what the project required. He'd neglected to mention that this account paid him a sizable bonus rather than contributing to legitimate operating expenses.

The project barely got off the ground before Noble ducked out of town with all the promotional funds, leaving Buford with little to show a potential horde of angry investors. Somehow, it didn't bother her that Noble had taken the money, but it left her having to clean up Buford's mess. Without telling him, she transferred the money from his bonus account back into the general operating funds for the project. Then she closed and erased any trace of what he'd done.

Buford hit the roof when she told him.

"I saved you from going to jail," she'd argued. "Not to mention possibly losing our home. As it stands now, Sam Noble will take all the blame."

"You cooked the books. That's a federal crime," he shouted.

Buford twisted the whole logic of the situation and, for Skippy, it was the last straw. She told him she was packing her bags and moving out. But he just laughed.

"If you do, your next home will be the penitentiary."

"But what about what you did?"

"There's nothing illegal about having a subcontractor account, and there's no way for you to prove it was anything other than legitimate – particularly since you erased the computer files." He held up the passbook. "I still have the physical evidence that you illegally erased an account. So we're partners in crime now – unless you do something stupid, like try to leave me."

Skippy had been furious as Buford closed the walls of her life around her. Everyone remembered the event as Buford's Folly, but she remembered the time as a dark hole in her past.

Now the name Noble was back in her life, and she wondered if Billy and Sam were related.

How ironic that another Noble showed up just as she had committed another federal crime.

PART THREE

JULY

CHAPTER TEN

Grady

He hated those women barrel racers. Bitches, the whole lot of them. Grady tried his best to look congenial as the two women argued about the placement of the barrels. He followed them around with a 300-foot tape measure and a shovel as they paced the distance between each turn of the race. Howard tagged along a few steps behind, carrying sections of yellow rope and a bag of lime.

"Here, bury that rope right here," barked one of the women.

Grady had participated in this ritual for close to forty years – as long as he had been a part of the rodeo. He could set up the barrel racing course with his eyes closed. First, measure out the triangle pattern, dig a hole at each corner, bury a rope to mark where each barrel would go, and then sprinkle white lime over the rope so the arena help could find the marker after the previous events had mucked up the dirt.

But these women just couldn't be satisfied. One would pick a spot and the other one would always disagree. Of course, not until Grady and Howard had dug the hole and buried the rope.

Grady pulled his pocket watch from his Levi jeans. Still an hour before the rodeo started.

"Grady! Grady!"

Buford loped towards him over the plowed furrows in the arena dirt. The advancing man looked as ridiculous as ever. More than likely, Buford had made a special effort to dress for the evening event, but he couldn't quite pull it off. For one thing, his jeans were rolled up in cuffs, a style no real cowboy would ever wear. A fake red leather vest decorated with fringe and sequins covered Buford's western shirt. His hat was way too clean.

"What?" Grady didn't look up. He started digging the last hole for the pattern.

Buford was puffing so hard he couldn't speak at first. But after a few seconds, he wheezed, "It's them! … The Hell's Angels … they're eighty miles away!"

"Yep."

"But, but they'll be here in time . . . in time for the rodeo," Buford said, waving his arms.

"Can't stop 'em." Grady motioned for Howard to drop one end of his rope in the hole.

"Don't you think we should tell everybody?"

"How 'bout Carl?"

"He already knows. He's the one who told me."

"Then I'd go take a seat in the grandstands and enjoy the rodeo."

Across the arena to the west, people had already begun to find their seats. By seven o'clock the stands would be full. Grady did a double-take. "What the hell?"

Raising a hand to shield his eyes from the setting sun, he squinted at the crowd. An odd jumble of people dressed as aliens dotted the seats between Friday night cowboys and cowgirls, tall silver cone heads mixing with western hats. He shook his head and swore under his breath.

"This is your fault, Buford."

But Buford couldn't have heard him. He was already running to alert another group of rodeo workers about the Hell's Angels.

Finally, the barrel racers seemed satisfied with the pattern and marched from the arena. Grady followed them out, Howard at his heels, and then walked over to a small holding pen full of sheep.

"Mr. O'Grady, are they sick?" Howard asked.

It was the first time Grady had seen the herd since the stock contractor had delivered them for the kid's mutton busting event. The sheep looked like they'd seen better days, and he hoped they'd have enough life left in them to give those youngsters a wild ride out of the starting chute.

Grady shrugged. "They're just old, Howard. We wouldn't want them too crazy for them little kids."

"Can I pet the sheep?" Howard moved closer to the flea-bit flock. They parted like the Red Sea and smashed into the fence rails to get away from him.

"If you can catch any of 'em," Grady said.

He left Howard in the pen. With the barrel pattern in place and the sheep ready, Grady had nothing else to do for the time being and he headed over toward the corral full of roping steers. It was easier to cut back across the arena and climb the fence than exit through the gate. He passed the bucking chutes along the way and heard a cowboy cuss as he tried to cinch up a rank saddle bronc. The fellow looked like he didn't have enough help, but Grady kept walking. His left shoulder still smarted from 'Ole Moss's shenanigans with that buffalo; wrangling wild horses was better left to younger limbs.

The aroma of cotton candy and corn dogs blended with the pungent odor of cow manure. It was a comforting smell that reminded him of many a rodeo. Of course, this year local vendors provided the concession instead of the usual carnival setup. With that damn theme park in town, the rodeo board decided not to renew their long-standing contract with StemWinder Attractions. Now nobody was frying up funnel cakes, much to Grady's disappointment.

When Grady reached the south end of the arena, he placed his boot on the first wooden rail of the fence, hoisted himself up, and swung over to drop into the pen of roping steers. Two other rodeo board members had lined up the animals single file in a narrow chute so workers could wind protective wraps around the steers' horns.

"Need a hand?" Grady asked.

He didn't wait for a reply. There was never enough help just before a rodeo, and Grady pulled a wrap from a pile on the ground and walked over to the chute. He took special care to avoid the steers' tossing heads. He'd seen more than one cowpoke cold-cocked by a hard bovine skull, and it paid not to get in a hurry. But with four men, the job didn't take long. Leaning over the last steer, Grady heard Buford's voice shouting his name from the other side of the fence. This time Grady didn't answer, hoping Buford wouldn't spot him. No such luck.

"Grady, I just heard a report that the Hell's Angels killed two people as they passed through Beaver Junction, and now they're only fifty miles from here!"

Beaver Junction, a place with only an abandoned railway depot and a boarded-up gas stop, lay south of Silverville a good hour away. How the bikers could have found even two people in that town on a Friday night was a mystery to Grady.

"Goddamn it, Buford, can't you see I'm busy? Mutton bustin' is going to start in fifteen minutes. If you got a problem with the Hell's Angels, go talk to Carl and leave me alone."

Buford began to speak but must have thought twice about replying. He closed his mouth and disappeared behind the fence.

Grady crossed back through the arena to the sheep pen. There he found Howard on his knees, cooing at the old ewes. Didn't look like he was having any luck getting friendly with them. Grady motioned to Howard for help as he started driving the herd into the north-end starting chutes. On the other side, eager youngsters with their parents in tow began to form a line to wait their turn at riding the sheep.

Grady always liked mutton-busting. The event gave kids a taste of what it was like to rodeo. Many a fine bronc or bull rider had started a career on the back of a sheep. Even Grady himself in his own day. Course, with the ranch to take care of, he'd only ridden locally. Now seeing all those anxious little faces warmed his heart.

"Quit your crying and get over here!" a mother screeched at her young daughter. "We already paid for this event, and you're riding whether you want to or not."

Well, maybe it didn't always warm his heart. From his peripheral visual, Grady caught sight of a man running in the direction of the sheep chutes. Jesus, why couldn't Buford break a leg?

To his relief the man turned out to be Merle, the board's secretary.

"Howard," Merle shouted, "Carl says you and Denton need to get to the funeral home right away."

Howard just stared.

Merle continued, "You don't know where Denton is, do you?"

It was Grady who replied. "He's up in the sound booth getting ready. What's going on?"

"Carl says it's coroner's business. We'll have to find somebody else to take care of the music."

At that moment, Grady saw Buford headed his way for the

third time that evening. "Take Buford. He's seems to have a lot of time on his hands tonight."

Merle looked aghast. "Awww, no! I don't think –"

"Buford!" Grady hollered. "We got a job for you."

§   §   §

"Welcome to the one-hundred-and-first annual Silverville Rodeo Days," the announcer blared over the loud speakers. He sat atop a borrowed horse in the middle of the arena. "For over a century, this town has celebrated the western heritage and the brave men and women who pioneered this great land to help make America what it is today."

As he directed his horse before the grandstands, he continued, "We'd like to thank our local sponsors and the cowboys and cowgirls who work hard each year to put on this great show.

"Before we begin, we'd like introduce our own rodeo queen, Miss – "

The queen spurred her horse in a large circle through the arena over the din of cheers and clapping. In the sheep chute, Grady squatted beside a trembling little girl. A wild-eyed ewe squirmed against Grady's knee as he pinned the animal against the gate rails.

"Now little miss, don't you be scared. All you gotta do is lay down on this ewe and wrap your arms around her neck. When that gate opens, she's gonna tear across this arena like a bat out of he – I mean, heck. And you just hold on 'til you hear that buzzer."

The little girl twisted the tails of her pink gingham shirt that hung over the waistband of her jeans. Her blue eyes stared back at Grady with the innocent trust of a child despite her terror. "But what if I fall off?"

It was a distinct possibility; most kids never made it two feet past the chute. "Don't you worry, honey. The sheep is short and the dirt is soft."

"Should I get on now?"

"Not yet. They gotta sing the 'Star-Spangled Banner' first."

She reached out to run her fingers over the surface of the sheared sheep. This might be the first time the little girl had ever touched mutton on the hoof.

A woman hung over the sheep fence. Grady figured she had to be the mother, but he didn't recognize her. A tourist, most likely.

"What happens to these sheep after the rodeo?" the woman asked.

Damn, Grady wished the board didn't open up mutton-busting to outsiders.

"Well ma'am, this ewe will head home with its herd to grassy meadows," Grady lied, knowing full well the whole bunch would be loaded on a truck and headed to slaughter before morning.

She nodded, seeming satisfied.

The ear-splitting squelch of the loud speaker interrupted the conversation. A teen-aged girl standing in the middle of the arena began her rendition of the "Star-Spangled Banner." In the grandstand, both cowboys and aliens placed their hands over their hearts. As she started the second stanza, her microphone cut out although her tiny voice continued bravely with the song without the help of the loudspeakers. But no one heard her finish. A sudden blast of "Honky Tonk Women" blared out from the sound system. That idiot Buford had tripped the music they played during the bucking events.

People across the stands didn't seem to know what to do or if they should keep their hands over their hearts as the Rolling Stones belted out, "Give me the Honky-Tonk blues," drowning out the national anthem. Grady put his hat back on.

By the time the singer walked out of the arena, Buford must have figured out how to turn the music off. The announcer on horseback addressed the audience.

"Is everyone ready to rodeo?"

As the crowd cheered, Grady turned to the girl and said, "It's time to saddle up."

Still pinning the ewe, he lifted her fragile frame and sat her down on the sheep. "Now remember. Lean forward and wrap your arms around her neck."

The little girl dutifully did as she was told. The rodeo worker on the arena side opened the chute, and Grady turned loose of the sheep. The animal bulleted out the gate, leaving the little girl in the dirt just a few feet from the start.

He walked over and picked up the fallen rider as he'd done so often before at mutton-busting. She cried, as many of them did, each sob showing a mouth full of arena grit. He carried her back to her mother and then closed the gate for the next sheep and rider.

The next two kids, both local boys, didn't have much better luck. But every ride earned hardy applause from the stands. Maybe these sheep were healthier than they looked. Grady shuffled back into the chute to help the fourth rider, another youngster he didn't recognize. He bent down to lift the boy onto the sheep. The kid yanked away from him.

"Naw, I can do it myself."

The boy scrambled onto the ewe as Grady held it steady. Before the gate even opened the kid started kicking and screaming at the sheep.

"There's no call for that. That sheep'll run out on its own," Grady said.

"Shut up," the boy replied, and stuck his tongue out.

Just as Grady reached over to pluck the kid off the back of the animal, the gate flew open and the ewe sprung out and ran hard toward the center of the arena. To Grady's chagrin, the kid stayed on. About fifty feet out, the ewe dropped to the ground without warning, pitching the youngster forward into a tumbling roll. The boy jumped up but the sheep lay motionless. Two cowboys ran out to inspect the ewe.

One cupped his hands around his mouth and called out to Grady, but loud enough for everyone to hear, "It's dead!"

Grady winced as a gasp arose from the crowd.

While the cowboys dragged the sheep away, the boy started back to his waiting parents, who stood by the chute.

As he got within earshot of his parents, he began to wail, repeating what the cowboys had said. "It's dead! It's dead!"

When he passed Grady beside the chute, the boy stopped just for an instant and once again stuck out his tongue. Then he resumed his crying, running into his mother's arms. She knelt and unbuckled the child's helmet and then hugged him close to her side.

She shot an icy glare at Grady and said, "Look at the trauma your rodeo has caused my child."

Grady held her glare for just a moment and then spat a thick wad of tobacco juice on the ground. Then he turned back to the chute and hollered out to the rodeo hand who led up the next little girl, "Rider up!"

The last nine rides went without a hitch. Except for Merle's news that quite a few upset spectators had left the grounds, complaining of cruelty to animals. Someone even swore at Merle.

"Them kind of people ain't got no business being here anyway," Grady had told him.

With the mutton-busting finished, the rodeo proceeded in typical fashion, thrilling what was left of the crowd with a line-up of bucking, roping, and barrel-racing events. But the big draw that everyone waited for was the bull riding, the last event of the evening.

Halfway through the rodeo, the events stopped for the featured specialty act. This year the board had to make a last-minute substitution because the scheduled act cancelled. It disappointed everyone. They had all looked forward to seeing Legendary Lorenzo, an accomplished Roman rider who specialized in simultaneously riding two horses – one foot planted on the back of each animal at the same time while the horses ran an obstacle course. At another rodeo earlier that season, Lorenzo had hit his head on one of the burning rings his two horses jumped through. The man hadn't been seriously hurt – he'd only suffered a mild concussion – but he cancelled all future performances until his singed hair had a chance to grow back. The substitute act consisted of a former bullfighting clown named Mickey and his miniature horse, Ricky. By all accounts, they were supposed to be pretty good, but no one on the board had ever seen the act.

While a tractor dragged and groomed the arena dirt, Mickey tried to tie his five-year-old miniature stallion to the fence alongside the north-end gate. Ricky wasn't cooperating.

"Somebody give me a hand here while I go get the rest of my gear," Mickey called out to the nearest rodeo hand, who just happened to be Grady.

About that time, Earl Bob walked by and Grady handed him

the lead rope of the Saint Bernard-sized steed, saying, "Got a favor to ask you."

Then Grady stepped back to watch the fun with the greenhorn. Earl Bob looked around as though he expected someone to tell him why he was holding the little horse. "What do I –?"

A hoof-blow to Earl Bob's chest stopped him in mid question. Ricky reared, challenging Earl Bob eye to eye. Grady was sure that all Earl Bob could see was black rubbery lips framing a mouth full of teeth. The cantankerous little animal clenched onto the lapel of Earl Bob's jacket, pulling him forward until the two smacked heads with a loud crack. He stumbled backwards still holding the rope, dazed.

Grady belched out a gut-splitting laugh as he moved up to give the reluctant horse-wrangler a hand. But by then, Mickey had returned with the props for his act.

The clown collected his horse from Earl Bob while the announcer introduced the specialty performance. Mickey tore into the arena on foot at a dead run, Ricky right on his heels with his ears flat and teeth bared at the clown's backside. Two young boys trailed behind with the props and began to set them up in the center of the arena as Mickey and Ricky duked it out in a mock fight. All the while, the horseback announcer bantered with Mickey, feeding him cues for the usual bad-clown jokes. Mickey replied through a wireless microphone attached to his collar.

"You look like you need some help," the announcer started. "Did you bring your wife along?"

"Naw, she won't leave her mother. They're at home driving my new car around."

Ricky bit at the clown's arm and pulled the sleeve off his shirt, which seemed to delight the spectators.

"Do you know what you call a Buick carrying my wife and my mother-in-law?"

"I don't have any idea, Mickey. What do you call a Buick carrying your wife and your mother-in-law?"

Mickey picked up his sleeve and slapped off the dust against his knee. "You call it a car equipped with two airbags."

A groan swelled up from the crowd. Grady thought this guy

was pretty good.

The act continued throughout the halftime, finally ending with Ricky kicking his trainer in the gut with both hind legs. Mickey doubled over and pretended to die while the horse tossed his head and stomped on him a few times. At the crowd's applause, both performers took a bow and trotted out of the arena.

Grady, still impressed with the show, waited for Mickey by the gate. "How did you train that little horse to do all that?"

"Train him? Hell, he's just mean. I couldn't stop him so I just made it part of the act." Now clear of the arena, Mickey limped over toward his horse trailer with Ricky bounding behind him.

§   §   §

Except for the sheep dying and Buford screwing up the music, things had gone pretty well so far. Of course, Grady wasn't happy about the woman who'd won the barrel racing. Some of the rodeo hands had remarked on "what a fine set of lungs" she had, but all Grady could remember was how she'd used those lungs to bitch him out when they'd set the barrel pattern. Grady couldn't see the justice of it when she came in with the fastest time. And those Hell's Angels never did show up either. All in all, it had been a damn fine rodeo, and Grady was proud to be part of it.

Now it was time for the grand finale, bull riding.

The air seemed charged with excitement before the final event. Riders got hurt but they seldom got killed, and everybody waited to see what would happen this year. Just to be on the safe side, the medical emergency crews rolled their ambulances up close to the gate in case they had to pull an injured cowboy out of the arena. Duke Fine jumped out of one of the two ambulances, and Grady figured the boy must be volunteering to work with them for the evening. That pleased Grady. More folks in town ought to get involved in this annual event. The whole crew climbed atop the fence boards to watch, their feet dangling inside the arena. Earl Bob, his face a little puffier and bluer that the last time Grady had seen him, sauntered over to the crew and climbed up beside them. Plenty of cowboys were on hand to help with the bull riding, and all

Grady had left to do was enjoy the rest of the show. He clambered up the fence to join Earl Bob and Duke.

Bullfighters, dressed as clowns, rolled large reinforced barrels into the arena – a safe haven for them to duck into when faced with a charging bull. Everyone agreed that those fellas had the most dangerous job out there, trying to lure the one-ton animals away from fallen riders. The bulls themselves provided plenty of background noise as they slammed their massive heads against the chute rails while they waited for cowboys to mount up. The day before, Grady had watched as the bulls unloaded off the trailer. They looked like a mean bunch of Brahma crosses, every bit as big and rank as the stock contractor promised.

From Grady's position on the fence, the bull chutes were a clear shot across the arena. He'd be able to see every cowboy who didn't make the eight-second ride hit the dust. The announcer was still bantering with one of the clowns when the first chute sprung open. Two-thousand pounds of beef charged from the gate, head down, body twisting and spinning as it tried to throw its rider. The cowboy managed to stay on for a full four seconds before the bull leaped what must have been six feet into the air and landed with a ground-shuddering pound. The contestant crumpled to the ground while the bullfighters rushed in to distract the animal. Pick-up men spurred their horses toward the bull, trying to herd it toward the exit gate. The bull would have no part of it and trotted along the fence line. Panic-stricken rail-sitters flew off the boards like a falling row of dominoes when the bull passed each one. You never knew what these foul-tempered critters would do. And even with all their bulk, they could jump like thoroughbreds.

The animal turned away from the fence, and it must have spotted the open exit gate because it headed in that direction and disappeared from the arena. By this time, the fallen cowboy had gotten back on his feet; the crowd was clapping and cheering – the only payback he'd get that night.

Grady had just plopped himself back down on the fence when the next bull shot out of a gate. *Damn, this wood is hard on an old butt.* He squirmed, trying to find a comfortable spot, when he saw out of his peripheral vision a riderless bull running straight in his direction. It had outrun the rodeo clowns and seemed to be moving with a purpose. Long ropes of snot flew from its nostrils and slapped onto the animal's shoulders as it thundered forward. A fine specimen of a bull, he was, too. Massive chest, thick legs, and spring-loaded muscles that rippled like waves under the brindle hide. A six-foot spread of horns swung wildly in each direction as though the bull were trying to sweep the arena clean of rodeo cowboys.

The pickup men, in hot pursuit, threw their lariats at the bovine locomotive, but he was a crafty son-of-a-bitch and dodged them every time. Grady would've laughed, except those eyes black with malice seemed to have singled out the row of cowboy-spectators where he sat. And the closer the beefy steamroller got, the bigger and meaner he looked.

He and the line of spectators beside him dove off the fence, all but Duke, who struggled to free himself. He had hooked the toes of his boots under one of the wooden slats and he couldn't twist them loose fast enough to make his escape. Grady reached over to help him, but he knew he was too far away. For a second, it looked like the boy was going to fall forward right into the arena.

Then, quick as a two-bit whore, Earl Bob smacked the heel of his palm at the back of Duke's boot, hammering at the leather heel until it dislodged. Earl Bob yanked the terrified kid back behind the fence, and the two of them fell to the ground together with a hard thud. Grady looked up to see the bottom side of the bull sailing over the barrier and into the crowd outside the arena. He could tell exactly where the bull went from there. Bodies sprang up like a mess of jackrabbits, people trying to get out of the way.

"Close call, Duke," Grady said, still squatting beside the fence boards.

"You okay?" Earl Bob asked.

Breathing hard and shaking, the boy nodded. "Thanks to you, Earl Bob."

Grady stood up, took his can of chew from his hip pocket, and rubbed his butt at the same time. "Well, better go help them boys catch that bull."

He left Duke to the medical crew, who would walk him over to the ambulance for a check-over. That bull had to be caught quickly; there were still some riders to go.

§   §   §

About eleven o'clock, Grady walked through the back door of his house. Leona had stayed up to wait for him. Forty years of watching rough stock and beat-up cowboys had lost its charm for her, and she hadn't bothered to go to this year's show.

"How'd it go?" she asked.

He sat down in the mud room and pulled off his boots.

"Oh, same as usual, I guess."

CHAPTER ELEVEN

Denton

The light was fading when Denton and Howard arrived at Poverty Pass. Denton parked the hearse beside Carl's Chevy Blazer and a state patrol car. Not as much commotion as Denton had expected. It seemed like law enforcement officers tended to congregate in droves for these kinds of things. But then, the area was remote, and no one could ever agree on who was in charge when an incident occurred on top of the pass. The county line cut right across the summit. When something happened on the east side, Placer City took care of it. When it happened on the west, jurisdiction fell to Silverville.

The problem was, there were bones on each side.

Before Denton even switched off his ignition, the Placer City hearse rolled up. Not far behind him, the sheriff and deputy from that county guided their vehicle into the narrow parking area alongside the road. Carl and his deputy leaned against the Blazer, joking with the state patrolman when Denton and the other coroner walked up.

"Well, fellas, we got another one," Carl said.

From time to time, a body turned up in the backcountry after the snow melted. Some were accidents; others were suicides. Occasionally, it turned out to be a murder. A lot of times, it was hard to tell, and no one ever found out.

"Where at?" Denton asked.

Carl pointed toward a ravine about fifty yards below the road. Denton grimaced, wondering if his hip would allow him to make the descent. He sent Howard back to the hearse for pairs of rubber gloves.

"Better grab some of those evidence bags, too," Denton called after him, noticing the other coroner had also pulled out similar equipment from his vehicle.

Carl led the way down the hill, sliding on loose gravel and rocks. The rest of the men followed, dodging patches of spring snow and mud that had survived in the forested shade of the high country. Denton trailed behind, wincing with each step. He barely heard Carl's words since the sheriff only now and then turned his head away from the treacherous descent to explain the situation.

When the party finally reached the bottom of the ravine, Carl was finishing his account. ". . . and by the time the hikers realized what they had walked up on, their dog was trotting off with part of a hand."

Carl pointed to a few bones half-hidden in a thicket on the Placer City side. "There might even be more on our side of the line. Predators pretty much picked them clean and scattered them all over the place."

The eight men split up to survey the scene, careful not to disturb any potential evidence. Denton and Howard began their own part of the investigation. Coroners always conduct an inquiry independent of law enforcement. The theory is it's better to have two sets of eyes at an unattended death, each working to figure out what's happened. No one was likely to get a clear picture of this particular death, Denton thought. Pulling on his gloves, he squatted down to look at a gnawed and splintered femur.

Carl walked up and shined his flashlight at the ground. "What you got?"

Both men studied the leg.

"Pretty big bone," the sheriff remarked.

"Must be a man. Too thick to be a woman's."

Under the dimming sky, the other men in the party flashed their spotlights over the shadowed terrain, their voices echoing off the sides of the ravine. Denton and Howard continued their meticulous search for more bones. Already, a pumpkin-colored moon peeked up over the summit, casting welcome light onto the scene. Before long, Denton could feel the mountain cold seep through his light summer jacket, and he wished he could wear something heavier than rubber gloves over his aching fingers. Somewhere from a safe distance, a coyote scolded the human intruders.

A thrashing sound accompanied by cursing caught Denton's attention, and he saw a flashlight sail through the air.

"I found the pelvis!" shouted Willy, the Placer City deputy.

Carl came back over to Denton and asked, "Any luck?"

"It's too darn dark out here. Maybe we should finish this up tomorrow morning."

"Maybe we won't have to. Looks to me like there's more bones on the other side of the county line." Then he called out loud enough for the rest of the party to hear, "Anyone find a head yet? Hey, Willy, what'd you just drop?"

Carl marched over to the deputy and shined his light on the ground. Denton and Howard followed. There by Willy's feet rested the missing skull.

"Goddamit, Willy, I saw you move that thing over to our side."

"Just what is your side?" the deputy asked, his voice sounding like he'd been caught red-handed and knew it.

At that point, Carl aimed the tunnel of his light toward a rock formation to the south and traced an imaginary line with the beam to a huge Ponderosa pine up the hill to the north. "It runs up that cliff wall," he said, "and back along a line toward that big tree. Oh, and by the way, Willy, judging by that line, I don't think you did drop that head on our side. Those bones are all yours."

The Placer City group started grumbling all at once. The expenses for the investigation and a possible burial would fall to whoever had jurisdiction.

Howard walked up to Carl, Willy, and Denton. "I think I found his teeth."

He held up his hand, which clutched a broken set of upper dentures. Willy snatched the teeth from Howard, and all the men clustered around the skull as Willy tried to fit them against the upper palate. They might have fit if the man's gums had still been there. The skull had other missing parts as well. The lower jaw was completely gone, and the back of the skull was bashed in. Teeth marks frayed the edges of the hole, making it nearly impossible to tell if the wound came from a predator or something else.

"What do you suppose this fellow died from?" asked the Placer City sheriff as he rubbed his chin.

"Well, he didn't shoot himself in the head." It was the other coroner who spoke now. Jacobs, Denton recalled his name to be.

"He couldn't have gotten his gun angled that far back on his skull."

"Maybe somebody else shot him from behind," Carl's deputy offered.

"I don't think so. That's a big hole," the Silverville sheriff said, and then he pointed to the front of the skull, "but there's no exit wound. Maybe he shot himself in the heart. There's no back pack and no identification. This guy didn't come up here hiking and die from natural causes. I think it's a good chance this was a suicide."

Howard spoke up, "Maybe somebody pushed him off the cliff."

Everyone seemed to think about this for a moment.

"It's not Silver County's problem," Carl said at last.

"Wait a minute!" the other sheriff objected. "You guys found as many bones on your side as we did."

"C'mon, Andy, you've got the skull," Carl said. "That officially gives you more bone mass than we have."

"Yeah, but you guys have the teeth."

"We don't know for sure those dentures are that fellow's teeth. Maybe somebody was out here hiking and dropped them." Carl looked pretty satisfied with his deduction.

"Oh man, that ain't right. We had to bury one earlier this spring. You haven't had one in a couple of years."

They argued back and forth for several minutes until Andy turned to the highway patrolman. "Dan, what do you think? Who has to claim those bones."

The patrolman backed away, raising his hands as if he were trying to escape the whole problem. "Don't put me in the middle of this."

"Somebody has to decide, or else we'll all have to come back tomorrow," Carl said.

They formed a half-circle around Dan, shining their lights in his face and waiting for a decision.

"Aw, shit." Dan turned away from the group and walked a couple of paces before stepping back. "I'd say it goes to Placer City. After all, you guys got the skull."

Andy let out a sigh of resignation. "Let's go home, boys. Looks like we're coming back tomorrow."

§   §   §

Starting the hearse, Denton waited for Howard to climb in the passenger side. His helper leaned against the open door, scraping his shoes against a rock to clean off the mud.

"Don't worry about it, Howard. I've already got my side dirty."

While Carl started down the pass ahead of them, Howard continued to wipe his shoes. He finally climbed into the vehicle and said, "Mr. Fine, I found—"

"Howard, I expect you to help me keep an eye out for deer on the way down." That past spring, Felicia had hit one that jumped up out of nowhere from the borrow ditch beside the road, and Denton remembered all too well the expense of repairing the fender and hood to their car. The windshield had cracked into a spider web of fissures when the deer's body rolled over the car, but at least Felicia had suffered no injury. Her accident wasn't unusual. Deer carcasses littered the highway between Silverville and the pass, all unfortunate victims of wildlife clashing with traffic.

Shifting into second gear, Denton began to guide the hearse down the curvy mountain pass. He didn't want to burn out his brakes on the steep grade. The highway didn't have much for guard rails, not that they'd stop a car careening off the road and dropping hundreds of feet. Probably just as well. Folks might get too cocky if they thought these rails would stop them from going over the edge.

Carl's taillights occasionally disappeared around a bend then came back into sight along the few straight stretches in the road. But the Blazer took the corners better than the hearse, and the sheriff's vehicle soon outpaced them.

Howard turned on the radio. After trying the usual stations, he settled on an evangelist talk show. Denton rolled his eyes at Howard's selection, not protesting because the young man's night had already been ruined by missing the rodeo.

The preacher droned on about the end of time and the need for repentance. *The time is at hand. It's time to take stock of your life and ask the Lord what you can do to make the world a better place.*

Can I treat my neighbors better? Can I work harder at my job? Can I make a generous donation to keep the Word of God alive? The answer, dear listeners, to all of the questions is yes! And you can start by sending your check or money order to the Word of God Ministry, in care of this station.

Howard turned to Denton and asked, "Should I send them a check or a money order?"

Denton shook his head. "Now you heard what he said, Howard. Seems to me you've already made the world a better place by being kind to everyone."

Howard nodded. "Mr. Fine, I've got something important to ask you."

Fearing Howard was about to ask him a theological question, Denton replied, "Well, I'll do my best to answer."

"How come they put that runaway truck ramp ahead just on the other side of a sharp curve?"

Denton paused for a moment, relieved the conversation wasn't going to involve the meaning of everlasting life. He'd sort of wondered, too, why the highway department built the ramp they now approached. The steep grade and winding curves on the Silverville side of the pass would more likely sling a brakeless truck over the cliff long before it could reach the sand and gravel incline.

Before Denton could speak, Howard started humming along with "Rock of Ages," a melody that alternated between radio static and a blaring chorus, depending on the reception.

The road finally began to straighten out as they came down the pass, and Denton felt the tension of mountain driving leave his shoulders. By this time, Howard had replaced his humming with sniffling.

"What's wrong?"

"Nothing, Mr. Fine. This church music always brings tears to my eyes."

Denton glanced over to see Howard dabbing his eyes with something he had wadded up in his fist. Even in the dim light of the dashboard, Denton could see that Howard's tear-catcher was leaving muddy smudges on his cheek.

"What are you wiping your face with, Howard?"

"The rag from my shoe." He dangled a scrap of dirty cloth.

"What?"

"I was trying to tell you when I got in the hearse. I found something stuck to my shoe."

Denton switched on the dome light to inspect the muddy fabric, but he couldn't tell what it was.

"Do you think you might have picked it up down in the ravine?"

"Maybe. I don't know."

"Do you mind if I take it?"

Howard dutifully handed him the soiled, snotty rag, which Denton jammed into the pocket of his jacket.

Before them in the distance, an island of amber light rose above the town of Silverville. Ranch yard lamps began to pop out of the darkness as they got closer to home. About ten miles from the city limits they met a string of cars probably heading out after the rodeo.

"I'm sorry you missed the rodeo, Howard. But thanks for helping me out tonight."

Howard smiled. "I like to help."

"Hopefully we'll have a quiet weekend with no more calls."

At the four-mile marker, Denton turned a sharp left onto a gravel road to take Howard back to his cabin. He dropped him off, told him good night, and continued the short distance home.

As he pulled the hearse into the garage, Felicia poked her head through the entrance that led into their kitchen. He turned off the ignition and stepped out to close the garage door. Behind him he heard Felicia's anxious voice.

"Wait'll you hear what happened at the rodeo tonight!"

§   §   §

"Stop right there," Felicia demanded as she eyed the trail of mud Denton's shoes left behind him on the kitchen floor. "You're a mess. Give me that jacket. I'm going to throw it right in the washing machine."

He peeled off the jacket and handed it over. Then he settled into a chair to remove his shoes.

"First of all, Duke is okay," she said as she returned from the laundry room.

He snapped his head in her direction. "What?"

"Duke, your dad's home," she shouted toward the living room. "Come in here and tell him what happened tonight."

The boy appeared in the doorway, a flush of excitement on his face.

Felicia and Duke both began to speak at once, and Denton couldn't make anything out of the garble.

"Whoa, whoa. One at a time."

"You tell it, Duke," Felicia said.

"He saved my life. He saved my life." Duke used dramatic emphasis the second time he said "life."

"Who did?"

"Earl Bob. I was almost crushed by a bull, and Earl Bob saved me."

Denton looked from one to the other. They both sounded like they were about to burst at the seams. "What are you talking about?"

"You knew that I went out with the EMTs at the rodeo tonight, right?"

Duke rushed on to tell his story as he pulled up a chair to the kitchen table where his father sat.

"Well, me and Earl Bob and Grady were sitting on the fence watching the bull riding when this big bull came charging over to our side of the arena. It came right at us. I thought it was gonna kill us. Earl Bob risked his life."

Duke rocked back on the hind legs of his chair, all the while letting his hands wave to punctuate the tale he was telling.

"I was stuck on the fence – my boots were stuck, I mean – I guess between the rails. Anyway, Earl Bob jumped up and started trying to help me get loose. I just knew that bull was going to kill us both. But Earl Bob stayed right there with me, even though his life was in danger, too. Then all of a sudden, my boots came free, and Earl Bob and I fell back just in time. The bull went right over the fence above us, Earl Bob shielding me with his own body. If that bull had landed on him, he would've been crushed."

Felicia paced back and forth in front of the table until Duke paused for a breath. "Do you believe it, Denton? Earl Bob saved our boy's life."

Denton sputtered, "Well, is everyone – are you okay?"

Duke continued. "That bull had blood in his eye. He's the biggest one I've ever seen. It was running around snorting and chasing people in the crowd. Grady and the other guys had a lot of trouble catching it. Boy, it was sure a good thing Earl Bob was there to save me. He's a hero, I really think he's a hero."

When Duke began the story all over again, Denton interrupted him. "Duke, I asked you, are you okay?"

"No!" the boy exclaimed. He hoisted up his pant leg and proudly displayed two small patches of scraped skin on his calf. "And you should see Earl Bob. He really got hurt. The bull must have kicked him in the eye because he's got a helluva shiner."

"Duke Fine, you don't have to swear when you tell a story," Felicia admonished. Then she turned to Denton. "We have to have Earl Bob over to dinner one night soon to repay him for what he did. Not that that would ever be enough!"

"Good golly, do you suppose I should call him up and thank him?" Denton asked.

"It's too late," she said as she got up to check the wash. "He's probably in bed by now."

Getting some sleep sounded like a good idea. Denton's hip had been throbbing for the past two hours, and all he wanted to do was lie down. Duke, on the other hand, was still wound up from his close call, and he pulled out a bag of popcorn and shoved it into the microwave. Felicia didn't look like she was ready for bed either. She hauled out a fresh basket of dirty laundry and disappeared into the wash room.

"Do you want some popcorn, Denton?" Duke asked. "I can't tell you how scared we were when that bull came charging at us . . ."

After listening to the third retelling of Duke's narrow escape, Denton stood and moved toward the stairs. No one had asked him about the coroner call, but Denton didn't feel like talking anymore that night anyway.

Before he reached the first step of the staircase, Felicia called out to him.

"Denton, I found this in the washing machine. It must have been in the pocket of your jacket."

She held up a white handkerchief. "Look. It's got initials on it."

He turned around and headed back into the kitchen. Felicia spread the handkerchief on the kitchen table and they both examined the embroidered letters.

"E.B.J. Who could that – oh, Earl Bob Jackson. This must be Earl Bob's."

At first, what she said didn't register. It couldn't be Earl Bob's. This had to be the rag Howard found on his shoe up at the pass and then used to wipe his face. Confusion roiled through him. Why would Earl Bob's handkerchief be up on the pass? And why was it near the bones they'd found?

Denton picked up the cloth from the table and turned it over in his hands. There couldn't be too many people in the county with those initials. And at the moment, he could think of only one. Earl Bob. Could there have been some relationship between him and the corpse on the pass? Surely this didn't belong to the man his family had just described as a hero.

He had to get the handkerchief to Carl; it might be evidence.

"I'll have to get this back to Earl Bob tomorrow," Felicia said.

"No!" Denton snapped. He lightened his tone. "Give it to me. I'll take care of it."

CHAPTER TWELVE

Buford

He couldn't find a place to park within three blocks of Main Street, and the parade would begin in fifteen minutes. Cars, pickup trucks, and motorcycles lined the curbs wherever Buford looked. He might miss the first part of the Saturday morning event, but what difference did it make, anyway? This year might be more novel with the UFO theme playing a large part in the festivities, but Buford still took his time.

Skippy and Felicia had gone downtown earlier that morning to help line up the floats. They had invited him along, but he declined. The pressure of running the rodeo sound system the night before still weighed on him. How could he help it if those old tapes had unraveled and there was no music during the second half of the show? His forte was masterful planning – not the minute-by-minute drudgery of execution. They should have asked him to organize the vendors or coordinate the media packets. Those were jobs where he excelled. But as it stood, now everybody was mad at him.

Buford pulled up to a stop sign and heard the engine of a Harley-Davidson roaring next to his car. When he turned his head to look, he came eye to eye with a grizzly Hell's Angel. The rider smiled back with only half a mouth of teeth, a red bandana holding back greasy strands of long gray hair.

But what really caught Buford's attention was the gun the Angel pointed right at him. For just a moment, Buford froze, nearly wetting his pants. *My God, I'm going to be killed!* Then he slammed his foot down on the accelerator and shot through the intersection. The Angel stayed right with him, laughing and keeping the gun trained on his victim's head. If only there were someone else on the road to help him, but everybody was at the parade. Buford drove faster; so did the biker. Buford swerved onto a side street; so did the biker.

Maybe he could make it to the police station, two more blocks away. He gripped the steering wheel so tight his fingers hurt. Sweat rolled down his forehead and into his eyes as he tried to close the gap separating him from safety. Couldn't that crazy biker see the City Police building up ahead? Buford didn't slow the car as he jumped the curb. He aimed his vehicle for the front door, finally skidding to a halt. The biker stayed beside him the whole time.

Afraid to leave his car, Buford pounded on his horn while the Angel dismounted and walked over to his door still holding the gun.

"The police have you covered! The police have you covered!" Buford shouted, hoping it was so.

The biker laughed, pulled the trigger, and saturated Buford's window with a spray of water. He then hopped on his bike and left.

Buford sat motionless in his car for a good minute, trying to absorb what had just happened. He released a sobbing, crying laugh when he realized he had only been assaulted with a squirt gun. Wiping the tears from his face, he stepped out his car door. The police ought to know these Angels were scaring decent folks half to death. As he approached the building, Buford rehearsed his report.

Officer, a Hell's Angel just chased me to the police station pointing a gun to my head the whole time.

Are you injured?

Well, no, but ...

Did you get a license plate?

No.

Did you at least see what kind of a gun he had?

Buford spun on his heels and walked back to his car. After last night's rodeo fiasco, he sure didn't want a report like that getting around town. He backed the car off the police station lawn and parked. Since he was only three blocks from Main Street, he decided to walk to the parade route.

He hardly noticed his feet hitting the pavement. Thank goodness he didn't report his own encounter. The Angels never did show up for the rodeo, but later that night they had streamed into town and headed for a local bar. Almost immediately, there had been trouble, and Buford was one of the first to hear about it. Just that morning, an irate father called to chew him out because the bikers had beaten up his son at The Water Hole. At least, that's what old man Dickinson told him when he called to complain that it was

Buford's fault the Angels were in town. What Buford did manage to get out of him was that a bunch of Silverville cowboys had taunted the bikers until tempers flared. Buford got on the phone to the tavern owner and found out that no one was beaten up. After much harassing, one of the bikers tripped Dickinson's son, who was pretty drunk anyway. And the kid fell on his face and broke his nose.

A motorcycle engine growled beside him in the street. In an involuntary reflex, he leaped sideways.

"Kind of jumpy, ain't ya?"

With much relief, he turned to see Carl next to him.

"Those motorcycles are sure loud," Buford said. He fell in step with the sheriff. "Are you headed to the parade, too?"

"Yep, me and the twenty-five extra uniforms in town right now."

"Been busy since the Angels rolled in last night?"

"A few tickets, but most of them have gone to locals."

"Locals?" Buford picked up his speed to keep his short legs in stride with Carl's.

"That's right. Illegal u-turns, jaywalking, failure to stop – that sort of thing. These extra law enforcement boys we hired are getting pretty bored. And that damn self-appointed cowboy vigilante group is causing more trouble than the Hell's Angels. The bikers are keeping mostly to themselves."

"Huh," Buford said, and didn't mention his own recent biker encounter. "I guess the City overestimated how much protection we needed."

"More a nuisance than anything else," the sheriff shouted at Buford as another pair of bikers rode past.

"Maybe you should give them a fine for noise."

Carl shook his head. "Never needed a noise ordinance until now."

He left the sheriff and worked his way through the crowd to the Main Street curb. The first float was just coming down the street but he hardly noticed it. The people standing around him were far more interesting than the parade. Cowboys jostled elbows with tourists wearing Hawaiian shirts; the same kinds of "aliens" he'd observed in the grandstands the night before edged away from tough-looking bikers. Besides the locals, several hundred other folks lined the street – folks who were spending their vacation dollars in Silverville.

The second float moved into view. Buford did want to look at this one since it was the main one promoting the theme park. On a flat-bed trailer pulled by a pickup truck, local children dressed as little green men sat around a large silver UFO. They waved at the spectators. Buford waved back. Howard trailed the display, smiling and throwing candy to the kids in the crowd.

Buford stepped off the curb and shouted, "Hey there, Howard!"

Howard grinned and trotted over with a fist full of green and yellow jelly beans. "Hi, Mr. Price. Would you like some candy?"

"Huh? Oh, no." Buford pulled him to a stop, leaning close to his ear. "You're gonna remember the message by Labor Day, right?"

A wide-eyed Howard nodded. "Okay, Mr. Price."

Buford stepped back to the curb as Howard jogged after the float. *You better remember, you idiot.* A lot of hype was hinging on those words, and Howard would have that message – whether he thought of it himself or not.

Multiple floats paraded by, each displaying a theme related to either Rodeo Days or UFOs. Buford had had to fast-talk the rodeo committee this year to convince them to split the traditional western theme with Silverville's new enterprise. Grady, the old fart, protested the loudest but by then several school groups had floats in the making. Nobody wanted to disappoint those little kids, and the committee reached the compromise of letting both themes enter.

The loud clap of horseshoes on pavement reached his ears. Turning the corner onto Main Street pranced a group of horses carrying riders with Rodeo Days flags. Grady and several other old geezers led the entourage. A fancy horse-drawn carriage followed the mounted cowboys and cowgirls. In a blur of red, white, and blue, they filed past him, all of them still wearing the same parade shirts they'd purchased twenty years ago. Grady looked at Buford and gave him a somber nod, and Buford returned the greeting with a salute. The presence of horses always signaled the end of the parade since nobody wanted to step in the deposits the animals left in their wake.

Several people started to turn away from the curb and leave when a motorcycle fired up somewhere ahead. At the same time, someone screamed and people scattered. The carriage horses were running the wrong way down the street, their panic-stricken driver unable to control them. The team weaved from one side to the other and then scooped up an unsuspecting bystander who flailed on his back atop the wagon tongue between the horses. As the team raced past Buford, he caught a glimpse of the unwilling passenger, his face white with fear.

"Stop that team!" somebody shouted.

It wasn't going to be Buford. He scrambled toward a store front and hugged the wall, giving the horses plenty of room to pass. A motorcyclist followed behind the carriage at a distance, probably unaware that his engine urged on the runaway. Above the noise of the bike, Buford heard the three-beat clip of a loping horse and then the words, "You damn fool!"

Like a white knight emerging from the fog, Grady burst through the chaotic throng of people, spurring his horse and swinging his lariat. Buford stood on tiptoe and strained his neck to follow what happened next. The hapless biker never saw Grady coming. With a fluid, practiced hand, the old cowboy dropped the loop of his rope over the biker's shoulders and leaned back in the saddle as his horse hunched down into a stop, sparks flying up from the hooves that raked over the pavement. The lariat jerked the biker to the street, and he landed hard on his backside. At the same time, the Harley tipped and slid to a stop on its side. The Angel struggled to his feet, yanked off the rope, and ran to his motorcycle.

"Look at my bike! You scratched the chrome!" he shouted, ignoring the rope burns around his bare shoulders.

But Grady paid no attention. He urged his horse back into a lope to pursue the runaway horses, all the while re-coiling the lariat that trailed behind him. No one in the crowd seemed willing to make eye contact with the biker, least of all Buford, who pretended to hurry after the runaway team as though he intended to help.

Buford marched quick time down the street until the commotion of people along the post-parade route had drowned out the sound of the biker's tantrum. Up ahead, Grady had already roped one of the horses and brought the carriage to a standstill. The man who'd been snagged on the harness tongue was just climbing down with the help of bystanders. When an ambulance finally arrived, the EMTs pushed through the crowd to assess the tourist's injuries. To Buford, he seemed fine. Plenty of assistance was at hand so he left to look for Skippy.

By now, the street had pretty well emptied since there was no longer anything to look at. He made a beeline toward the Lazy S. All the excitement made him hungry.

A line of other hungry people had formed outside the door, and he peered through the window to see who he could join. He recognized the back of his wife's head over a booth.

"Excuse me, excuse me," he said, striding past an irate line of people and into the diner.

No sooner was he through the door when somebody stood up from the counter and blocked his way. "Hey, fat boy, I've got an issue with you."

It was Lars Jorgensen, a lowlife who lived off his wife. He poked a dirty fingernail at Buford's chest and snarled, "I just lost my home because of your damned theme park."

Buford tried to look from side to side past Jorgensen's bulk to Skippy's booth. But every time Buford's head leaned either direction, the man shifted his weight and thwarted the view.

"The City's making me move my trailer next week for that new parking lot. Where are me and the old lady supposed to go?"

At the risk of being shoved, Buford slid past Jorgensen and maneuvered around the tables toward Skippy's booth.

"Hey, I'm talking to you!" Jorgensen called out.

Several people sat huddled with Skippy deep in conversation. When Buford approached, they all straightened up and fell silent. Next to Skippy was Felicia, of course, and also Denton. Earl Bob and Lela sat across from them. Was it Buford's imagination, or did they look guilty?

"Well, this is a cozy little get-together," he commented.

Fingers gripped his shoulder from behind. "Hey, butthead, I said I'm talking to you."

Buford ducked the grasp and backed away from the booth. He made a quick exit, calling out, "Y'all have a nice lunch. Sorry I can't stay."

Billy

They stared at Buford running out the door, Jorgensen following close behind.

"I wonder what that was all about," Lela remarked.

"Who knows?" Skippy shrugged, turning back to the topic. "I think I have to agree with Felicia. The whole summer has turned into a fiasco. I don't know how much more we can take."

"At least there's not going to be a lawsuit from the ride accident," Billy added. "I took care of that."

Felicia threw up her hands. "But how long will it be until the next one?" She turned to study his face. "Say, Earl Bob, that's a beauty of a shiner you have. Does everyone know he got that when he saved Duke's life last night?" Felicia beamed as she spoke.

"We heard a bull charged Duke, and you jumped between them," Skippy added and turned to Felicia. "I bet you and Denton are ever so grateful."

"You better believe it. Aren't we, Denton?"

It took a beat for Denton to respond. "What? Oh, yes, of course we are."

"Fawn," Felicia shouted over the din, "we're ready to order."

Billy wasn't sure he wanted to eat. Denton kept staring at him, and everyone in town knew the undertaker-coroner had been up on the pass the night before examining a dead body. Townspeople speculated about who the corpse could be, but Billy had a pretty good idea already. When he'd heard the news, his first reaction had been to duck out of town. But making a fast exit would have been a sure sign of guilt, and it might have sent Buford running to the police to tell them "Earl Bob" was an imposter. But if they suspected his involvement, why hadn't Carl come to question him?

Denton had called right before the parade to set up an

appointment to talk at the diner. What did he know – or thought he knew? Neither of them expected the three women to show up before they'd had a chance to speak.

"Earl Bob, it's your turn to order," Felicia said.

He told Fawn to bring him a slice of lemon meringue and a Diet Coke while the others continued to talk about Silverville's current state of affairs.

The mayor spoke up. "Revenues from sales tax receipts are way up, but it looks like everything we make this year will go back into street improvements and the need for more infrastructure. Sewer upgrades, trash disposal, and landfill enlargement – the list goes on and on."

"Is it true," Skippy asked, "that someone's proposed to tear down the old theater and put in a strip mall?"

Lela nodded. "And don't forget about the Big Box. It hasn't been finalized yet, but I can tell you, that discount store is coming. It'll bring more people to town, and that means more housing, bigger schools, and even more public facilities." She dropped her head to the table in a gesture of defeat. "I need a different job.

"What's more, there's a faction in town that doesn't like the increased tourism, and I can't say that I blame them. Carl is meeting himself coming and going trying to keep the peace between the locals and the summer tourists."

"Gosh," Skippy said, "I wonder why some towns seem to be able to grow while Silverville finds it so hard."

"You can't buy quality of life." Lela glanced toward Billy. "No offense, Earl Bob."

"None taken," Billy said. But he couldn't focus on the conversation. He said to Denton, "What do you think?" *Say something. Don't just sit there staring at me.*

"Maybe the problem's that it's all happening too fast," Denton said at last.

Lela sighed. "Somebody should do something about this." They all turned to her. "Well, not me. But somebody. I want my old life back."

§   §   §

They finished eating and the women got up to leave. Billy started to rise, but Denton reached for his sleeve, motioning for him to sit back down.

"I need to ask you something," Denton started, "but it's too crowded in here."

Dark circles rimmed the undertaker's bloodshot eyes, and it didn't look like he'd slept for the past twenty-four hours. Maybe it had been Duke's close call that made him look like one of his own clients, but Billy suspected it wasn't going to be that simple.

"Let's go to the funeral home where we can talk in private," Denton whispered.

Billy sucked in a quick breath. This could be a trap, and Carl could be waiting there for him. His daddy would have said, *Always watch your back.* "I have a better idea. Let's go to my motel room."

Denton showed no objection, and Billy wondered if he was being paranoid. Together they left the diner and walked the half block to the yellow Cadillac. Denton remained silent the whole way to the Galactic Inn, which was fine with Billy. He needed time to think, to plan how this might play out if he was accused of killing Earl Bob. A dozen times he'd seen his father fast-talk himself out of tight situations. Albeit Daddy was never accused of murder – at least as far as he knew. Billy had the Pisser's identification and his car, but it wouldn't take many phone calls to find out about the stolen identity. Then it would be a short leap to figure out he had killed the real Earl Bob. He would deny everything, of course, trying to give himself enough time to blow town.

When they reached the room, Billy offered Denton a chair. He cleared the dirty clothes off the bed and sat down to face the coroner.

"What's this all about?" Billy asked, trying to project as much innocence as he could muster into his voice.

Denton reached into his pocket and held up a monogrammed handkerchief, the letters "E-B-J" displayed across the bottom. "I found this on the pass last night. Would you know anything about it?"

Like a broken elevator, Billy's guts plummeted toward the

floor, and within seconds a film of sweat seeped through his shirt. It was Earl Bob's alright; Billy had found a full set of them in the Pisser's suitcase.

"I hope it's not yours." Denton paused, as though he were giving his words time to register. "Someone with these initials could have a connection with the dead body we found."

Billy took the piece of fabric, pretending to turn it over in his hands like he'd never seen anything like it before. Then he realized Denton was staring past him to the dresser on the other side of the bed. Billy turned to see what his visitor looked at, and there lay the other two matching handkerchiefs in full view.

Paralyzed, Billy watched Denton move toward the dresser and compare the handkerchiefs.

"This is yours, isn't it." It was a statement, not a question, and the tone was full of regret.

Possible alternative explanations raced through Billy's mind. Maybe he could convince Denton the hankie had blown out the window the first time he crossed the pass, driving into town. But who would have had their car window open during a snow storm? *Think, think!* He looked over at Denton, who appeared truly distraught.

"Before you answer," Denton said, "I want you to know this is really hard for me. I'm not out to frame you, Earl Bob. I like what you've done for our community and I'm grateful for what you did for Duke. But I feel compelled to cover all aspects of the investigation, and this is the only concrete evidence that we've found."

"Does Carl know about this?"

"No. I was up all night, debating whether to talk to you first or hand it over to him. And then I thought, if you were guilty of murder, the morale of the town would collapse. Things seem pretty shaky as it is around here lately."

"What do you think, Denton? Am I capable of killing somebody?"

Denton walked back to his chair and sank deep into the seat. His long face seemed to hang lower than usual. "I think you're capable of saving a life – like you did last night. But we've all just known you a few months." Denton still toyed with the handkerchief. "I need to know if you had anything to do with the body on the pass. Tell me if this is yours."

The anguish in Denton's voice startled Billy. It was clear the man was struggling with the idea of turning him over to the law. And really, the only crime he was guilty of was accidentally killing the Pisser and falling victim to Buford's scheme. But would it be enough reason to keep Denton on his side? And then it occurred to him what he had to do.

"No, the handkerchief isn't mine. It belongs to Earl Bob Jackson."

Taking his eyes from Denton's perplexed face, he retrieved the Pisser's suitcase from the closet and returned to the bed. "I hit Earl Bob Jackson on the pass the night before I got to Silverville. It happened during the middle of a snow storm, and neither one of us saw it coming. All of a sudden, there he was, standing in the middle of the road beside his car. There was no way I could avoid hitting him."

Before he could finish the account, Denton interrupted. "Why didn't you report it?"

It was a good question – although it never occurred to Billy to report the accident. After all, he had been on the run at the time. *Never look a gift horse in the mouth.* But that's not what Denton would want to hear. "I don't know why I didn't report it. My car wasn't going to make it much further, and I took his Cadillac, it's true." He didn't mention he'd riffled through the Pisser's pockets and rolled him over the side of the road. "By the time I got to town and stopped at the diner, you and Buford met me at the door. Before I knew it, the whole thing had snowballed and suddenly I was Earl Bob."

"The right thing would have been to report this."

"Probably true, but not everyone always does the right thing." Billy reached into the luggage sitting beside him on the bed and pulled out the yellowed newspaper clipping. "Let me show you something."

He handed Denton the article and gave him time to read. When the undertaker let the clipping fall to his lap, Billy continued, "I found this in the Pis—in Jackson's things."

"What does this mean?"

"I'm not sure. I've been wondering about it ever since I found the article, but I think Earl Bob Jackson was the one who hit you. If he wasn't the one, then why did he keep the newspaper clipping all these years?"

"This doesn't make sense. Did he know I lived in Silverville?"

"Maybe, but I don't know. There was no mention of you in any of the correspondence with Buford. Just the clipping."

If any man looked beaten, it was Denton. He reread the newspaper article, shaking his head with disbelief.

"So many years ago," he said with a sigh. "Did you know about my past?"

"Yes. Skippy told me. That's why I kept the article. It seemed like too much of a coincidence. Earl Bob runs over you, I run over Earl Bob, and we all end up in Silverville."

"And you planned to just continue posing as Earl Bob?"

"I had no choice. Buford figured out I'm an imposter, and he threatened to go to the police if I didn't play along in his little venture."

"Buford's blackmailing you?"

"I guess you could call it that."

Denton frowned. "This is inexcusable, even for Buford. Obviously, he thinks he needs you. The whole town needs you."

The two men sat without saying anything for several minutes. Then Denton stood up to leave. "Who are you, anyway?"

"Nobody. Until I got to Silverville."

Still clutching the handkerchief in his fist, Denton replied, "Well, I don't need to know. To me, you're just Earl Bob."

"So you're not going to turn that handkerchief in as evidence?"

The coroner leaned toward the bed and dropped the cloth on Billy's lap.

"What handkerchief?"

CHAPTER THIRTEEN

Howard

Howard liked to pedal. He didn't have to think about anything else – just push the right foot down and push the left foot down. Sometimes he went so slow his bike would wobble, but then he'd stand up on his pedals and pump until he sped up fast enough that it felt like flying.

In some ways, it reminded him of messaging limbs. Whenever he helped Mr. Fine embalm bodies, Howard's job was to squeeze the arms and legs so the blood could come out and the embalming fluid could go in. At least, that's what Mr. Fine said it was for. First the right leg, and then the left leg. Just like pedaling.

He couldn't wait to get home because his stomach had started to growl. Mr. Fine had needed him later than usual that afternoon because they'd had to pick up Mr. Outhouse from the nursing home. Mr. Fine kept reminding him that the man's name was "Oh-thoose," but to Howard, it looked like "Out House." The poor man died during his nap and no one had noticed all day. Howard wondered what it would be like to die during your nap. Would you dream you were dying? Would God say, "Wake up, Mr. Out House, you're dead now"?

It made him think of the man they'd found up on the pass – or what was left of him. He knew from the Bible that on the Last Day, the trumpets would sound and the dead would sit up. But what would happen to the man on the pass? His bones were scattered all over the ravine. A week or two after they discovered him, Howard had asked Mr. Fine if they ever found out who he was. Mr. Fine seemed concerned about that, too, and he'd called the sheriff several times to ask. But the sheriff had told him he didn't think they'd ever know.

Howard's bike wobbled, and he stood up to pedal harder. When he got home, he was going to open up that can of chili he'd been thinking about eating all week. He especially liked chili with Ritz crackers and dill pickles. First, he'd line the bottom of the bowl with sliced pickles, and then he'd top them with crumbled crackers. Next, he poured on the hot chili. But not too thick. Pickles tended to get soggy if they waited too long on the bottom of the bowl.

R-r-r-ring, ring, ring. He squeezed on this handle-bar bell to let Fawn know he was right behind her on the side of the street. She was probably walking to work at the Galactic Inn. Portia ducked between her legs at the sound of the bell.

"Sorry!" he yelled as she tripped on the dog.

He steered around the pair and continued along the road. Up ahead, some men were standing around a backhoe. Howard thought they were digging a well for the new campground. He'd been watching the construction all week, and so far they had started building a shower house and plowed a path for a winding road. When they got done paving, He planned to ride his bike on it.

Braking to a stop, he slid off, put his kickstand down, and walked over to see how deep the hole was.

"Hey, Howard, don't get too close!" one of the workers shouted as he started to pack up for the day. Howard smiled and waved back.

"Boy, this well goes way down." He kicked a clod of dirt over the edge.

"There's not going to be a well. This is a drainage culvert for the sewer we're installing." The man pointed to a silver pipe that ran along the bottom of the trench.

Culbert, that was a new word to Howard. "How come it's so deep?"

"It's only eight feet, but it looks that way because it's so narrow. It has to be deep enough to go below frost line." The worker pulled off his hard hat and wiped his forehead. "Well, time to get home for supper. You be careful not to get too near the trench."

As the man walked off, Howard backed a respectful distance from the opening in the ground. Even though he hadn't dug the hole himself, he felt proud. All the changes in Silverville were because of him, because of what he saw. That reminded him. He had to remember the UFO message by Labor Day. Mr. Fine told him not to worry. The message would pop into his head when he least expected it. But he did worry about remembering. The message had been important, special. Maybe the UFO had given him advice for Silverville, or maybe Colorado. Maybe even the whole world.

Something poked him in the butt. He swung around to find Portia wagging her tail behind him. In her mouth, she carried a half-chewed tennis ball, which she dropped at his feet. The dog barked and jumped forwards and backwards at the ball. Over on the street, Fawn continued toward the Galactic Inn.

"You better go with your owner," Howard told the expectant dog. "You want me to throw this first?"

He reached down and picked up the ball and tossed it away from the street. He didn't want Portia to get hit by a passing car. But just as the half-ball left his hand, the edge caught on his fingernail and sailed straight into the open trench.

"Portia, don't go in there!"

Too late. The dog leaped into the hole and disappeared. He ran over to the rim and peered down. Portia was nowhere in sight.

"Portia," Fawn called from the street. "Portia! Get back over here!"

"She went in there," he explained, pointing at the trench.

By the time Fawn walked over, he was already on his hands and knees trying to figure out what had become of the dog. Then he heard a whining echo from the end of the pipe.

"Where's my dog?"

"She's in the culbert. She won't come out."

One of Fawn's eyes stared at him, but the other one seemed to look down into the hole.

"Come on, Portia. Come on," she coaxed.

The whining turned into whimpers as they heard thrashing sounds coming from the pipe.

"I think she's stuck. Help! Help!" Howard shouted, but the workers had already left for the day.

Fawn scrambled down into the ditch, a cascade of falling dirt trailing behind her.

"You can't go down there! You can't go down there!" he shouted as he paced back and forth along the trench.

"I'm going in," she said. Her face looked white as the sheets at the funeral home.

"It's too skinny. You won't fit."

He hadn't been this scared since the accident at the theme park. The men had told him it was dangerous to go in the hole, and here was Fawn trying to squeeze into the pipe. He watched with horror when her shoes disappeared from sight. Squatting next to the edge, he listened to the sound of her body scraping against metal. It was the same sound his model car had made when he'd shoved it into the tailpipe of his father's truck. Howard had only been nine at the time, but he still remembered how his dad had to break the model into pieces with a screwdriver to get it out.

He got even more scared, and shouted, "Fawn, come back out!"

It was a few seconds before she answered. "I can't. I'm stuck."

Billy

As he pulled out of the museum parking lot, Billy took a deep breath and turned the yellow Cadillac toward the Galactic Inn. He'd spent the better part of the afternoon with Mrs. Watson, who had become disillusioned with her job as curator. For most of the summer, she had survived visits by church camp kids, Hell's Angels, and UFO followers. But when a group of teenaged tourists broke a display case and stole her prized meteorite, she became livid. *That's it, she'd told him. I'm done, I can't take this anymore. If I see one more tourist, I'm going to have a stroke.* Billy had nodded, pretending sympathy, listening to her rant and rave until she finished.

Phrasing it fifteen different ways, he'd assured her that no one in town was as qualified as she to hold the position. If she stepped down, the town would suffer a great loss. Finally, she calmed down enough to agree with him, particularly when he promised to find the teenagers and retrieve the meteorite. The tourists, of course, were long gone, but would she notice if he replaced the space rock with something he found lying along the road?

Just as he approached the new campground site, he saw a man running in circles and wringing his hands. Billy pulled his car over to the curb and rolled his window down. It was Howard, and he was shouting, "Oh no! Oh no!"

Switching off the ignition, he stepped out of the Caddy and walked over to him. It was obvious, but Billy asked the question anyway. "Something wrong?"

"In there!" The young man jabbed his finger toward an open trench. "It's where I threw that half ball. And now it's my fault. They need help."

"Who needs help? What's your fault? Howard, calm down." Billy reached for his arm and brought him to a quick halt.

Howard buried his head in his hands. "Oh this is terrible. I think we're going to have to break them."

"Huh?"

About that time, a muted voice shouted from the culvert at the bottom of the trench. "Would somebody please get me out of here!"

Billy leaped down into the hole and peered into the culvert. "Fawn, is that you?"

"Portia crawled in here, and I was trying to get her out. Now we're both stuck."

He'd never heard Fawn utter so many words at one time.

The culvert only looked to be about fourteen inches in diameter. Way too small for him to climb in after her. He thrust an arm into the opening anyway, but couldn't reach her. "I can't help you, Fawn. I'm going to go call the fire department."

"No! Don't you leave me!"

The panic in her voice startled him. He asked, "Are you hurt?"

"I can't breathe. I'm claustrophobic. Can you do something fast?"

"Can you go backwards or forward, either direction?"

"I can wiggle forward a little, but I can't back out."

Standing up, he rubbed his chin, looking at the stretch of pipe. Twenty feet from the open end, a sleeve joined another section. If he could pull it away, Fawn might be able to crawl toward the other end and get out. There could be a chain in the trunk of the car. At least, he thought he'd seen one there.

He couldn't resist saying, "Don't go anywhere. I'll be right back."

"Very funny."

He turned toward Howard, who stood looking down at him. "Give me a hand and help me out of this trench."

Once he scrambled up, he jogged over to the car and popped the trunk. Sure enough, there lay a chain curled up against one side. He climbed into the Caddy and backed the wheels over the curb, getting as close as he dared to the open hole. Once he'd found a spot on the undercarriage to hook the chain, he called out to Howard to find a sturdy stick or a flat rock to wedge under the culvert. Then he jumped back into the trench.

"Fawn, you still with us?"

"Where else would I be?"

"Here's what we're going to do. Howard and I will wrap this chain around the pipe and try to pull it forward with my car. When it breaks off from the sleeve, you try to crawl forward."

"What about my dog?"

"One at a time."

By then, Howard arrived with a broken two-by-four.

"That'll work. Climb down here and give me a hand."

Howard shook his head. "The man told me not to."

Trying to be patient, Billy said, "I can't get Fawn out unless you help me."

The young man stood at the edge, as if he were debating what he should do. Then he handed Billy the board and slid into the hole.

"Good boy. Now, you jam this two-by-four under this pipe while I try to pull it up a little bit."

Billy gripped the curved rim of the culvert and heaved upward. It moved a couple of inches. "Now! Stick the board under."

It worked. With the leverage from the board, Billy slipped the chain under the pipe and snugged the links against the ribbing.

"Okay, listen, buddy. I've got a real important job for you to do. You're going to have to drive the car forward while I guide this pipe back."

His eyes opening wide, Howard said, "I can't drive."

"Come here. I'll show you what to do."

Once again, they climbed out of the trench and Billy guided his helper into the driver's seat. "Nothing to it. Just put your foot on this pedal, that's the brake, and push this lever to the 'D.'" Billy tapped on the display above the steering wheel. "Then put your foot on that pedal, and press lightly until the car moves forward. But go slow. Got that?"

Howard nodded his head.

"Okay, get in there and roll this window down so you can hear me. When I say 'go,' you do what I tell you."

When he'd returned to the trench, he gave Howard the signal. At first, the culvert didn't budge although Billy could hear the Caddy's engine humming louder. "Press the pedal harder!"

With a lurch, the culvert broke free from the sleeve and tipped vertically as the car yanked it up over the side of the trench. As the far end flew past Billy, he heard Fawn screaming from inside. The pipe paused for a moment as it snagged on willow roots near the top, and down and out she tumbled.

"Stop, Howard, stop!"

But the pipe disappeared over the edge, banged against the ground and, seconds later, screeched over the pavement as Howard drove away. Billy shot a quick look at Fawn. She was standing and seemed no worse for the wear, so he leaped out of the ditch and ran after his car. Lucky for him, Howard wasn't going very fast and Billy caught up to him in seconds.

Running alongside the Caddy, he shouted, "Put your foot on the brake!"

Howard did, but he must have forgotten to take his other foot off the accelerator because the vehicle stopped and pitched forward in intermittent jerks, the culvert skipping and banging behind. As the car lost momentum, the pipe slammed into the rear end.

"Howard! Open your eyes," Billy gasped, still running to keep up, "and turn off the ignition."

When Howard obeyed, the car rolled to a halt.

"I'm sorry, Mr. Jackson. I told you I didn't drive."

Giving him a thumbs-up, Billy spun on his heels and ran back to check on Fawn. Portia met him at the mouth of the trench, dirty but wagging her tail.

"I got her out," Fawn said, climbing up the steep side. "She was at the front of that next section."

Billy collapsed on the grass, still out of breath. Fawn and Portia came over and sat down next to him. Soon, Howard joined them. He yanked free his shirttail and used it to wipe his glasses.

"Guess I'm going to be late to work," Fawn said. Her monotone voice had returned.

How typically Fawn. Billy fell on his side and laughed so hard that tears rolled down his face. Within a few minutes, Fawn stood and batted the dirt from her jeans. She started off toward the Galactic Inn, but after a couple of steps, swung around.

"Howard, free diner meals next week."

"Huh?"

"I'm buying your meals next week, get it?"

Howard gave her a broad grin and a thumbs-up, like Billy had done to him earlier.

Then she turned to Billy. "You stop at the desk when you get to the motel." She didn't explain; she just turned and walked away, Portia at her heels.

Still weak from laughter – or maybe the aftermath of all the excitement – Billy pushed himself upright. "Boy, Howard, I gotta talk to these construction guys about covering these holes before they leave at night."

They both stood and stared down at the open trench. Billy slapped Howard on the back. "Hey, buddy, you really helped save the day. And you get free meals at the diner. What a deal."

"For next week," Howard clarified.

"If I were you, I'd take advantage of that right away."

Howard smiled but shook his head. "I'm having chili tonight." He waved good-bye, walked over to his bicycle, and pedaled away.

Billy hiked the half-block up the road toward his car, where the culvert still lay chained to the undercarriage. A deep crescent-shaped dent creased the rear bumper. He should call Earl Bob's insurance company. The documentation was in the glove box with the registration. On the other hand, maybe it wasn't a good idea to start a new paper trail that involved the real Earl Bob. Unhooking the chain, he rolled the pipe into the ditch. Let the workmen pick it up; it was their fault anyway.

He hopped in the Cadillac and drove the short distance to the motel. He went inside and stepped over to the desk, where Fawn was already reading the evening newspaper. When Portia saw him, she shoved her snout against the back of his hand, asking for a pat. He dropped to his knee and took her head in both of his hands. "Well, you sure had an exciting day." The dog wagged her tail, and licked his chin.

From above him, he heard Fawn say, "This is for you." He straightened back up to see her holding out a large brown envelope.

"Don't open it here," she said. "Take it up to your room."

"What is this?"

"Buford dropped it in the diner the day you came to town. I found it under a booth." She sat back down and returned to her paper.

He wondered why she didn't give the envelope back to Buford, and why she'd held onto it for so long, but he took it anyway, told her thanks, and climbed the stairs to his room. What an odd duck she was. She hadn't even told him thanks for helping her. Guess he still had a thing or two to learn about Silverville locals.

Back in his room, he kicked off his shoes and plopped on the bed. He tore the seal on the envelope and fished out what looked like a gray bank passbook. Flipping it open, he saw it did, indeed, belong to Buford. But when he skimmed the entries, he began to understand why Fawn had given it to him. Maybe she'd thanked him after all.

It was more leverage than he could have hoped for.

PART FOUR

AUGUST

CHAPTER FOURTEEN

Denton

In an hour and a half, no one had won the argument. The Citizens for a Better Silverville had brought the community together – at least under one roof. But tempers were getting hot.

"Sure, you realtors love this," an angry man shouted, "but the locals can't even afford to own a house around here anymore!"

It was the president of the Board of Realtors who responded. "It's a sellers' market, Roy. We can't fix prices just to accommodate you. And if you went to sell your house, you'd be singing a different tune."

"If I sold my house, I'd have to move out of town."

"You can't stand in the way of progress. People have bitched for years that this was a stale little town. For the first time in decades, Silverville has a chance to really make something of itself, and all you can do is whine."

"You call higher prices 'progress'? Progress for who? What happens when my property taxes go sky high?"

Denton hadn't said anything all evening. He considered everybody in the room a friend, and he'd made funeral arrangements for just about every family there. For his part, more people in the community meant more business in the long run. On the other hand, a growing community would inevitably attract another funeral director. But aside from his personal gain or loss, he hated to see Silverville so divided. Only some of the business owners in town seemed happy about the newfound "progress." Most of the others resisted seeing their home town turn into a tourist destination.

He felt the pressure of someone looking at him and turned to see Lela staring his way. She scribbled on a note pad, and then she singled out other people with her gaze, each time pausing to write on the pad. What was she doing? For once, she wasn't at the podium leading the meeting. That job had fallen to Alonzo Haney, chairperson of the citizens group who'd called this unofficial gathering. And the turnout was good – from the garbage collector to the mayor, a good share of the townsfolk came to voice an opinion, or at least to hear what others had to say.

All heads turned when the next person stood to speak. It was Fawn. Denton had never heard her say much of anything except "More coffee?"

"The average wage in this town is twenty-four thousand a year." She paused as though she surprised even herself by speaking up. "I work two jobs for minimum wage, and last year I made twenty-thousand dollars. There's lots like me who can't save enough for a down payment on a home on those kinds of wages. It's hard to find a house now in Silverville under $140,000. With the twenty percent down bankers want, a person would have to come up with almost thirty-thousand dollars."

A voice called out, "Is that true?"

All eyes turned toward the local banker. "Well, twenty percent down is standard procedure. With house prices going up because of all the newcomers, Fawn is pretty accurate."

Loud grumbling arose across the room.

"But these rich folks coming in here are a higher class of people," Buford blurted. "They'll give our town a better image."

Lela snapped around to face where Buford sat. "Shut up before you get tarred and feathered."

To that, a dozen people clapped while others hooted Buford into silence.

The woman who owned a jewelry store on Main Street stood. She wore a smart, navy blue business suit that complemented a glittering brooch and matching silver earrings. "I, for one, like this new influx of people. My profits are up, and I'm thinking about expanding my store."

Her comment startled Denton. Like many other shopkeepers in town, she'd complained not two weeks earlier that she felt overwhelmed by the increase in trade. Up and down Main Street, sales clerks had become surly, even with the locals who entered places of business.

"But who around here can afford to buy anything in your store?" a woman asked.

Another person chimed in, "Yeah, prices have gone up all over town. Even our own grocery store thinks we're all millionaires. We're thinking about going to Placer City to buy our food."

The battle of pros and cons about Silverville's growth continued for another hour as Alonzo tried to moderate. Teachers complained of overcrowded classrooms, but a doctor countered that because the hospital serviced more people, it could now afford to build a new surgical facility. Now the community had a movie theater, but someone complained that the lines were too long. New residents had helped fund Silverville's failing art center, but only the patrons could afford to attend any functions.

Denton finally decided it was his turn to offer an opinion. Too stiff to stand up, he raised his hand. Several minutes passed before Alonzo called on him, and when he did, Denton kept it short. "Seems to me we made the decision to promote Silverville two years ago. People have already found us, and like it or not, there's nothing we can do about it."

Some people nodded; others looked grim with the realization that they'd made their bed. Now finding a way to get along with their new bedfellows presented the biggest challenge.

"It's getting late," Alonzo said to the crowd. "Do we want to talk about this at a later date?"

A flurry of dissenting voices erupted, each offering their own version of "hell, yes!" and "leave it be!" Alonzo closed his notebook and scanned the departing audience, his face twisting into a mirthless smile that said it all: The town was at a stalemate.

Waiting while people shuffled from the room, Denton watched Earl Bob walk over and sit down on the empty folding chair beside him.

"Thanks again for that favor. I owe you."

Denton shrugged. "It's a done deal. No need to talk about it again."

Earl Bob started to speak, but he stopped when Lela moved in their direction. He stood, pressing Denton's shoulder with a knowing squeeze and walked out the door. With Earl Bob gone, Lela positioned herself in front of Denton and leaned down to whisper in his ear.

"You said there's nothing we can do. Maybe there is. Come to my house tomorrow at six."

And she left.

Buford

Price's Gun Paradise had had a good month already. Buford ran his finger down the ledger and smiled at the totals at the bottom of the page. The new line of "horseshoe art" seemed popular with the tourists. And what he didn't sell in firearms, he made up the difference with worthless curios. Those out-of-towners now flocked to his new and improved inventory – bookends, lamps, and coat hangers made out of welded horseshoes, courtesy of the local farrier, who was just one more person making a profit from Buford's brainchild.

Looking at his watch, he wondered what was keeping Earl Bob. The "consultant" had called him first thing that morning and said he needed to talk. He'd be there at eleven.

The buzzer in the backroom announced someone coming in the door, but it wasn't Earl Bob. A man and little boy stopped at a display case and studied the binoculars under glass.

"Can I help you?"

The child ducked behind his father at Buford's booming voice.

"We're looking for binoculars," the man said. "I want something my boy here can use to get a good look at wildlife."

Buford waltzed behind the counter and unlocked the case. "Well, we got plenty of those. How long you folks going to be around?'

"For the next two weeks. Maybe through the first part of September."

"Are you planning to attend the big UFO celebration on Labor Day?"

"We're thinking about it."

Reaching behind him, Buford grabbed a flyer, facing it toward the tourist. "You're not gonna want to miss all this stuff. We're planning a community barbecue and discounted theme park rides all day. Later that night, there's going to be a street dance and fireworks."

"Uh huh." The man's attention strayed back to the assortment of binoculars.

"And best of all, Howard Beacon," Buford tapped on Howard's picture in the brochure, "the man who started it all, will reveal the aliens' message."

That got the tourist's attention. "This guy talks to aliens?"

"All the time. Why, Beacon is the pipeline between ETs and Silverville. You know, people around here see UFOs just about every night," Buford lied.

"No kidding?" The man pointed through the counter glass. "How much are those binoculars on the end?"

"You're not going to want that little pair of Nikons. You need this Swarovski spotting scope." Pulling a twelve-inch optical from under the case, he continued, "This baby has a zoom eyepiece with twenty to sixty magnification. You'll be able to look those little green men right in the eyeballs."

"How much?"

"And it's filled with nitrogen to prevent fogging. It's also covered in rubber armor so you don't have to worry about your little boy dropping it."

"How much is it?"

"Thirteen-hundred and ninety-nine dollars."

The customer gasped and shook his head.

Buford could feel the sale slipping through his fingers and added, "That's the list price, not the Silverville price. We appreciate folks who come out of their way to visit our special little town. So how about eleven-hundred dollars?"

"You'd discount that scope three-hundred dollars?"

"For you, yes. You seem like a nice fellow, and I want this little guy of yours to say he saw his first UFO in Silverville."

Reaching for his billfold, the tourist muttered to his son, "Your mother's going to kill us."

Buford took the credit card and was ringing up the sale when Earl Bob walked in. The tourist took his new scope and led the youngster out the door.

"We'll look for you on Labor Day!" Buford called out, but the door had already closed. He turned to Earl Bob. "That was an easy sale."

"Easy come, easy go, eh, Buford?"

"What do you mean?"

"Sales must be pretty good." Earl Bob walked toward the back office.

Following along, Buford bragged, "I just have to mention 'aliens' and I've got them eating out of my hand. Oh yes, it's been a very good month."

He stepped into his office and settled into the chair behind his desk before he realized that Earl Bob had closed the door behind them.

"How good of a month?" Earl Bob asked.

Buford let a self-satisfied smile flow over his face. No reason to hide success. "Let's just say, enough to make this all worthwhile."

"Enough to stash ten-thousand a month over the last year?"

The statement sucked the wind out of Buford. He leaned forward in his chair and clasped his hands together. He smiled. He hoped he looked congenial. "Excuse me?"

Earl Bob held up the gray passbook and said nothing.

"I'll be damned. You found it. I've been looking all over the place. Here, I'll take that." He stood, stretching over the desk to take the passbook, but Earl Bob yanked it beyond reach.

"I don't think so. Not until we have a little talk."

A slow panic seeped through Buford's chest. This was his money. He had earned it and he'd taken it. Who else had worked as hard as he? He'd wined and dined the fat cats who'd bankrolled the theme park, coordinated promotion and the subcontractors, and overall kept the ball rolling. There wouldn't be a project if it weren't for him.

Siphoning the money from the cash flow had been easy, just like he'd done before when Sam Noble rolled through town a few years back. No one except Skippy had ever noticed then, and no one had suspected this time either. Until now.

He had to get that passbook back. He pulled out a handkerchief and wiped his brow.

"This money's so hot it's making you sweat," Earl Bob said.

"That's a legitimate account, and you can't prove different."

"Looking at your business and this account, I bet an auditor could."

Buford sat down. Maybe he could still figure out a way to convince Earl Bob the money was legally his.

"That's a contingency fund for emergencies."

"Then why's it in your personal name? And why aren't there any debits?"

"Well a lot of that money is my fee for acting as general contractor for the project."

"You can't have it both ways. It's either a contingency fund or it's your personal fees."

"Maybe the bank messed up and accidentally combined the two accounts. Ask Skippy. She'll tell you," Buford said, knowing his wife would cover for him even though she was unaware of the account or the purpose of the passbook.

"You're trying to tell me you've got an account that accumulates ten grand a month and you never checked to see if it was a mistake? Nobody's going to buy that."

Buford's shoulders collapsed. There was no sense in trying to fool Earl Bob; the man had to be some kind of con artist himself, and one fox could always spot another. "What do you want?"

"I want control of my own life again."

"Keeping that passbook isn't going to change anything."

"No, but taking it to the UFO Economic Development Committee might."

Okay, Earl Bob hadn't turned him in yet. That much was clear. But if he did, Buford might end up in jail. Even with time off for good behavior, he'd probably get ten years, ten years of living in an eight-by-eight foot cinderblock cell with a metal toilet open for anyone to see through the bars. A menial job making license plates would fill his days, and he'd eat bad food in a dirty cafeteria, a place where big burly guys picked fights and knifed each other.

One of the burly guys was bound to be his cellmate, and Buford would become his bi-bi-bi – there might still be time to cut a deal with Earl Bob.

His voice changed to a more pleasing tone. "Now, Earl Bob, you saw the balance in that passbook. That's a lot of money. Enough for the both of us."

Without saying a word, Earl Bob kept his eyes locked on Buford's. Was he thinking about it? Buford built on the momentum of his sales pitch. "And this is just the beginning. There's no telling how much we could add to the kitty. Especially if we work this thing together."

Earl Bob opened the gray book and paged through the entries.

"You're just here for the money anyway, aren't you, Mr. Imposter? Come on," Buford added, "what do you say?"

Rising to his feet, Earl Bob lazily sauntered around the desk and over to Buford. Then with the quick grace of a pouncing panther, he clutched Buford's collar and jerked him up until the two were only inches apart.

"You think I'm some kind of idiot?"

Fearing for his life, Buford stammered, "I thought you and me– I mean, I thought we were alike."

"No one's as big an asshole as you are, Buford." Earl Bob released him and pushed him back into his chair. "If I took the money, then you'd have two things over me."

"Then what do you want?"

"I want out, with my bonus and the rest of the money coming to me, as soon as the Labor Day celebration is over."

"Sure, Earl Bob, no problem. I can live with that." Buford sighed with relief. This guy was becoming a liability. The sooner he left, the better.

"Oh, and one more thing. You don't get to keep all that money." Earl Bob slapped the passbook against the palm of his hand and then slid it into his rear pocket. "If you do, I'll report it."

"Do that and I'll turn you in for fraud. Besides, I can't turn that much money back or they'll know I stole it. And if anyone finds out, I promise, we'll sink together."

Earl Bob returned to the other side of the desk, smiled and said, "You don't understand. This is the deal. You keep half the money, and the other half is an anonymous donation for Denton's surgery."

"Why would you let me keep half?"

"That gives us the same number of chips in this poker game. I may be an imposter, but don't ever forget who knows you have sixty-thousand dollars in stolen money."

Skippy

She strolled through the Auto Roundup's outdoor lot until a metallic steel blue T-Bird caught her eye. *Oh yeah, this is what I had in mind.* Admiring the wide sixteen-spoke rims on the tires, she opened the driver door and slid inside. She loved the smell of new leather, and the bucket seat made her feel like she was sitting in a cockpit. Power windows, tachometer, and even an Audiophile sound system with a six-disc CD changer – this little baby had it all. And the two-seater convertible fit her like a tailor-made glove.

When Skippy was a teenager, her girlfriend's father owned a '59 Thunderbird convertible. Born eighteen years after her two sisters, Marsha was an unexpected addition to the small-town doctor's family, and she got everything she wanted, including free access to the vintage sports car. Marsha would pop by Skippy's home in Daddy's T-Bird on a Saturday night, and they'd be off to the movie theater in the next little town, the wind whipping at their long tresses as they rocketed into the night. Those were heady times – hot boys, under-aged drinking, and two teenaged goddesses in a fast car.

"You look right at home in there, Skippy."

Dex Johnson's voice pierced the bubble of memories. Too many years of heavy smoking had raked the tenderness from his vocal cords. But he was a natural born salesman. In the years Skippy had lived in Silverville, she'd seen him selling televisions, insurance, cemetery plots, and now cars.

He dangled the keys before her. "You wanna take it for a little spin?"

Of course, she wanted to. It had been years since she'd been behind the wheel of Marsha's car, and she remembered how exhilarating it was to tap the accelerator and feel the T-Bird shoot away like a sprinting racehorse. She stepped out of the car and walked around it.

"It's got a 3.9-liter V8 under the hood, a lot of power for this sized vehicle," Dex continued. "And those heated seats will be mighty nice this winter."

Skippy nodded and leaned down to read the sticker price pasted on the passenger door window. A little more than forty grand. She made a quick mental calculation and decided she could afford it.

"If you don't like this color, we can custom order something else. This model also comes in Torch Red, Evening Black, Cashmere, and Bronze."

"No, no, this color is just fine." When she finished circling the T-Bird, she reached for the keys. "Yeah, I do want to take it for a drive."

"I'll just run and get a plate and be right back."

While she waited, Skippy popped the trunk. Not much storage space, but she probably wouldn't need it once she left. At that moment, she saw Earl Bob's yellow Cadillac roll to a stop next to the lot. He waved before opening his door and walked in her direction.

"Hi, Earl Bob. What are you doing here?"

"Looking for you," he answered as he approached. "I saw you from the road."

Dex returned with the temporary license plate and attached it to the car.

"Wanna go for a test ride?" Skippy asked Earl Bob, and then turned to Dex. "If that's okay."

The salesman threw out his hands as though pushing them out of the lot. "Not a problem. You two have fun."

They climbed in and Skippy eased the T-Bird out of the lot and then gunned it down the street. The feel behind the wheel was everything she remembered. Minus the excitement of youth. Still, she had something else to look forward to now.

"Are you going buy this car?" Earl Bob asked.

"Thinking about it."

"What about the Beamer?"

"That's Buford's. I think it's time I got my own wheels." *And my own life.* "So, why were you looking for me?"

"Do I need a reason to see you?"

Skippy squealed around a corner, leaving rubber on the pavement. She gave Earl Bob a wicked smile. "Did I scare you?"

"You do, but not with your driving. What scares me is that I'm not sure I want to leave town without you."

It took a second to absorb his words. "So you're escaping Buford, too."

"What are you talking about?"

"That's what this T-Bird is all about. It's my getaway car."

He started to laugh.

"What's so funny?" she asked.

"I was going to ask you to leave with me."

She brought the sports car to a stop at the side of the curb and twisted in the seat to face him. She'd been so anxious to escape Buford, she didn't realize until that moment that she might miss Earl Bob. Then again, he was a complication. She recalled the advice of her counselor: Solve one problem at a time.

"Earl Bob, I would like nothing better than to leave with you, but I've got to establish a new life and shed Buford before I can consider a new relationship."

"I think we'd make a pretty good team."

Yes, they might. However, there was something about this Noble that reminded her of the older one who had inadvertently caused her to commit her first federal crime. And here she was, involved with a second Noble just as she had committed her second federal crime. Could the two men be related? The coincidence seemed too unlikely.

"If and when I get my life in order, we can talk about this again."

Earl Bob looked disappointed. He readjusted his long legs as though he were trying to find a comfortable position in the cramped confines of the passenger seat. "I wish you'd think about this some more. I'm leaving Silverville right after Labor Day."

"Why after Labor Day?"

"I want to stick around long enough to make sure Buford makes an anonymous donation to Denton."

An anonymous donation. What did he mean? "Okay, I'm

completely lost."

"It's the other thing I wanted to talk to you about. Your husband has been skimming money from the theme park funds. A lot of money, actually."

How could Earl Bob have found out? A groan escaped from her throat.

He raised an eyebrow but continued, "By a fluke, I wound up with the passbook, and I threatened to expose him unless he returned the money."

She pressed the back of her hand to her forehead, sure her face must look flushed. Buford would never be able to return the money because she had also discovered his secret account and transferred every last dollar into an account of her own.

Just like before, it was easy for a bank employee to manipulate the electronic records. She thought she had a few weeks to use that money and still get out of town before Buford found out. He would know right away what she'd done because he'd seen her do it before. But he wouldn't be able to turn her in without implicating himself.

It had been a good plan.

She weighed her words carefully as she spoke. "Buford will never turn that money back." For once, she was counting on his greed to work for her. "Besides, I know how his mind operates. If you expose him, he'll expose you."

"He's already agreed. We cut a deal. He's keeping half the money."

"Why would you let him do that?"

"It's my insurance policy. Buford doesn't turn me in as an imposter, and I don't turn him in for being an embezzler. It's the only way I can get free. As far as the other half of the cash goes, I owe Denton a favor, and I'm going to pay him back with Buford's money."

Skippy slumped in the seat. She could see no way to hold onto the funds. If she took the money and skipped town right now, her husband would probably expose Earl Bob and get him arrested. Buford might even claim she and Earl Bob planned this together. Buford, on the other hand, would be free and clear. With Skippy having tampered with the electronic records in her favor, there'd be no trail to implicate him. And then there was the question of personal guilt. Could she live knowing she'd deprived Denton of money he needed for surgery? Felicia talked to her about it constantly, worried that without the surgery, Denton wouldn't be able to walk.

There was nothing left to do but replace the funds. She'd never get free. A bottle, she needed a bottle to help her rinse the taste of defeat from her mouth. But the thought made her burst into tears. No, that would never do; she'd need all her wits to figure this out.

Earl Bob reached over and placed his hand on her shoulder. "You're feeling bad because I'm leaving, aren't you? We'll work this out. Even though we're both leaving, we should promise each other we'll stay in contact."

"Okay," she said absently. There had to be another way to fund her escape from Buford, even if she couldn't leave town. After all, she had a good job and she could afford a small room someplace. At least it would be a start. The other choice was that she could go with Earl Bob after Labor Day. But what did he really know of her? Once he found out she was a recovering alcoholic and an embezzler, would he still be interested?

"Look," Earl Bob said, "I know you don't know anything about my past, so I don't blame you for not wanting to come with me. But we've hit it off so well, and I'm pretty sure we can make a go of this when you're ready. Who knows? Maybe we'll find out we have more in common than we thought."

"I guess," she sniffed, and started the car. "I better get this T-Bird back. Maybe I won't be leaving after all."

"What? But you just said—"

"I know what I said. I'm leaving Buford – that's settled, but ...." But she wasn't ready to come clean with Earl Bob. Some secrets were just too private, too complicated to share. Instead, she added, "But maybe I have ties to this place that run too deep to leave."

They rode in silence the rest of the way back to the Auto Roundup.

As they got out of the car, Earl Bob asked, "So what do you

think?"

"I told you already what I'm probably going to end up doing."

"No, no, I meant the car."

She studied the sleek lines of the T-Bird one last time. Without Buford's secret stash, she'd never be able to afford a sports car. She looked around the lot until she spotted a Ford Escort. And it was brown, not Cashmere. "I think I'd better keep looking."

Dex met them as they walked away from the Thunderbird.

"Should I put a bow on it?" Dex asked, a confident tone in his voice.

"Do you have anything in brown?"

Dex stood there scratching his head while Earl Bob started toward his car. By the time he reached his Caddy, he turned and called out to Skippy, "Will I see you at Lela's for the meeting tonight?"

She nodded and then motioned Dex over toward the Ford Escort.

CHAPTER FIFTEEN

Billy

"We'll have to run a quick credit check on you, Earl Bob," the clerk said. "No offense. Even if it's a small town and we know you, the phone company requires it."

This was one more reason why he needed to get out of town. Earl Bob Jackson was a ghost who could materialize at any time. Like now. At last night's meeting, Lela had delegated the communication job to Billy, which meant he'd need a cell phone. They assumed, of course, he already had one, and maybe the Pisser did. But it wasn't among his personal affects.

"I'll need the phone by Labor Day," Billy said.

"Oh, that won't be a problem. Credit checks don't take long." The clerk handed him a form. "Just need to fill this out."

Billy took the Pisser's wallet from his pocket and looked for the Social Security card and other information he might need for the form. He felt lucky that Silverville had a Radio Shack, even if it was tucked in a corner of the hardware store. The store didn't offer much in the way of electronics except cell phones and a limited range of DVD players and speakers.

When he finished the application, he asked the clerk where the Christmas lights were. The hardware salesman gave him a quizzical look.

"You know," Billy prompted, "the kind that hang on your house."

"Oh man, I don't think we've got anything like that in stock this time of year, but I'll go look in the back."

"I want the kind that blink," he called after him.

While he waited, he meandered over to the plumbing aisle to look for duct tape, the next thing on the shopping list he'd been assigned at Lela's meeting. The closer they got to Labor Day, the more excited everyone in the secret planning group seemed to become. Lela had doled out jobs to each one with the same finesse she showed as a mayor. The only difference was that the "employees" for this public service weren't on the city payroll.

The clerk reappeared while Billy squatted near the rolls of tape. "Sorry. We don't have any Christmas lights and probably won't until after Halloween."

"You can still use mine." The voice was Carl's. He stood at the end of the aisle, probably there taking care of his own list for the plan.

Billy thanked the clerk and waited until he left before walking over to Carl. "Thanks, but like I said last night, I don't think blinking chili peppers are going to work for this."

"Well, suit yourself, but I don't know what else you're going to use since you can't find big-bulb lights in town any time soon. They're better than nothing. And besides, I still say chili peppers fit right in with the plan."

Just then, someone else rounded the corner and moved through the aisle, and both men fell silent and pretended to look at the tape. When the third shopper left, Billy asked, "Do you think your wife would notice the lights are missing?"

"Not until December first."

"Okay, could I pick them up this afternoon?"

"I'll meet you at the house at one-thirty. We'll want to do it when my wife goes back to work after lunch."

They shook hands and parted, each leaving the aisle at opposite ends. Billy felt an unexpected tingle of excitement. A secret agent on a clandestine mission. An undercover spy about to save the world with feats of daring – or, at least, with Christmas lights and duct tape.

But what if the plan failed?

As far as Billy was concerned, it didn't matter. He left the store, got in the Cadillac, and drove toward his next stop. Turning onto Main Street, he passed the storefronts, counting how many shop owners he knew on a first-name basis. *Suckers waiting to be fleeced*, his daddy would've said. He thought about the passbook – his passport out of Silverville. He'd intended to use it as soon as he'd finished his role in Lela's plot. Or at least that had been his original idea. He'd been sure Skippy would agree to join him. But when she turned him down, he wasn't as anxious to get out of town.

He could still take the money they'd paid him and run, but would it be worth it if he never saw Skippy again? That was a part of his own plan that he didn't want to fail.

Billy had experienced plenty of failures in his life, some in schemes but most in personal relationships. Even his parents had left him, first his mother and then his father. Why would Skippy want to stick with him when his own family hadn't? Maybe there was something in his personality that eventually pushed people away. When his mother had disappeared with his little brother, Billy had taken it hard. He used to think she left because of something he'd done. But Daddy had told him that nobody was perfect and you couldn't always guess what people were going to do. If his mom couldn't take that kind of life, then he and his dad were better off without her. Billy had accepted what his father told him at the time, rolling with the punch and considering it a lesson in life. Still, it didn't change his feelings for his mother. After she left, he missed her tucking the covers around his neck at night, kissing his scrapes and bruises, and singing lullabies when he was sick. Even now, he still missed the framed photo that Daddy ran off with the night Billy found himself abandoned by the last member of his family.

Maybe he'd followed Daddy's philosophy for too many years and figured he was always better off without anyone else. Billy was, after all, the first one to run when relationships got too close. However, this time he wasn't sure he wanted to run off without Skippy.

He stopped at Hangar 18 for a quick burger, which still didn't deliver on their promise of "out of this world" cuisine. The same squeaky-voiced girl, who'd served him the first day he arrived in town, met him at the drive-through window.

"Yeah?" she asked without looking up.

The peppy attitude she'd had at the beginning of the summer had evolved into dour impatience.

"I'd like a burger and fries."

"Right." She turned away from the window, presumably to get his order.

While he waited for his food, a van with out-of-state plates pulled into the drive behind him. Through his rear-view mirror, he watched kids bob up and down from the back seat. The driver-father reached an arm back and popped one on the side of the head.

The drive-through window reopened and Little Miss Peppy threw him a sack. He fished in his pocket for the right change, but the van driver must have decided it was taking too long and honked his horn.

"Come on, buddy. You got your food. Let's move things along here," the tourist shouted, leaning out his window.

Billy paid for his meal and pulled ahead into a parking space to eat. Behind him, he heard the van's horn again and looked up in time to see the driver flip him off. He munched on his burger and tried to envision what would happen on Labor Day evening. Not that the plan was all that complicated, but there was no way to rehearse what would happen. Of course, the beauty of the plan was that it depended on imperfection – something this crew would have no trouble with.

Even if they got their cues mixed up, it didn't matter. But the whole thing stood no chance unless they could keep it secret, particularly from certain key people in the community who would try to stop it cold. He tossed the sack and the largely uneaten fries in the trashcan near his car and left the drive-in.

At the appointed time, Billy swung into Carl's driveway. Without missing a beat, the garage door rolled up and the sheriff motioned his car in. No sooner had he eased inside than Carl pulled the door down with a slam.

"Pretty cautious, aren't you?" Billy asked.

"Why take chances? I've got a nosy neighbor who's sure to ask questions."

Carl dug into a box planted on the floor beside the Caddy and yanked free a long tangled string of chili peppers. He dragged the wad of wired lights into Billy's trunk.

"You think this will be enough?" Carl asked.

"How far do they stretch around your house?"

"All the way across the front – maybe sixty feet."

"Should be plenty, but I'll be sure to ask." Billy closed the trunk lid.

Carl pointed at a plastic reindeer that stood eighteen inches tall. "That nose blinks. You want it, too?"

Staring at the sheriff for a just a second to see if he was joking, Billy ventured, "Are you serious?"

"Well, it blinks."

"No. The lights'll do fine."

He got in his car and started the ignition after Carl raised the door. He backed out and headed north of town. Billy almost missed the turnoff to Up, Up and Away, Bob Hardin's place, the last stop on his list. Trees flanked the upwind side of the acreage, and a small duck pond separated a modest one-story bungalow from the road. He parked near the office, which was attached to the house. Taking the lights from the trunk, he walked toward the building while clamoring geese flocked around his feet, looking for a handout.

"Watch out for that big one," Bob shouted above the honking din from the doorway. "He bites."

Billy kept a wary eye on the evil-looking gander as he quick-stepped over to the office and slipped inside the door. "Don't those things drive away customers?"

"I keep hoping. There's too damn many tourists around here as it is."

"Business is good then."

"Too good. I was enjoying retirement until Buford sucked me into this thing."

Billy had wondered why Bob was willing to help Lela's gang, but his attitude answered that question.

"Where do you want these?" Billy asked.

"Chili peppers?"

"It's what we got."

"Just drop them on the desk there." Bob picked up the dangling end of the string of lights and held up the plug. "This looks like AC."

"It's what we got," Billy repeated. "Is this string long enough? Can you make it work?"

At this, Bob replied, "I'll figure out something."

"You all set then?"

"Yep."

"No questions?"

"Nope." But then he added, "This is really a stupid plan."

"That's the whole idea."

Buford

Walking through the funeral home's garage, Buford sidled around the hearse. He heard noises coming from the door leading to the preparation room but barged in anyway. In the past, Denton had scolded him for that.

"You can't be in here when we're preparing someone," Denton had said, ushering him from the room. "What if that had been your mother lying on the table? Would you want just anybody coming in?"

Buford had laughed it off, countering, "That'd depend on which one of my mothers you were talking about."

But Denton had been adamant and always shooed him from any room that wasn't open to the public. Today, however, Buford wouldn't let his undertaker-friend intimidate him from finding Howard. Time was running out.

As it happened, Howard was alone and cleaning an empty embalming table. The young man looked up, startled by the intrusion, and said, "You're not supposed to be in here, Mr. Price."

Buford gawked at the open shelves neatly stacked with rows of embalming fluid bottles, instruments, and linens. He'd never been in the room long enough before to get a close look at the mysterious equipment kept there. Picking up a cardboard box, he plucked out a small pink disc that was shaped like half a hollow marble.

"What are these?"

Howard dropped his towel into a hamper. "They're eye cups. We stick them under the eyelids after someone dies." Then he added, "So the eyes won't sink."

Buford took two of the little cups and raised them to his own eyes, squinting to hold them in place like two plastic monocles. "Like this?"

He heard the door open behind him and turned, blindly, in that direction.

"Buford, what are you doing in here?"

Opening his eyes, Buford felt the cups slide down his cheeks toward the floor. Denton stood with his hands on his hips, and he didn't look pleased.

"You know you're not allowed in here."

"I'm going, I'm going. I just needed to talk to Howard for a minute. Besides, there's no body in here right now. What's the big deal?"

"Inspectors are coming today."

"Ocean inspectors," Howard offered.

"OSHA," Denton corrected. "And I don't want them finding someone in here playing with the embalming supplies."

Denton stooped to retrieve the plastic cups but had to struggle to straighten up.

"You schedule your surgery yet?"

"When I do, you'll be the first to know. Now you better get out of here."

Before Buford could protest, a buzzer sounded from someone opening the front door.

"That might be the inspectors now. Maybe you and Howard should go out through the garage." Denton turned and shuffled out the door.

Buford could swear he was dragging a leg. His friend needed the operation, and soon. Too bad he'd never know it was Buford's generosity that was destined to pay for it. Hell, he'd probably have given that money to Denton anyway. Or at least he'd have thought about it.

He and Howard stepped into the garage, and Buford leaned against the hearse. "Well, Howard, tomorrow's Labor Day, and tomorrow night you're going to announce the alien's message. Right?"

Howard pursed his lips and his face turned red like a man fighting constipation. "I'm sure going to try."

"You've got do more than try. Let's see if I can help jog your memory."

"Okay."

"It'll probably be something that just comes into your mind – like something you've heard before."

"Okay."

"Let's explore the possibilities. Maybe the aliens told you Silverville is the center of the universe."

Howard shook his head. "No, I don't think that was it."

"Well, maybe they gave you the formula for an inexhaustible source of energy."

"They didn't really say anything, Mr. Price. It was just a feeling I got."

"Come on, what kind of feeling?"

"Like I had to throw up."

How could he have ever placed himself in a situation that depended on Howard? Buford patted his pockets looking for a piece of paper but all he could find was an old parking ticket crumpled in his jacket pocket. He smoothed the ticket against the hood of the hearse with the heel of his palm and fished out a pen.

"Those aliens did tell you something. I'm going to write it down and this is what you're going to read out loud to everyone." Buford thought for a moment and then scribbled down two sentences. *We have come to save your planet. We have made Silverville our headquarters.* Elegant. Simple. Now for the coup de grace. He wrote, *Next summer, through our ambassador Howard Beacon, we will reveal the meaning of life.* Perfect, keep them begging for more.

Buford went over the first two sentences, making Howard repeat each one.

"Now Howard, this third sentence is the most important of all. 'Next, summer, through our ambassador Howard Beacon, we will reveal the meaning of life.'"

"They will?" Howard's jaw dropped open.

"Of course. It might even happen sooner than you think. Those aliens work in mysterious ways. They could even send you the message from a source you least expect." Buford was sure he could arrange that when the time came. He slipped the parking ticket into Howard's shirt pocket. "Now you go home and practice these lines."

"I will, Mr. Price."

"Ata boy, make me proud." He gave Howard his best winning smile, patted him on the back, and left the funeral home.

Driving home, he marveled at his own genius. Despite the dimwit he had to work with, Buford had made it easy for Howard. All he'd have to do is stand up and read the words on the parking ticket to an audience who wanted to believe. The town didn't know how instrumental Buford had been. On his own, he'd even arranged for most of the speakers throughout the summer. He didn't need Earl Bob. He'd been doing most of his job anyway. Buford had been forced to give the man credit for everything he'd done himself. Besides, the blackmailing s.o.b. was far too friendly with Skippy, too popular in the community, and starting to act like too much of an equal partner. All from an imposter. The sooner he was out of town, the better off they'd all be. And good riddance.

Skippy's car wasn't in the driveway when he got home. Just as well, since he had a private phone call to make. He tossed the car keys on the kitchen counter and marched back to the den. He didn't have to look up the number – he'd dialed it often enough over the past couple of weeks.

A voice at the other end of the line answered on the third ring. "This is Larry."

"Buford here. Is everything set for tomorrow night?"

"Yep. We'll be there around nine-thirty."

"Perfect. And everybody will be able to see you, right?"

"Don't worry. Nobody's going to miss us."

"That's all I needed to know."

Buford hung up without saying more. Unlocking the cabinet behind his desk, he poured three fingers of Scotch into a crystal tumbler. He laughed quietly to himself about the special surprise he'd arranged. Then he looked into the mirror above the cabinet and raised his glass to the reflection. "Here's to you, Buford. This grand finale is going to keep Silverville on the map."

Howard

"We should all try to eat at both restaurants."

Mr. Fine's advice made sense to Howard. They'd been sitting in the reception room of the funeral home, visiting with a caller paying respects to the deceased Mr. Winkler. For the past two nights, Howard had spent the evenings helping Mr. Fine receive friends and family. People had come and gone, signing the guest book, and offering their condolences. A few stayed longer to visit with Mr. Fine, like the man standing by the chapel doors now. He talked a lot, but not very much about The Deceased. Mostly he seemed unhappy with some of the new folks moving into town.

For every old timer we bury, we get two new ones in town who can't speak English," the man said.

Howard had heard the complaint before, but he didn't understand why other people in Silverville felt that way. He liked hearing the different languages these newcomers spoke. He liked Spanish the best, especially the Rs. He also liked that they spoke fast, not like the people in Silverville. And the Spanish had pretty names, like the time he overheard a woman in line at the checkout stand at the grocery store who kept repeating her husband's name, "*Estupido! Estupido!*"

But he didn't think the man paying respects at the funeral home agreed.

"Too many foreigners in this town. It's getting harder to find a good steak, there's so many Mexican and Chinese restaurants."

"Homer, there's only one of each. They're new businesses trying to keep their heads above water, and we all should try to eat at both restaurants."

"Well, I prefer American food." The man blew his nose and looked at his watch. "It's getting late, and I gotta be getting home to dinner. The wife is making spaghetti."

After he left, Mr. Fine pulled a twenty-dollar bill from his pocket and handed it to Howard, "You get out of here, too, and go get something to eat."

Howard thanked him and walked out to his bicycle, which leaned against the side of the garage. His free dinners from Fawn at the diner had run out, and he was glad. For five nights in a row, he'd ordered chicken fried steak at the Lazy S, the only thing he liked there. But now he could eat where he wanted. He thought about going to the grocery store to buy some cans of chili and then remembered the two new restaurants in town.

Should he go to the Mexican or should he go to the Chinese? He pedaled first toward the Chinese restaurant, and then he turned around and started toward the Mexican restaurant. But he'd never tried Chinese food; maybe that was the place he should go. On the other hand, if he went to the Mexican restaurant, he could listen to those pretty Rs. Now he didn't know what to do. He stopped his bicycle to think it over.

As he dropped the kickstand to the ground, Mr. Fine's words popped into his head. *We should all try to eat at both restaurants.* Of course, that's what he would do. He would eat at both restaurants. Already facing the direction of the Mexican place, he decided to go there first.

He pedaled the few short blocks and parked his bike on the sidewalk. Music and singing voices met him at the door. He looked around but didn't see a band.

"Just one, amigo?"

Howard looked up at a short smiling waiter who wore a white ruffled shirt and black pants.

"One what?"

"One for dinner?"

Howard thought about it and replied, "I might want two."

"Do you have anyone with you?"

Now Howard got it. "Just one."

"So they'll be two of you eating?"

The waiter seemed nice but not very smart. Howard replied, "Just me."

He followed the man to a booth and sat down. When the waiter asked him what he wanted to drink, Howard ordered a root beer. He looked around at the dining room. It didn't look like anything else in Silverville. The walls were all pink and covered with colorful pictures of dancing people and Mexican hats. From the ceilings hung birdcages with green parrots. Howard knew they weren't real, but he thought they were neat.

He picked up the menu lying on the table to see what he could order. Nothing sounded familiar and he wasn't sure what to do. Just then, to his relief, the waiter brought him his root beer, a basket of chips, and little bowl of red soup. This was probably what he would have ordered anyway.

"What would you like this evening?" the waiter asked.

"This is just right. Thank you." He handed the menu to the waiter, who shrugged and walked away.

Howard dipped his spoon into the little bowl of soup and swallowed a mouthful. Immediately, tears began to flow down his cheeks and he grabbed the root beer to wash the taste of the hot soup from his tongue. He wouldn't order that again. Munching on his chips, he reached into his shirt pocket and pulled out the piece of paper Mr. Price had given him. He needed to practice what he was going to say the next evening. Every time they'd asked him to talk in front of people, he couldn't think of anything to say. He was glad Mr. Price had written it all down for him this time.

He mouthed the words on the paper. *We have come to save your planet. We have made Silverville our headquarters.*

"How are your chips and salsa?"

Without thinking, Howard looked up at the waiter and said, "We have come to save your planet."

"¿Perdón? How is your food?"

Howard nodded his head. "These chips are good, but this soup isn't."

"¿Como?"

"The soup is too hot to eat."

"Ah, not soup, amigo, salsa. You dip in your chips." The waiter leaned over, took a chip from the basket, sunk it into the bowl, and then handed it to Howard. "Eat it like this."

Howard took a bite. It tasted a lot better that way. After the waiter moved on, Howard ate chip after chip, covered with "salsa," until the basket and bowl were both empty. When the waiter returned with his bill, Howard was surprised at how cheap it was to eat at the Mexican restaurant. He'd have to come here again.

He paid and walked outside to his bicycle. Now he needed to go over to the Chinese place, and he pumped against the pedals as he steered onto the street.

When he got to the restaurant, he parked his bike and went

inside. A waitress greeted him.

"Just one?"

This time Howard thought he would be ready, but before he could say, "Yes, just me," the words stuck in his throat. All he could do was stare. She seemed like the most beautiful girl he'd ever seen. Her long, black hair came all the way down to her waist, which wasn't that far since she stood no taller than Howard.

"You okay, mister? You okay?" She smiled at him, her pretty oval eyes sparkling.

Howard thrust out an arm to shake her hand. "I'm going to eat here and I sure am glad."

She took him by the wrist and led him through the busy restaurant.

She handed him a menu and said, "You sit here. I be back."

As she turned away, he put his wrist to his nose. It smelled like her perfume, and he felt the pit of his stomach tingle. He watched her walk through the room and pick up a tea pot. Then she stopped at a corner booth to refill somebody's cup. That's when he noticed that the couple was Mrs. Price and Mr. Jackson. They sat on the same side of the booth, huddled together writing in a notebook. Howard waited for them to look up, and he waved when they saw him.

Still glowing from the warmth of the waitress's touch, he adjusted his glasses and looked at the menu. Just like the other restaurant, this one listed food he'd never heard of.

"You leady to order?"

He smiled at the waitress and shrugged.

"You no eat Chinese food before. Ret me help you." She leaned over the menu and ran her finger down the choices. "This one good, and this one, too."

He breathed the cloud of her perfume and looked up, but his eyes never made it past the scoop of her blouse's neckline. There, a little piece of white lace peeked out between the gap of her buttons.

"Oh no!" Howard gasped, throwing his hands over his eyes in embarrassment.

"You no rike what you see?"

"I'm not supposed to see!"

"Then how you order?"

Howard handed her back the menu, saying, "You pick it, you pick it."

"Okay. You want tea with dinner?"

"No. Root beer."

"No have loot beer. I get you tea." She winked at him and left. He continued to stare at her until she rounded the corner. He even liked her tennis shoes. *This is a happy place*, he thought, as he tapped his feet under the table. That must be why Mrs. Price came here to eat. He looked over at his friends and saw they were holding hands under the table. *Yes, a happy place that makes people want to hold hands.*

"There you are!" Mr. Price's booming voice shouted across the room. Howard sunk in his chair because he hadn't learned his lines yet. But Mr. Price pushed past Howard's table and walked over to the booth where his wife sat. "Getting ready for tomorrow night, I see."

Mrs. Price pulled her hand from Mr. Jackson's and scooted over a little closer to the wall. All of a sudden, the place didn't seem to be as happy for everybody there.

The waitress returned to his table and poured his tea. "That roud man eat here before," she said, nodding her head in the direction of the corner booth. "He a plick. I go get your food now."

A minute or two later, she came back with a plate covered with rice and vegetables and handed him two wooden sticks.

"What are these?" Howard asked.

"No fork. Use chopstick." She slid onto the seat beside him. "Here, I show you how." Placing the two sticks between his thumb and fingers like a couple of pencils, she then put her hand over Howard's. "You use them rike this."

She dipped the sticks into the rice and brought them up to his mouth. "Okay, now you do it."

Howard tried, several times, and when she laughed, he did, too.

"More you come here, more you get hang of it. When you through, I bring you fortune cookie." She got up and left.

He set down the sticks and picked up his fork to finish his meal. All around him, people were using their forks, too. Maybe

Mrs. Price and Mr. Jackson knew how to eat with chopsticks, but they and Mr. Price were already gone.

When the waitress came back with his check, she said, "Now for special treat." She unwrapped a fortune cookie and broke it in half, pulling out a pink piece of paper from the center and handing it to Howard.

"This your fortune." She winked at him again, and added, "My name Kim. You come back."

After she'd gone, he put the paper and crumbled cookie in his shirt pocket, and then he placed on the table the remaining money Mr. Fine had given him for dinner. She'd told him to come back, and he sure would.

After he stepped outside he reached into his pocket for the fortune and read it for the first time. Howard smiled and then dropped the paper back in his shirt pocket. Yes, this was a happy place after all.

CHAPTER SIXTEEN

Howard

Throughout the day Howard walked around, watching the people who'd come for the Labor Day celebration. He didn't go into the theme park, but he listened from the gate to the children laughing and screaming as they whirled around on the rides. He had a little time left before four o'clock, when he had to get over to the picnic grounds to dish up food for the barbecue.

Even though he was looking forward to the street dance that evening, he didn't want to give his speech after the barbecue. Hard as he tried, he always got the words mixed up.

We have come to your saved planet. No, that wasn't right. *We have made Howard Beacon our headquarters.* That didn't sound right either. He fumbled in his shirt pocket for the instructions and read how Mr. Price had written them. Something fell from his hand while he recited the lines. At his feet, he saw the pink cookie fortune, and he knelt and picked it up. He smiled. The words reminded him of Kim and the happy restaurant. He'd have to look for her at the barbecue and street dance.

Picking up his bike, he pedaled through town toward the picnic grounds. On Main Street, he braked for a band of children with faces painted to look like clowns and aliens. They skipped through the crosswalk and stopped at one of the many outdoor booths, selling everything from snow cones to shoes. He walked his bike along the street, dodging groups of people. Half down the block, Brother Martin shouted his name and ran toward him. Howard pretended he couldn't hear the holy man and picked up his pace, hoping to get lost in the crowd. All summer, Brother Martin had asked him to come and talk to his congregation, but Howard always managed to find reasons why he couldn't go. He just didn't like talking in front of people, even when the audience was small. Which reminded him of what he had to do that night. The thought made his stomach hurt.

On the other side of Main Street, he got back on his bike and pumped over to the picnic grounds, which were only a couple of blocks from downtown. Already the organizers for the evening events had set up a podium and strung it with ribbons. He tried not to think about his speech. He waved at band members setting up their equipment and wheeled over to the barbecue pits. On the far side of the grounds, city workers had roped off a paved side street for the dance that would start after the evening line-up of special speakers. Mr. Price had said Howard would go last. After that, he could relax and enjoy the dance and fireworks.

"Howard! Come help me set up these tables," Mr. Fine shouted. He wore an apron and stood by one of the pits holding a large spoon.

Howard looked at the four long tables under a tent and wondered if those would be enough. "Is everyone going to sit here?"

"No, these are just for the food. People will sit on all those straw bales." He pointed to rows of bales sitting outside the tent. There must have been a hundred of them.

They lined the tables up end to end and covered them with plastic tablecloths. Mr. Fine handed him a box of mustard and ketchup bottles and told him to set them out. By the time they'd placed the salads, buns, and platters of corn-on-the-cob, it was almost five o'clock.

"People are going to start coming anytime now. What I want you to do is spoon the barbecue beef onto people's plates as they come through the line. Be sure to keep it on the bun." Mr. Fine handed Howard a ladle and left him at the table.

About fifteen minutes later, people started to arrive. Just a few at first, but then in a steady flow. Howard mostly kept the barbecue on the buns, but it took all his concentration. He didn't look up from his job until somebody spoke his name.

"Ready for tonight, Howard?" Mr. Price said as he thrust his plate under the ladle. Mrs. Getty-Schwartz stood beside him, her hair piled on her head like a bee hive. Next to her stood the tall man Howard always thought looked like a ghost.

He plopped a spoonful of barbecue on Mr. Price's plate and

then scooped up another serving for his friends. Just as he reached over the table to drop a helping on her bun, Mrs. Getty-Swartz jerked back her plate. The barbecue fell on her purse.

"Hans and I don't kill animals," she said, picking up a napkin to wipe the meat off her leather purse, which was shaped like a little saddle. "Look what you've done." She stomped one of her ostrich boots to knock off another piece of barbecue from her foot.

Before Howard could say he was sorry, she, Mr. Price, and the ghost man moved down the line. He didn't have time to worry about it because the next person shoved a plate toward him.

Scoop, plop. Scoop, plop. Howard's arm was getting tired feeding an endless line of people.

"There you are, Howard. I tried to get your attention downtown but you didn't hear me."

Of course, Howard had heard Brother Martin, and now he couldn't look him in the face. He felt like he hadn't been honest with the church leader.

"Anyway, I know you're busy with the celebration, but I'd really like to set up a time for you to talk with our congregation."

Howard dropped a spoonful of barbecue on Brother Martin's bun.

"Maybe we could tentatively set up a time for you to come a week from this Sunday."

Another spoonful of barbecue hit the bun.

"You may not know this, but the Earth is covered in ley lines, energy fields. And when these lines converge, it forms a vortex. A place of real power."

Brother Martin never moved his plate away, and Howard continued to fill it with barbecue.

"Silverville is one of those places. It's a vortex that draws together events, and sometimes people, for special purposes. We think your UFO sighting may serve such a purpose."

Once again, Howard reached over to place another helping of meat on Brother Martin's bun, but this time the minister pulled back his plate. "Think about it. We'd love to talk with you."

Another person stepped up in front of Howard and said, "Not quite so much on my plate, please."

After a while, not as many people waited in line and most sat on the bales eating. When the last person came by, Mr. Fine walked over and told Howard he'd better grab something to eat before everything was gone. He filled his own plate and found a seat on an empty bale. But he wasn't very hungry. What if he couldn't remember the words he was supposed to say? What if Mr. Price got mad? He patted his shirt pocket to make sure he still had the piece of paper. Maybe it would be okay if he just read the words instead of memorizing them.

"You need chopsticks for that?"

Howard twirled around at the familiar voice.

"You not able to eat with those anyway," said Kim from the Chinese restaurant. She giggled and sat down beside him.

"I get to talk tonight at the celebration. Are you going to stay for that?"

"Sure, what you talking about?"

For the first time all day, Howard felt proud that he was one of the speakers. "Important stuff."

"Oh, you must be important person."

He nodded. "There's a vortex on me because I saw a UFO."

"Oh, you the one who see frying saucer! You big shot."

"Yes," he said as he took a bite out of his sandwich and felt a clump of barbecue hit his collar.

She laughed and took a napkin to wipe his shirt. "I go now. Maybe I dance with big shot rater." She waved and walked away.

They would dance together! Now Howard couldn't wait to give his speech. Then she'd really know he was an important person. He took his paper plate to the trashcan and walked over to Mr. Fine, who was talking to the sheriff.

"Carl, I'm still worried about what will happen to all these new businesses after tonight."

"Lots of folks have come through here this summer, and I bet some will be back next year just for the camping and fishing."

Howard cleared his throat to get their attention, and Mr. Fine turned to face him. "Yes, Howard?"

"When does the talking start?"

Mr. Fine looked at his watch and said, "In about ten minutes.

You'd better go on over and take a seat behind the podium."

"When will I know when it's my turn?"

"Earl Bob will announce you."

Howard went over to sit on one of the folding chairs set up for the speakers. There were only two, and the other person was already there. He stood when Howard walked up.

"I'm ..."

But Howard wasn't paying much attention because his stomach began to churn again. Then he remembered he was going to read the words instead of trying to memorize them, and that made him feel a little better.

When it came time to start, Earl Bob announced the first speaker. The other man stepped behind the podium and began to talk.

"As a UFO historian, I want to give some context to the events here in Silverville," he said.

Howard looked at the crowd and started counting heads, but he gave up when he reached ninety-something because latecomers were filling in the seats and he couldn't keep track. He squinted against the sun, now falling directly behind the audience, trying to spot Kim. They were going to dance together later after he talked. Then it struck him that he didn't know how to dance, and he felt like throwing up. He'd seen people dance on TV, and it didn't look that hard. They mostly jumped up and down and swung their arms. He studied his feet as they moved around in a practice dance pattern. In his head, he tried to keep time to the only song he could think of at the moment. *Oh, I wish I were an Oscar-Mayer wiener. That is truly what I like to be.*

A wadded ball of paper struck him in the chest and Howard looked up to see Mr. Price sitting in the front row, shaking his head. He ran his finger straight across his throat twice in quick, sharp movements. Howard stuffed his feet back under his chair and tried again to listen to the speaker.

"Even in Renaissance art, painters depicted strange objects in the background of portraits of the Madonna and Child..."

His stomach sure hurt, and he wished he'd had a bowl of chili instead of the barbecue. Beads of sweat rolled down his face.

Taking in big gulps of air, he looked over at the huge "S" on the hill in the distance and tried to get his mind off the rumbling in his gut. The sun had turned the whole hillside a deep orange; a little breeze rustled the trees and a few leaves floated down beside him. It wouldn't be long until winter. Then all the tourists would leave and the town would be quiet again until springtime. Or at least that's what Mr. Fine had said.

"Howard. Howard? You're on!" Mr. Jackson stood before him and was lifting him by the arm toward the podium.

Looking at all the heads staring back, he cleared his throat as a wave of terror coursed through him. He stammered, "I've – I've got something important to tell you. It's a message from the aliens." He fumbled at his pocket. "It's right here. Just a minute."

To his dismay, he'd buttoned his pocket earlier so the paper wouldn't fly out. And now he couldn't pull the button through the hole. He poked a finger through the corner of the flap, trying to fish out the message. It wouldn't come. While his fingers worked at the button again, he looked out at the crowd. Everybody watched him; nobody talked. Finally, he grabbed the pocket, tore it off the shirt, and held out a pink slip of paper to read.

"When Fate closes a door, it opens a window." Then he turned his head and threw up behind the podium.

After a few seconds of silence, Brother Martin stood and shouted from the second row, "It's a voice of hope!"

Others nodded their heads and some started clapping. Mr. Jackson walked up and slapped him on the back. From the front row, Mr. Fine gave him a thumbs-up. Amid the cheers, Kim worked her way through the crowd and came up to give him a peck on the cheek. While people shook Howard's hand, Mr. Price pushed through the group. He looked mad.

But before he could get too close, Kim took Howard's arm and said, "Come on, Big Shot, we go dance now."

Grady

"Slow down, Grady," Leona scolded. "You won't be shooting off any fireworks if we don't get there in one piece."

He slowed the pickup to the speed limit. He'd already been to town once today, and he was ready to finish his job and get back home again. Serving as the mortar chief for the fireworks display was something he'd done for a dozen years with the Elks club, but that had always been for the Fourth of July festivities. Now the city expected the club to do it again for Buford's fool celebration. This afternoon, he'd run twenty-five-hundred feet of wire to the mortar tubes that contained the charges for the field show. All they had left to do was shoot them off during the dance.

He passed the city limits sign, but few cars met him on the road. Everybody must've been at the picnic grounds already. Good thing he could park near the display since all the parking spots were likely taken up close to the grounds.

When he arrived it was just as he thought. People milled around everywhere and cars lined the streets. He drove over the curb and stopped the truck as close to the display as he could get, which was a hundred yards away. That afternoon, they'd staked off the area so people wouldn't get burned by the sparks.

They got out, and Leona pulled on her sweater against the evening chill, saying, "I'm going over to listen to the music." She headed off in the direction of the street dance while Grady walked past the bleachers and over to a small group of Elks waiting by the electronic control board.

"If you hadn't showed up soon, I was going to start this thing without you," Merle called out.

Grady knew better; he was the only licensed mortar chief in Silverville. Still, there wasn't much danger since they'd started using electronic fuses. In the old days, lighting a mortar by hand could be as exciting as – well, sitting on a fence in front of a charging bull. You just never knew if the explosive that rocketed the fireworks into the sky would go off early and blow the whole damn thing up in your face. Now they could stand a fair distance away to detonate the mortar with an electronic control box. For some things, Grady reckoned, modern technology might be okay.

Merle said to one of the other Elks, "You go tell the band to give us five minutes before they announce the fireworks."

Grady stooped and checked the wires that led into the fuses for the ground display. Next he walked over to inspect the wires that set off the aerial show. They'd arranged the forty mortar tubes across the northern end of the picnic grounds opposite the bleachers.

Everything looked good to go, and he called over to Merle, "We're all set."

When the band finished their song, Grady heard one of the singers tell the crowd to get ready for an aerial show they'd never forget. He spat a spray of tobacco juice on the grass. *Damn right.*

He took one more look at the ground display to be sure everybody was clear and then shouted, "Fire in the hole!" It was the expression they'd always used on the ranch before dynamiting beaver dams, and it got the message across.

Buford hadn't put in his request for fireworks until it was too late in the season for a custom show. Of course, he'd wanted a UFO theme; instead, they got "Wonders of the Nile." It was what the Chinese importers had in stock. Grady twisted the electronic switch and waited for the delayed fuse to ignite the first part of the display. Seconds later, a brilliant spectacle of lights created the illusion of the Sphinx and Great Pyramid, not as big of course.

Between cries of delight from the audience, a voice shouted, "Egypt is a sister vortex to Silverville!" Grady snorted. Probably that crazy New Age preacher spouting off again.

As the sparks fizzled out, the scene flashed into what was supposed to be the image of a boat floating down the Nile. Except there was no water. Grady glanced at the script. It said, "Felucca traversing the Nile waters." Again, he squinted at the scene but it just looked like a boat floating in midair above the picnic grounds.

"Look, it's a UFO!" someone exclaimed. Several people in the crowd laughed as the felucca drifted across its constructed path, its lights dying along the way.

Annoyed at the quality of their hastily purchased field display, Grady watched the disappearing boat reach the end of its mechanical cable. He started to swear when a light above and behind the display caught his attention. The crowd must have seen it, too, because people began standing in the bleachers and pointing at the distant object. It glided, slowly and in silence, until it came within a hundred feet of the treetops past the picnic grounds. A line of arcing red lights twinkled on its hull, dimly showing parts of a massive craft above and below the glow.

Merle walked over to Grady. "What is that thing?"

Couldn't be a plane. Too slow and too quiet. Nothing he could think of right off hand could hover in place without rotor blades. And the shape suggested by the lights made it look like some kind of circular craft.

A rumble of voices rose from the bleachers. Several people hopped to the ground and stood in awe of the mysterious object.

"That really is a UFO!" a man yelled. At that declaration, people began screaming and flooding down from the bleachers. Some even jumped from the higher seats when the crowd bottlenecked at the bottom.

Grady shifted his attention from the crowd to the arc of lights and back to the crowd. Seemed like all hell had broken loose. Like coyotes worrying a herd of calving heifers, the presence of the lights in the sky started a stampede. Folks began running in all directions, smacking into the ones who stood and stared at the craft. Children cried and dogs barked, and his focus fell on a lone little girl sobbing, "Mommy, Mommy."

"I'll be damned," Merle said. "Somebody's got to do something."

But Grady was already moving as he shouted to Merle, "Grab the control box for that first mortar!"

"What're you gonna do?"

"Shoot that damn thing down! You get ready to throw the first switch!"

He raced over to the line of mortars. The tubes sent a burst that was set to detonate about four- or five-hundred feet up in the sky. He couldn't tell how far away the UFO was, but it couldn't be much further than that. He wrenched the first mortar tube from its stand and pointed it at the flashing red lights.

"You ready?" Merle called out.

""Throw the switch, damn it!" Grady braced his foot against the base of the cannon and tried to steady it in his hands.

"Fire in the hole!" Merle shouted.

For two seconds nothing happened. Then a fireball blasted

from the mortar, knocking Grady flat on his back. From the ground, he watched the starburst fill the sky, blocking his view of the UFO. But as the embers from the arms of the fireworks faded, the craft remained just where it had been, its red lights still twinkling.

He yelled at Merle, "Again!"

Grady scrambled to his feet and ran over to yank the second tube free from its platform. He braced again for the concussion to follow as he signaled to Merle to throw the next switch.

Another blast roared out of the tube and threw Grady to the ground. This time, when the embers died, he could see that the UFO was creeping upward and away from them.

"One more time?" Merle hollered.

Grady stood up and watched the receding object grow fainter in the night sky. "Naw, we've scared it away." Besides, he didn't think he could take another slam to the ground. He limped back over to the control box.

"What was that thing?" Merle asked.

Grady shook his head but said nothing.

"I know this sounds crazy," Merle continued, "but I could have sworn those lights looked like chili peppers."

"That's the stupidest damn thing I've ever heard."

Together they stood and stared up at the darkness while the frenzy behind them began to quiet.

"What do we do now?" Merle asked.

"We finish our fireworks."

But before they could begin, another frantic voice from the crowd reached Grady's ears.

"Oh my God! The UFO – another one's coming!"

Buford

Buford stood on top of the curb and tapped his foot in time with the band. Or maybe he tapped his foot because he wanted the fireworks display to start. He couldn't wait to see how people would react to his secret surprise.

In the dim light of the street lanterns, people partied to the rhythms of the Bad Booze Boys, and they were bad, as usual. Just like they'd been at the funeral for Chantale's buffalo. Buford marveled at the variety of dance styles, seeing everything from jitterbug to waltz to cowboy swing. And then there was Howard, who looked like he was having a seizure in front of some little Asian girl. One man's head bobbed way above the others, his long white ponytail snapping like a bullwhip that Chantale dodged with every step. Hans High Horse's techno-war dance kept people at a distance, particularly when he let loose an occasional whoop.

Buford released a satisfied belch. Absolutely no significant glitches so far this evening. Sure Howard dropped a little barbecue on Chantale's purse, but it was a ridiculous accessory anyway. And Howard didn't quite get the words right in his speech, but the crowd responded more favorably than Buford could have hoped. That "open window" part of the message wasn't half bad, and he figured he could work with the phrase in his promotion for the coming year.

When the song finished, the band leader took the mike in his hand, saying, "We're going to take a thirty-minute break for the fireworks, courtesy of the fine city of Silverville. They want to remind you it'll be an aerial display you're never going to forget. Now go get a seat at the bleachers, but stick around 'cause we'll be here the rest of the night." Then the microphone squelched so loud that everyone had to cover their ears.

A large herd of dancers moved in a ragged wave toward the bleachers and shuffled Buford along in the flow. He made a half-hearted attempt to spot Skippy but knew he'd never find her in the crowd.

He stepped behind a fat man, someone who could plow the way, and followed him to the second row of seats from the ground level. People took one look at his new friend and scooted down rather than let him step over them. It cleared enough space for both Buford and the fat man to sit down.

"The name is Terrance," the man said, swinging an arm toward Buford once they had a seat. "Want some popcorn?"

"No thanks." *Or maybe I should. One more bite of junk food for this fellow and our end of the bleacher might flip over.*

Terrance shrugged just as the first images from the ground show began to sparkle. Everyone applauded when the outline of the

Sphinx and Great Pyramid lit up the field. Not quite the theme Buford had hoped for, but the crowd seemed to like it nevertheless. By the time the cheering from the bleachers died down, the fireworks crew launched the next image; it was a boat sporting a tall sail and it appeared to float across the sky.

"Look, it's a UFO!" someone behind him shouted, and everyone laughed. The disembodied boat seemed to fly rather than sail across the end of the picnic grounds. Too bad they couldn't have gotten a custom flying saucer display since everybody came to Silverville to see UFOs. *Little do they know they're about to get one*, he thought to himself.

Just as the sparks from the boat disappeared, a horizontal line of red lights began to peek between the tree limbs, moving slowly closer. At first, Buford sniggered. Right on time. It had to be his little surprise for all the fool idiots who wanted to believe in UFOs. But something was wrong. Shouldn't a glider be swooping over the heads of the crowd rather than drifting at a snail's pace? To hear the guy he'd hired, the craft would soar without a sound and vanish before anybody realized what it really was. And the glider company said they'd attached a row of white lights, not red.

Within several minutes, the blinking lights seemed to loom above the trees just beyond the grounds. The fat man sitting beside him dropped his popcorn, standing and pointing at the growing object in the sky. Several others in the bleachers leaped to their feet.

"That really is a UFO!" a man yelled.

The hair on Buford's neck hackled. People began flying off the seats, and someone's knee struck him in the back of the head during the scramble. Some screamed; some sobbed; one person threw up his hands, exclaiming, "It's the mother ship!"

Buford felt Terrance's pudgy fists shoving him off the seat.

"Hey, buddy," Buford complained, "what's the hur—" They tripped off the step at the same time and the fat man slammed on top of him as they hit the grass.

A loud crack echoed through the picnic area, creating even more hysteria.

"What's going on? What's happening?" Buford shouted from his pinned position under Terrance.

His rotund friend rolled off him and struggled to his feet just as a second boom resounded. "They're shooting at it, but it's getting away!" Terrance gasped.

Rubbing the man's sweat from the side of his neck, Buford stood just in time to hear a panicked voice behind him. "Oh my God! The UFO – another one's coming!"

He looked up to see a V-shaped string of white lights streak overhead. It made no sound and was gone seconds later. Buford's glider had arrived, but his little surprise seemed unnecessary when faced with the reality of the first unknown craft.

"Must be a scout ship!" It was one of Brother Martin's followers, and the man dropped to his knees and clasped his hands together. "A mother ship and a scout!"

The preacher also fell to his knees, proclaiming in a loud voice, "Our brothers from space have graced Silverville with two visitors from beyond the stars!"

Most of the members of the New Age church cheered and clapped with apparent joy. They ran over to Howard, who stood at the edge of the crowd next to Lela and the Asian girl.

"You really are the pipeline between the aliens and planet Earth," one said. "The message they gave you is prophetic. Silverville truly is the open window to the universe."

By now, those not euphoric with the arrival of the Mother Ship darted one way or another, trying to escape the grounds. Out on the streets, tires squealed and horns blared; the sound of colliding fenders rose above the ecstatic singing of Brother Martin and his group. The sheriff was running from one accident to another.

But Buford paid little attention to the melee. Instead, he stared up into the dark night.

"I'll be damned," he murmured to himself. "There really is a UFO."

Billy

The evening light had faded while Billy and Bob Hardin waited by the side of a desolate dirt road just outside town. He glanced at the luminous dial on his watch. Nine o'clock. The fireworks should start in about thirty minutes.

From a distance, he saw the twin beams of an approaching car. *That had better be Skippy and Felicia.* The last thing they needed was a lost tourist stumbling on their set-up. He'd have called on his new cell phone to make sure, but he couldn't hear anything over the roar of the burners from the propane tank. When the vehicle neared, the headlamps switched off and the car rolled up with only its parking lights on.

Skippy stepped from the driver's side of a brown Ford Escort. Felicia got out the other side.

"Were you able to hook up Lela with Howard?" Billy asked. The timing had been tight, but with such a small planning group, everybody had assumed multiple roles. Carl and Denton were on hand at ground zero for crowd control in case of a panic. That left Skippy and Felicia to help Lela locate Howard during the street dance. The mayor's job was to guide his reaction when the "UFO" landed at the picnic grounds that night. How Howard reacted when the craft crash-landed on site had become the key part of the plan.

"Yeah, we found him. Tell me how your lunch went with Howard," Skippy said.

"Just like we hoped. First, I worked the conversation around to his sighting two years ago. And then I pretty much reminded him of what he saw – a circle of red lights at a distance."

"And he agreed?"

"Howard doesn't really remember that night very well. Whatever I suggested, that's what he saw." While Billy had planted memories in Howard's head, Daddy's words came to mind. *You can lead a horse to water and you can make him drink, if he's dumb enough.*

Billy walked over to check on Bob Hardin's progress. Over the past couple of days, Hardin had rigged his hot-air balloon to look like a home-spun UFO. Credible enough at a distance. The made-to-fail plan would be to maneuver the balloon close to the crowd and then to fake a malfunction that set the balloon down in the middle of the celebration.

"This all sounds confusing," Billy had told Lela when she first proposed the idea.

"No, it's not," she insisted. "We make a UFO that we try to pass off as real. And when we have a 'forced landing,' people will think we tried to pull something over on them. We'll make sure Howard believes this is the same thing he saw before. People will then see that Silverville's UFO culture is contrived. They'll be pissed," she smiled, "and they'll leave. So it's all very simple. In order for our hoax to succeed, it has to fail."

Howard, of course, would have to be the sacrificial lamb in this plan. The whole town would be mad at him if they thought they'd rebuilt their economy around a mistake. Some people in the group had seemed bothered by Howard's unwitting role, but Lela agreed to step forward after the landing and admit she'd also seen the red lights in the night sky. No one would dare ridicule Lela.

The balloon began to inflate, giving it the appearance of a long sausage.

"Where are the lights?" Felicia asked.

"They're attached about a third of the way up," Billy said. Hardin had assembled them around the base of the balloon just below the swell but high enough not to illuminate the basket. Once aloft and headed toward the picnic grounds, Hardin would turn the burners off and plug the lights into a battery. The balloonist had chosen the launch site based on the westerly winds, which would carry the craft directly over the picnic grounds.

Within thirty minutes, the tethered balloon stood erect. Billy looked again at his watch. They needed to be in position during the ground show, well before the aerial detonations posed a threat to the balloon.

Skippy's cell phone rang. It had to be Lela. After a brief conversation, she hung up and turned to Billy.

"It's time to get this show off the ground. They're starting."

Hardin jumped inside the gondola, his cell phone holstered at his hip. He'd stay in continuous contact with Billy during the flight while Lela relayed updates to Skippy.

The two women released the ground lines, and the balloon ascended with the thrust of the roaring propane burners. When it reached about two hundred feet, Hardin turned off the furnace and switched on the lights.

"Those look like chili peppers," Felicia said.

Billy shrugged. "It's what we had."

The balloon drifted to the east, its red lights pulsating. Soon, the wind pushed the craft's bulk and carried it toward the celebration.

Skippy touched her speed-dial button. "It's coming your way," she said into the phone.

At the same time, Billy called Hardin. "This is it, Bob. Good luck."

"Copy that. I can see the lights of the ground display. ETA in four minutes."

Billy paced back and forth, the phone glued to his ear. The two women nearby looked like black paper-cut silhouettes against the twilight. Felicia pressed clenched fingers into her cheeks and nodded to Skippy, who rocked nervously on her heels. They all stared at the receding craft, which really did resemble a UFO the further away it traveled.

"Still there?" Hardin asked.

"You're coming in loud and clear."

"I'm starting my descent, and it looks like people on the ground can see me already."

Billy called out to Skippy and Felicia. "He's making his approach."

Suddenly, a starburst exploded low in the sky, and a loud boom echoed across the valley. At the same time, Billy heard Hardin shout into the phone, "Son of a bitch! They're shooting at me!"

"What?"

"Somebody just blasted me with fireworks."

"Are you hit?"

"No, it just missed—. Damn, they just did it again!"

Another explosion sprayed streamers of light over the east side of town, followed by second boom.

"I gotta get out of here! I'm dumping my sandbags!"

"But the landing?"

"Screw the landing."

Billy heard a click followed by a dial tone.

"What's happening? What's going on?" Skippy asked as Billy

snapped the phone shut.

"The plan is a no-go." Before he could explain more, a low-flying wedge of white lights swooshed over their heads and made a beeline toward town.

They stared after the phantom craft as it soared over the treetops and disappeared.

At first, no one said a word.

Finally, Skippy turned to the others. "What was that?"

A breeze rustled the dry grass on the side of the road, and an uncomfortable silence surrounded them. Billy scratched his head, but he dared not say aloud what he was thinking.

I'll be damned. There really is a UFO.

CHAPTER SEVENTEEN

Billy

The end of summer barely thinned out the tourists, and news crews continued to trawl the town, looking for witnesses to interview about the Labor Day sightings. Silverville's notoriety vaulted into the national spotlight during the days following the appearance of the two UFOs. Billy knew, of course, that there had only been one, but he wasn't talking. Neither was anyone else in Lela's planning group.

Television coverage depicted the town as a UFO mecca, airing footage of the picnic grounds, the museum, and the theme park.

"This isolated Colorado hamlet," one newscaster had commented, "is the scene of remarkable celestial occurrences. Hundreds of people witnessed two UFOs, one said to be the mother ship, and the other, a scout looking for Howard Beacon, the man credited with telepathically attracting ETs to this community." The news report panned to the fleeing figure of Howard, who tried to dodge behind a tree. "Since that day, thousands of visitors have descended on Silverville, each hoping to find their own special answer to the universe's mysteries."

The reporter, like all the others, went on to interview Buford, happy to take center stage. Billy was equally happy with the arrangement since they both knew the town's UFO consultant could never show his face on national television – if he was going to be a familiar face in the community from now on. Buford had even resigned himself to the idea that Billy had decided to stay.

The Economic Committee had approached "Earl Bob" with an offer he couldn't refuse: official liaison to investors. It was an honest buck, which ran contrary to his nature. Maybe Daddy wouldn't agree he'd found The Big One, but Billy would milk this opportunity for as long as he could. And besides, he had more finesse than Buford in handling the public relations where money was concerned.

Buford had made a mess of the finances, and everyone was still trying to figure out the haphazard passbooks and accounts he'd used to track the project's income. They'd never know the half of it, thanks to Skippy. He managed to keep his status as town promoter, creating his own limelight, but he stayed out of Billy's way.

Billy thought about his new role as he transferred his few belongings from his car to the new house he'd rented. Way too big for one person with no furniture, but he hoped he wouldn't be there alone for very long.

"Need help with that one suitcase?" Denton called out from his car window.

Billy set the luggage down and walked over to the curb.

"How are things going?" he asked. "I heard through the grapevine you've scheduled your surgery."

"I wanted to talk to you about that. I got an anonymous certified check in the mail – enough to cover my operation and even start a fund for Duke's education. You wouldn't know anything about that, would you?"

Billy smiled. "Well, when Fate closes a door, she opens a window."

"Boy, I've sure heard that mantra around town lately."

"So who's going to cover for you while you're in the hospital?"

"The funeral director from Placer City offered to take his vacation and come over. Howard knows the fellow and gets along with him. Speak of the devil…"

As if conjured by the mention of his name, Howard pedaled down the street toward them. Kim rode another bike beside him. He grinned as they passed the car but didn't stop to chat.

"He's on a 'bike date,'" Denton explained. "No time for the likes of us old guys."

"At least he's got somebody to share all that chili with."

When Howard captured nationwide attention, one of the stories about him involved his love for a particular brand of chili. The company got wind of it and sent him a year's supply.

Denton said good-bye and drove away.

Taking his suitcase into the house, Billy closed the front door and went back to the Cadillac. If only he could find the title, he'd dump this crate and maybe buy the T-Bird. Maybe he would anyway.

He pulled out of the drive and worked his way over to Main Street. At a stop light, the square little figure of Lela strutted through the crosswalk, hand in hand with a distinguished-looking man, sixtyish and wearing golf shoes. She had surprised the whole town with her whirlwind romance and engagement announcement. And of all people, with a tourist. She met her new beau when he came to town for a golf tournament. It was love at the ninth hole, and the two had been inseparable ever since.

But stranger things had happened in Silverville; they had all summer long.

Billy passed Grady on the road to the Galactic Inn and waved. The old rancher lifted a forefinger off his steering wheel in acknowledgement. All hell had broken loose earlier in the summer when Grady's cows and heifers turned up their noses to his best bulls. When he'd had the herd checked, they all turned up pregnant. Had to be Chantale's buffalo. You could almost hear Grady cussing across three counties. He threatened to sue; he promised to kill the rest of her exotic beef; he swore he'd take that Juanabee Indian and wrap him around a fence post. And then someone pointed out the market price for beefalo. Grady could make twice as much on each little curly white calf, and that changed his attitude in a hurry. Billy had heard that Grady was now thinking of buying a buffalo bull himself.

He wheeled into the Galactic Inn to pay his final bill. Inside, Portia met him at the desk, wagging her tail. Fawn set down her newspaper.

"I came to settle up," he said, handing her a check. "Sure didn't take me long to move into my new house."

"I have a new house, too. Or I will have by spring."

She seemed particularly chatty that day, and Billy tried to preserve the rare moment of carrying on a real conversation with her. "That's great, Fawn. Were you finally able to find something?"

"Someone did a story on Silverville's rapid growth and the high cost of housing. So Habitat for Humanity made plans to build a few homes here, and I get one of them."

"Best news I've heard all day. Guess we both should start shopping for furniture."

From behind him, he heard Skippy's voice. "You're buying new furniture?"

She walked down the stairs, carrying a wrapped gift under her arm. She'd left Buford right after Labor Day and moved into one of the rooms at the Inn. That had made it convenient for her and Billy to spend more time together.

He walked over to meet her at the foot of the stairs. She handed him the package.

"Here, this is for you," she said. "It's a house-warming gift."

"I'd like my house to be your house, too."

She looked up into his face and said, "I'm a terrible house-cleaner."

"I like dirt."

"I eat crackers in bed."

"I don't have a bed."

"My Velouté sauce always gets lumpy."

"I don't have sauce pans."

She laughed softly. "You really do need a keeper."

"That's what I've been trying to tell you."

He held the door for her as they walked out. When they reached the pavement, he took her arm and swung her around to face him. "Skippy ..."

"Okay, okay." She paused, and then said, "I'll think about it."

EPILOGUE

Buford

Buford pulled a TV dinner from the microwave and climbed the stairs to his bedroom. He flipped on the television set and plopped on the bed with his Salisbury steak. In five minutes, one of the Denver news stations would air footage about Silverville, and he'd be the star spokesperson. It had taken only a few initial interviews for him to hone his rhetoric. He'd even managed to work in the lines Howard never gave on Labor Day.

The news program began with its normal preview of upcoming stories, including a teaser about UFOs in the state. Two weeks before, Silverville had been breaking news, but now the sightings had been relegated to short features and personality profiles that appeared later in the shows. Nevertheless, interest in the town persisted with the help of continuing news coverage. He picked up the remote and turned the volume down while the anchors talked about traffic, sports, and weather.

Jabbing a fork into a lump of meat covered with tomato sauce, he remembered more appetizing meals he'd eaten when he still had a wife. He took a bite and wondered what Skippy was having that evening.

Twenty minutes later, he saw on the screen the buildings of downtown Silverville and fumbled with the remote to restore the sound. The anchor was already talking.

"...the familiar setting of Silverville to viewers everywhere around the country, but tonight we'll highlight locals who believed from the start that their city was a destination for ET."

Guarded comments by Lela and Carl confirmed what viewers wanted to hear – yes, Silverville was the apparent host of alien visitations. The reporter asked if the town had adjusted to its new-found fame, to which Lela answered, "Fame has its price, but we're making the best of it."

The scene switched to a view of the picnic grounds while the journalist's voice-over asked, "The question now is 'Will they be back?'"

Then Buford's face filled the screen. "Of course they will. We've now had three sightings, and there's no reason to think they won't return. In my mind, the aliens probably consider Silverville a place of open windows, a place to communicate their wisdom of the universe."

He dipped into his TV dinner for a bite of cherry cobbler and thought, *Damn, I sure sound smart.*

When the feature ended, he turned off the set and dropped the tin tray on a growing stack beside the bed. He walked over to the closet and hung up his blazer. Then he unfastened his cufflinks and dropped them into the top dresser drawer. One bounced off a framed picture lying in the bottom. Plucking the photograph from the drawer, he laid it on the bed. He'd been a small child when his mother had taken him and fled from Nashville, later abandoning him in this one-horse town.

"Well, Mama, you'd be proud of what I did for Silverville." He traced a finger over the image of a green-eyed, auburn-haired woman standing by her two small sons.

At least he still remembered his brother's name.

And he wondered whatever had happened to Billy.

THE END
(OF BOOK ONE)

(An excerpt from Book Two of
THE SILVERVILLE SAGA follows)

All Plucked Up
Book Two of
The Silverville Saga
(An Excerpt)

PROLOGUE
August, 1602

Diego Cordova crawled to the edge of the cave and fingered the last of his coins. He'd thrown most of his *reales* at the blood-thirsty *bastardos* before they had begun to torture him. How stupid of them not to realize the value of money. How stupid of his scouting party to think these savages would ever have possessed any gold.

Now he was the only one left to ponder the consequences of such a misguided expedition.

The *indios barbaros* had stripped him of his armor, his finely crafted rapier, and even his boots, leaving him to die at the edge of the valley. He could still hear the laughter of the younger warriors as they loosed random arrows into his half-naked body. Eventually, they seemed to tire of the sport and turned their backs on the carnage of dead Spanish soldiers and their horses. It had given him the chance to gather his possessions and crawl away.

Cordova watched the cave floor grow red with his own blood, some dripping into a dark pool of water near his feet. Why had he volunteered to join the dozen men commissioned by Oñate to explore the uncharted regions above the Rio del Norte? It was a fool's errand, a costly venture that had brought them neither honor nor wealth. Most of his men were lucky, falling swiftly to the first volley of arrows from the ambush. But in his head, he couldn't quiet the last screams of his *compañeros*, or erase the look of terror in Bernardo's eyes just before their tormentors smashed his skull with a rock.

Diego Cordova, proud son of a governor of Spain, could no longer see the stamp of the Maltese Cross on the coin between his thumb and forefinger. Even the light filtering into the cave had become blurred. A rush of anger coursed though him, and he dropped the coin. He was dying and no one would ever know what had become of him. He would never again see his gentle *mamá*, his beautiful betrothed, Carlita. Gone were the tender moments with his beloved Isabella, the finest chicken in all of Spain.

His gut wrenched in spasms. Surely it was not the pinch of hunger that coiled his body into a painful ball – although it had been two days since he'd eaten even a crust of bread. Food had been scarce on the last days of the journey, yet no one was willing to butcher a horse. Not so for the savages. Gusts of wind now carried the scent of roasted horse flesh to his rock shelter as they sang and celebrated their victory on the sides of the arroyo below. Tormented by the heathen lyrics, Cordova clasped his hands to his ears and forced himself to mumble songs from his childhood. Anything to drown the clamor.

"Diego, what are you singing?" a voice asked him.
He stopped and looked up at his father's face, surprised that his vision had become so clear.

"Songs I heard on the street, *Papá*."

"Do not fill your head with such nonsense."

Then the lovely walls of his parents' *villa* dissolved into the cold granite of the cave, and the horror of the present returned. Cordova raised his fist and summoned one last surge of defiance.

"Damn this God-forsaken wilderness! I curse those who live here. And their children, and their children's children! May they suffer the same indignities as Diego Cordova."

Against the dim light of evening, a sudden flash lit the mouth of the cave. The silhouette of a robed figure limped toward him as Cordova struggled to speak.

"Help me, *Padre*. Can you give me communion?"
The robed figure stooped, reached into his cassock. He placed a small wafer on the conquistador's tongue.

The host tasted sweet to Cordova. "I'm dying!" he gasped.

"What is death but moving from one reality to another?"

"Our quest was for nothing."

"A game, my son. And you were only a pawn."
The words echoed off the rock walls as Cordova's eyes
closed for the last time.

CHAPTER ONE
Present Day

Pleasance stood atop the Pyramid of Kukulcán, hoping to
escape the sticky mid-summer swelter. The Yucatán jungle
stretched in all directions, islands of stone ruins occasionally
interrupting the monotonous green of dwarfed cedar and chakah
trees. Trying to ignore the sweat that pooled between her breasts,
she focused on the snatches of international babble that drifted from
the base of the structure seventy-five feet below her. Chichén Itzá,
an archeological wonder, could bake, broil, and roast people from
all parts of the world this time of year.

Nothing ever changed at the site. The heat, the humidity,
the hordes of people. Even the little vender shops still sold the same
kinds of ice cream they always had. The locals hawked the same
jewelry, terracotta masks, and Mayan figurines. On her first visits,
she was charmed by curios for sale along the walkway that
connected the museum to the ruins. But that was a long time ago,
long before her buying habits had become a little more
discriminating.

In an hour, she would meet Tomás by the parking lot when
he got off work. She'd caught a glimpse of him sweeping the
museum floor when she first arrived, but as usual they avoided eye
contact. She shouldn't have been in such a rush to get here. The
two-and-a-half hour drive from the Cancún airport had gone faster
than she anticipated, and now she could only wait until closing time
for her rendezvous.

Pleasance took a swig from her water bottle. Almost empty.
Skirting the rim of the pyramid, she stepped into the temple where a
Chac Mool and jaguar throne once stood, now displayed in a
Mexico City museum. Probably just as well – some enterprising
thief would have covertly whisked them away. She turned and

started for the stairway on the western side of the pyramid, sweeping past the tourists who clung to the safety rope that aided them during the steep descent. About a third of the way down, she caught sight of an old man leaning on a metal walker, the brim of his khaki pith helmet bobbing with each familiar-looking step.

"Shit," she muttered and darted back up the stairway towards the temple, elbowing past people who moved down the narrow steps.

"Sorry!" Pleasance called out as one of her long yellow braids snapped a man in the face while she bounded upward, two steps at a time. She rounded the temple and ran to the stairway on the north side. Fewer people had chosen this side of the pyramid for the climb since it had no rope. It gave Pleasance the chance to make her way to the bottom without running anyone down.

As soon as her feet touched dirt, she walked briskly toward the Temple of the Warriors. She hugged the line of trees situated to the south of the Group of a Thousand Columns, careful not to walk so fast that she'd attract attention. With any luck, she'd be able to get back to the site's museum without the old man noticing her.

At that moment she realized that in her efforts to use the pyramid as a blind, she'd placed herself on the wrong side of the open courtyard that would take her back. That meant she would have to cut north into the trees behind the warrior temple, bushwhacking past the Sacred Cenoté to reach the museum. She knew better than to let the courtyard get out of sight. Her track record in the jungles of Honduras had nearly been disastrous on a previous buying expedition. At least here the occasional glimpses of bright-colored tourist clothing helped her navigate.

Within fifteen minutes, she reached the outskirts of the Sacred Cenoté, a great sinkhole filled with water that the Mayans had used for human sacrifice. It was one of many wells dotting the jungle. She blended in with a troupe of sightseers, patiently listening to the guide explain the grisly ritual. When the speaker finished, she moved into the group's center and shuffled along the path until she could cut over to the museum.

* * *

Pleasance leaned against her rented Ford as Tomás approached.

"*¡Hola!*" she said. "*¿Qué tal?*"

"*Chido, y tú?*"

"*De pelos.*"

With the obligatory pleasantries finished, she switched to English. It would be Tomás's job to translate for her once they reached the village.

"You said it would be worth the trip. What've you got?"

Tomás lit a cigarette and blew a stream of smoke past her armpit. He seemed shorter than she remembered, but most men seemed short to her.

"Good stuff, *Señorita* Pantiwycke. Ceramic crocodiles, a death mask – "

"Jade?"

"Of course. Also an obsidian dagger, a stone jaguar. Maybe more. They bring much."

She nodded. The jaguar would be too heavy to smuggle out of the country, but she could probably manage everything else.

"One more thing. These are bad men. I brought you a gun."

At this, Pleasance groaned. An unpleasant aspect of her business, but often necessary. It was one of the tools of dealing in illegal antiquities.

"First, one more question," Pleasance countered. "You haven't seen an old guy in a walker come by here, have you? Trying to sell me to you?" The look on his face gave her the answer.

"Okay, guess not. Let's go."

They walked over to his rickety pickup truck, where he reached behind the seat and handed her a cloth bundle. Through the wrapping, she could feel the notches of the revolver's cylinder.

"You follow me in your car," Tomás said.

"How far this time?"

"Only a little ways," he answered as the pickup grinded to a start.

They pulled out of the museum parking lot and traveled a short distance down Highway 180 toward Valladolid. But within a few miles, Tomás turned south ahead of her onto a narrow paved road. He slowed as they passed a sign for the village of Xlohil and turned right onto a dirt corridor cutting through the jungle trees. Every so often, a little shanty stood off the road, its twig-lashed walls housing a large family by the looks of clothes hanging out to dry. Outside one of the huts, she saw a few ragged children playing in a mud ditch, an emaciated dog skulking at their heels. Her Ford bumped along, hitting more ruts the deeper into the jungle she traveled, and at one point the car lurched so hard her head bounced against the roof. As she slammed back down into her seat, her eyes fell on the rearview mirror and she thought she saw the front end of a blue van making the curve behind her.

"Oh, it can't be!" she said aloud. She studied the mirror, waiting for the vehicle to reappear, but saw no sign of it. It must have been a local who lived in one of the shanties.

She rounded a bend where Tomás had already stopped his pickup near a cluster of dilapidated houses. She pulled up behind him and stepped out of the car, tucking the revolver into her belt so that it snugged against the small of her back.

"Is this the village?"

"Only a suburb." He pointed to the various buildings. "Over there is where my nephew lives, and over that way is where my cousin lives."

They walked between the shacks, sidestepping the goat dung and empty cans that paved the way until they approached a clapboard house larger than the others.

"This," Tomás explained, "is the recreation center." Rusted sheets of corrugated metal covered the roof and several whole slats had fallen from the walls. Plastic covered the windows that weren't boarded up, and the door was gone altogether.

As they passed the building, Pleasance saw ripped mattresses through the gaps in the wall. She also heard a woman groaning to the cadence of a rhythmic thumping noise.

"¡Más, más!" the woman screamed.

They continued down the path several steps before Pleasance clutched her business partner's sleeve. "I thought you said that was the rec center. These people were . . ."

He shrugged and kept walking, saying over his shoulder, "Sí, that is recreation for Xlohil."

As the light began to fail, her other senses sharpened. A rich scent of dirt mingled with rotting vegetation. Occasionally, she caught the perfumed whiff of orchids. Buried in the canopy above her head, she could hear the calls of macaws and woodpigeons. They were deep enough into the jungle forest that she knew larger animals stalked nearby. Predatory animals, like the jaguars the Mayans had carved on their stone temples.

Pleasance picked up her pace, her long strides easily overtaking Tomás.

"So tell me who we're about to meet."

"They would not want you to know their names, but I will tell you anyway." Tomás never changed his gait. "There are three of them. The leader is called Mocoso. Short and ugly. Watch him the closest. And there is Lorenzo. You'll know him by his wild, curly hair. He only does what Mocoso tells him."

"And the third?"

"Rizoso. The bald one, fat and stupid."

She nodded, trying to fit names to the descriptions Tomás had given her.

"*Son tres necios*. Three fools. But unpredictable."

A twig snapped behind them and Pleasance wheeled around. Nothing but the gathering dusk. Raw-nerved, she always experienced a surge of adrenaline before sealing a deal. The trees thickened, creating an impenetrable awning over the footpath, and she struggled to keep her toes from hooking overgrown roots.

Within fifty yards, they came upon a low-ceilinged shed with a dim light shining through a single open window.

They stopped well short of the doorway, and Tomás called out to the men inside. She saw the silhouette of a man glance through the window, and a few moments later the door opened.

"Let me do the talking," Tomás whispered as they moved forward.

That was fine with Pleasance. She'd always found it useful to let a local liaison make the initial negotiations. More often than not, these characters ended up being petty thieves, undereducated peasants who were more likely to talk to a local than a blonde American woman. Of course, that wasn't always the case.

Once in Bulgaria, she'd dealt with eastern European Mafia types – high-class criminals counting on her contacts to broker ancient Egyptian stone reliefs to an Amsterdam museum. They may have been too good. They'd already covered the inscriptions with fresh paint so the relics would pass as fakes in order to get them out of the country. When she arranged for one of them to present the artifacts to the museum, the idiot courier failed to remove the new paint and the police arrested him for trying to sell forged pieces. His predicament grew worse when he insisted the reliefs were genuine and all they had to do was remove the paint. That, of course, landed him in jail once Egyptian Antiquities authorities discovered that true artifacts had left the country without proper documentation.

She let Tomás step into the shed's entrance first; she followed, having to duck under the doorjamb.

The short, ugly man – that had to be Mocoso – greeted Tomás and then his eyes grew wide at the sight of Pleasance. "*¡Qué mujer más grande!*"

Her Spanish was good enough to understand Mocoso's surprise at her size. But the comment didn't insult her. She'd often used this intimidation factor to her advantage. Mocoso's two sidekicks busied themselves further back in the room; with nervous jerks they unpacked boxes. One of them, obviously Lorenzo, arranged some of the loot on a table. He dusted off the priceless jade death mask and placed it under a dirty rag at the far end near the window. At the same time, the other – Rozoso, the fat, stupid one – hoisted a heavy stone jaguar out of an old trunk and set it on the dirt floor. Pleasance moved closer to the objects for a quick survey.

Everything looked authentic; she didn't think these three were smart enough to create anything on their own. Tomás had told her that The Three Fools had uncovered a mound at the far reaches of Chichén Itzá at a site that archeologists had not yet discovered in the thick undergrowth. Plausible enough, since the entire area covered over six square miles.

Mocoso leered at her. "You interested in old treasure, *señorita*?" he asked her in fractured English.

She returned his scrutiny and nodded toward Tomás. While her liaison stepped forward and began to barter for the goods, Pleasance became the observer, pretending she didn't know enough

Spanish to conduct business. During the course of the discussion, she would point to an individual object and Mocoso would declare its price. After hearing the cost of each, Pleasance and Tomás would retreat to the corner to consider the real value.

"Two hundred pesos," Mocoso announced when she touched a large ceramic bead on the table.

Pleasance pulled Tomás toward her. "That's only twenty dollars. Haven't these guys done this before?"

"They're small-time crooks," Tomás whispered. "Just out of jail. They got seven years for robbing a drive-up bank in Mérida. The teller wrote down their license plate."

Pleasance nodded and they moved the bead aside. She pointed to a sacrificial obsidian dagger with an ornate handle. Lorenzo jumped forward and with great emphasis declared, "Eleven hundred pesos."

Her breath quickened at the proposed price. The dagger would fetch at the very least a hundred times that on the market. But before she could agree, Mocoso leaped at his partner, slapping him across the head and unleashing a volley of colloquial insults.

"No, no, *señorita*. He gives a price too low." He scowled at Lorenzo and turned back to Pleasance. "It is *twelve* hundred pesos." She nodded again and they moved the dagger near the bead. Next she indicated her interest in a seashell buzzard that sat on a barrel near the door.

"Ah, this one is more, three thousand pesos."

She inspected the buzzard more closely. A number of the shells were chipped and still others missing. She had planned to have Tomás coat the artifacts in plastic and paint them in order to slip them out of the country as reproductions. But the buzzard was sure to lose even more shells in the process. "No, too much. It's damaged."

The three thieves exchanged glances and called Tomás over to them. They spoke in rapid and heated Spanish. After several minutes, Tomás turned to her and said, "They will give you a deal for cash right now."

"Now? No, once we've made the deal, I'll contact my client and meet them again to make the transaction."

At this, Mocoso exploded in anger. Pleasance reached behind her back to touch the reassuring revolver. No one spoke as each of them eyed the others, as though everyone was waiting for somebody to make the first move. Pleasance began to feel like Clint Eastwood in a bad spaghetti western.

She decided she'd better break the silence. "I can have the cash tomorrow, *mañana*."

Mocoso, Lorenzo, and Rizoso moved to the corner behind the table and seemed to debate what to do.

Pleasance leaned over to Tomás. "Are we in trouble?"

"They will likely kill us," he replied in a calm voice.

Before she could comment, Mocoso spoke, "*Está bien. Mañana.*"

Pleasance exhaled with relief. Tomás tried to ease the tension, joking in English, "Ah, women, they have no head for business dealings."

Mocoso started to laugh as did his friends, who obviously had no idea what Tomás had said. With disaster averted, Pleasance looked over at the rag covering the jade death mask on the table near the window. They had saved the best for last, and the most important of the negotiations. She mentally calculated its value on the open market as Rizoso plucked the rag.

His mouth fell open. "*¡Dios mío! ¡La máscara! ¡Ya no la tenémos!*"

Pleasance turned to Tomás. "It's gone?" That was impossible; she'd just seen it earlier when they set it by the window. She began to piece the day together – the old man in the courtyard, the blue van behind her on the road, the snap of a twig on the jungle path.

Where the mask should have been now lay instead a small rectangular purple wafer. She skirted around a wooden box and over to the table, snatched up the little wafer and bit into it.

"Maurice! It was Maurice, that old bastard!"

She sprinted out the door to see if she could still catch sight of him. Behind her, she heard Mocoso call out. "*¡Ladrona!* Thief! Stop her. She has the mask!"

Without thinking, she ducked back inside the door to explain and saw Tomás wrestling a gun from Mocoso's hand.

"Run!" Tomás shouted to her.

But when Rizoso and Lorenzo saw her, they dived in her direction. She snatched the seashell buzzard off the barrel, stuffed it in her pocket, and kicked the drum over to block her assailants. Pleasance turned and ran into the night.

All Plucked Up
Is Now Available

Watch for Book Three
The Magicke Outhouse
Coming Soon

About the Authors

Kym O'Connell-Todd is a writer and graphic designer. **Mark Todd** is a college professor and program director for Western State Colorado University's MFA in Creative Writing. They live in the Cochetopa Mountains east of Gunnison with more animals than most reasonable people would feed.

Visit the authors' Web site at www.writeinthethick.com